GOING UNDER

THE BLACKHAWK BOYS

GOING
THE BLACKHAWK BOYS
UNDER

New York Times Bestselling Author
LEXI RYAN

Going Under © 2016 by Lexi Ryan

All rights reserved. This copy is intended for the original purchaser of this book. No part of this book may be reproduced, scanned, or distributed in any printed or electronic form without prior written permission from the author except by reviewers who may quote brief excerpts in connection with a review. Please do not participate in or encourage piracy of copyrighted materials in violation of the author's rights. Purchase only authorized editions.

This book is a work of fiction. Any resemblance to institutions or persons, living or dead, is used fictitiously or purely coincidental.

Cover © 2016 by Sarah Hansen, Okay Creations
Cover image © 2016 by Sara Eirew

Interior design and formatting by:

E.M. Tippetts
BOOK DESIGNS

www.emtippettsbookdesigns.com

For Deb

About GOING UNDER

If I met Alexandra DeLuca for the first time today, I would only need one word to describe her: *MINE*.

She's everything she was when we said goodbye. Beautiful, stubborn, sweet…and off-limits.

After two years leading separate lives, our worlds have collided. Now that she's back home working beside me, she's bound to make me lose my mind.

She's all I've ever wanted, all I've ever dreamed of, and the one thing I can never have.

Not because she's my best friend's sister.

Not because all four DeLuca brothers would come at me with fists swinging if I hurt her.

Not even because she's way better than I will ever deserve.

I keep my distance because we didn't meet for the first time today. We met five years ago when I was a different person. When my demons ruled me. Even though I've changed—even though I've gotten my life together and become a better man—I can't change the past. And the secrets that haunt me would destroy her.

But I'm not the only one with secrets, and when the truth comes out, I don't know where to turn. What do you do when your world washes away beneath your feet and you feel like you're drowning? What do you do when the woman you promised yourself you'd never touch is the only thing that can keep you from going under?

GOING UNDER is a standalone novel and the third in the world of the Blackhawk Boys.

Football. Secrets. Lies. Passion. These boys don't play fair. Which Blackhawk Boy will steal your heart?

Book 1 - SPINNING OUT (Arrow's story)

Book 2 - RUSHING IN (Christopher's story)

Book 3 - GOING UNDER (Sebastian's story)

Book 4 – FALLING HARD (Keegan's story – coming summer 2017)

More Blackhawk Boys titles to be announced in 2017!

PROLOGUE
ALEXANDRA

Two years ago...

Are you awake? I'm at your front door.

The text message catches me off guard. It's just after midnight, and the house is quiet. My parents and brothers are asleep, and I should be too. We leave for the airport at oh-dark-thirty, but I'm too anxious to close my eyes. And now a text message from Sebastian Crowe?

I could count on one hand the number of times Sebastian has texted me in the last three years, but every other time it was about school or my brother.

I turn off the TV and flip on a hallway light as I go up front to answer the door.

And now I can add another mind-fogging emotion to my

anxiety, because Sebastian's standing on my front porch. I stare at him through the window by the door. His hands are tucked into his pockets, and he's shifting uneasily, his gaze drifting to the second story, where my bedroom is. I pause for a minute just to take him in—his broad shoulders and muscular arms, the well-trimmed beard that makes him look older than his nineteen years, the dark eyes with thick lashes girls would kill for.

Swallowing hard, I open the door. "Hey. What are you doing here?"

He looks me over, taking in my black yoga pants and the tank top that reveals more of my scars than I've ever shown at school. "I don't...really know." His chest rises on his deep inhale.

My pounding heart feels too wild for my chest. When you've had a crush on a boy for three years and he shows up on your doorstep in the middle of the night, I suppose it's normal for your heart to go off the rails.

Playing it cool, I lean against the doorway and survey him. "Are you ready for this?" I ask, not sure what else to say.

"Which part?"

"College? Leaving your family?" Shrugging, I lick my dry lips. "Goodbye?"

He leaves tomorrow too. While I'm boarding a plane for Colorado, he'll be moving his things into the dorms in Lafayette and begin playing for the Purdue Boilermakers. Is he as nervous about his new life as I am about mine?

I can't imagine Sebastian being nervous about anything. He's always so composed, so strong. After the fire, when my family was simultaneously falling apart and treating me like I was made of glass, Sebastian was a rock, solid and steady. He never said much during his visits to my hospital room, but that was what I needed—someone to be close without needing me to speak.

"I shouldn't be here." His voice is low, his features twisted with worry.

"Why not?"

His gaze skims over me again, and this time the skim of his eyes is so *hot* that I almost expect my clothes to start smoking. But no. That can't be right. This is Sebastian. Sebastian, who wants to be my friend and nothing more. Sebastian, who sees me as the sweet little girl who likes to work on cars with her brothers. Sebastian, whom I've wanted to look at me like this since day one, but who's kept me at arm's length.

"I'll miss you." I'm not sure if I say it to fill the silence or because it's so painfully true.

"Don't." He lifts his eyes to meet mine and shakes his head. "Don't give me another thought."

I back into the foyer and fold my arms to cover my chest. "That's why you came here? To tell me not to think about you?" I'm afraid he'll see how I feel in my eyes, but I can't look away.

"What do you want me to say?" Stepping into the house, he reaches for me but drops his hand before making contact.

I want to imagine I'm seeing so much in his eyes—lust, affection, heartache—but it's all in my head. It's late, and I'm worried about leaving my family and starting a new life. I'm seeing what I want to see. And if I stand here any longer, I'm going to make a fool of myself by telling him exactly how I feel. "Good night, Sebastian. I hope you have a good life." I start up the stairs, leaving the door ajar and Sebastian standing in the foyer. He can see himself out and close the door on his way.

I ascend into the dark second story. When I reach the top of the stairs, I focus on putting one foot in front of the other and moving in the direction of my bedroom. I'm second-guessing everything. I shouldn't have left him. I should have told him how I feel.

Was that click the front door? Is he gone? When will I see him again? *Never?*

"Alex."

The sound of Sebastian's voice is like a lasso around my heart, tugging me backward.

Slowly, I turn toward him and rest my shoulder against the doorjamb. He climbs the final stairs and treads silently forward. The only light in the hallway comes from my bedroom, but it's enough to confuse me when I make out the hurt on his face.

He slides his hand up my arm. It's not the first time he's touched me. We've spent the last three years in school together, so occasional contact is inevitable—a fist bump, the squeeze of an upper arm. And when he found me at Martina's grave months after her death, he pulled me into his arms. He was the first person to hold me after the fire. Everyone else was too afraid. But tonight, something about his touch is different, and it sends an electrified shiver along my skin.

He's still for a moment, his warm fingers unmoving while my

heart pounds so hard I'm sure he can hear it. Then, in one smooth motion, he spins me into my bedroom and backs me against the wall. He's close. Close enough that his heat becomes my own—a warm rush that follows the electric shiver and settles in my belly. His eyes drop to my mouth, and his lips part.

I'm afraid to breathe. Afraid to *blink*. I don't want to ruin this moment or do anything that might wake me from this dream.

His broad chest rises on a long inhale, and his dark eyes stay glued to my lips. I'm faintly aware of the tick of the second hand from the grandfather clock in the hallway and the soft hum of the ceiling fan in my bedroom. With every second that passes, the netting around my heart draws tighter. Mustering all of my courage, I lift my chin and tilt my face ever so slightly toward his.

He squeezes his eyes shut, and I think he lowers his head, but the movement is so slight that I can't be sure. When he exhales, his breath brushes across my lips. It's the sweetest thing I've ever felt.

The moment I'm convinced he's going to kiss me is the same moment he backs away. "I suck at goodbyes."

I want to lift my hand to my mouth, to run my fingertips across lips that feel wounded by his rejection. I keep my hands at my sides and my chin up, refusing to let him see what he just did to me.

I shouldn't have bothered. He's turning away, leaving my room, my house, and my life. I have no idea when I'll see him again, but my heart is firmly in his careless hands.

CHAPTER 1
SEBASTIAN

It's not every day you get to work and are confronted with your own personal wet dream, but when I step into Dad's body shop, I'm greeted by the sight of a white '65 Shelby GT350 restored to its former glory. The car is freshly waxed and shined, and even with an unsightly dent in the passenger door, it makes my mouth water.

The car alone might be enough to do me in, but it's nothing compared to the ass of the woman under the hood. It's a fucking perfect ass, molded into a tight pair of jeans that are almost indecent in the way they cradle her curves.

There are lots of guys who love cars, and lots of guys who'd say there's nothing hotter than a sexy woman lying on the hood of one. Me? I prefer the woman who knows what to do under the hood, and trust me when I say that's not some dirty sex metaphor. I'd choose the girl who isn't afraid to get her hands dirty over one who thinks she's a hood ornament every time.

Since she and I are the only ones in this service bay, I take my time to appreciate the view. Maybe this makes me a creep of the highest order, or maybe it just makes me a red-blooded male who's got a thing for beautiful cars and sexy women. Either way, I take a breath and slowly run my gaze from the curve of her hips down to her black tennis shoes. I put everything from my mind but the fantasy of her.

As she works, she sings along to the pop song playing on the stereo overhead and sways her ass just the slightest bit to the beat. The rich, sultry tone of her voice isn't helping my attraction. Those legs. That voice. That car. Something like déjà vu niggles at me, and then the realization smacks me in the face—I'm not standing here attracted to a strange woman in Dad's body shop. I'm standing here getting turned on by the fantasy that Alexandra DeLuca is back in town. She's the only girl I've ever known to love cars more than I do. The only girl who's ever kept me up at night aching for things I shouldn't want and can't have.

Maybe it's been too long since I've gotten laid, because my imagination is damn near running away with possibilities. Fantasies where Alex isn't just back in town and within arm's reach, but in *my* arms—her ass propped on the hood of the car, her legs wrapped around my waist. Fantasies where she's humming for altogether different reasons.

It can't be her, of course. Alex moved to Colorado two years ago and only comes home at Christmas—not that I ever see her on those brief visits. Last I knew, she was still angry with me for what happened the night before she left. So it's both good and bad that the woman whose ass I've been ogling for the last two minutes isn't who I want her to be. Good, because Alex is a temptation I don't need in my life right now. Bad, because two years later, I still think about that night and am gut-punched with a cocktail of need, regret, and relief, and that's not the kind of cocktail you want to indulge in too often. It's the kind that mixes sweet shit and hard liquor and promises to leave you with one hell of a hangover the next day.

A metallic clang yanks me from my thoughts, and I turn to see Dante DeLuca coming through the door that divides the service area from the body shop. He'd kick my ass clear to Chicago if he knew his little sister plays the starring role in my seriously dirty daydreams. He'd throw in a bonus punch to the junk if he knew how often I've had those fantasies.

I'd like to be the kind of guy who could say he never looked at his best friend's sister that way, that I always saw her as one of the guys. But that would be the biggest fucking lie I've ever told. I knew Alex before I knew Dante. I fell for that sweet smile and the way she chews on her thumbnail when she gets nervous before I even knew she was into cars. And even if I've done my best to hide it, from the first day I met Alex I've wanted more from her than I should.

"You could get off just looking at her, couldn't you?" Dante says, walking my way.

Fuck yes, but you don't say that shit out loud. "What the hell, man? Lower your voice." Hopefully the girl isn't offended. Who is she, anyway? She's probably one of the random women Dante brings into the shop trying to impress with fancy cars, though in reality, Dante's women have never been the type to get their hands dirty.

He grunts. "Nothing wrong with speaking the truth." Stepping forward, he strokes the top of the Mustang, and the woman backs out from under the hood and turns to me.

It's in that moment that my lust-addled brain registers two pieces of information simultaneously. One, Dante was talking about the car, not the girl working on it. And two, Alexandra DeLuca isn't in Colorado anymore.

Alex wipes her greasy hands on the rag tucked into her skintight jeans. Reaching up to close the hood, she lifts onto her toes, and my gaze lands on the strip of skin exposed between her waistband and the hem of her shirt—that soft skin my fingers itch to touch. I caved to that itch once. One dark night in the hallway of her parents' old house when I wasn't sure if I'd ever see her again.

I was sixteen years old when Alex took the seat next to me in English class and instantly caught my attention with her big blue eyes, long, dark hair, soft skin, and a set of curves straight from my horny teenage fantasies. When I learned of her unapologetic love for all things muscle car, you could pretty much stick a fork in me.

"Sebastian." Dante's firm tone makes me think I missed something. Like maybe he was asking me a question while I was ogling his sister.

It's been so damn long since I've seen her, and I want to soak her up, drink her in, swallow her whole. I tear my eyes off Alex and turn to her brother. "What?"

"I asked if you were responsible for us getting this job. People with cars like these usually take them to specialty shops in the city." He eyes the dent. "Does it belong to one of your fancy football friends?"

I drag my hand through my hair and shake my head. "If this belongs to any of the guys, this is the first I've seen it."

Alex's eyes meet mine and she cocks her head to the side, concern wrinkling her brow. "You okay, Sebastian? You look upset about something."

"Not a thing." *A lot of things.* But I'm not upset. I'm *reeling*—from my body's reaction to seeing her again, from this ache in my chest that feels like my lungs are in a trap two sizes too small, from the fact that no one fucking bothered to tell me she was coming home. I need to prepare myself for this, to give myself a pep talk that includes a list of ninety-nine excellent reasons I should stay away from her.

"Welcome home," I say as she saunters toward me. No. She doesn't saunter. Alex isn't the type to saunter. She walks with purpose, like a girl who has no fucking idea that her every move is my sexual fantasy.

"Thanks." Her mouth stretches into a wide smile. "When do you head back to Lafayette?"

I flinch. If she'd ever bothered to ask about me, she'd know that I moved home and transferred to BHU a year ago. If she'd ever bothered to contact me, I'd have told her myself.

Then again, communication is a two-way street, and I've personally been sticking to the detour since the night I pinned her against her bedroom wall and came so fucking close to taking exactly what I wanted. Some lines you just can't cross.

"I'm at BHU now," I say. "I came back when Mom was sick."

Some of the color leaves her cheeks. "I didn't know that."

"She's all better now. It's okay." Of course, with cancer, doctors never say "all better." They prefer the word "remission," which always sounds foreboding as hell to me.

She nods. "Oh, good. So you…live here again?"

"I can't seem to stay away." I swallow and attempt a smile. "For better or worse, this is home."

Dante grumbles something under his breath that I can't make out, but I catch the words "until the draft" and "pro ball." When it comes to my football career, my buddy likes to put the cart way ahead of the horse.

"How long are you visiting?" I ask Alex.

She looks at Dante and back to me. Her lips are bubblegum pink, and I wonder if they taste as sweet as they look. "I enrolled at BHU. Didn't Dante tell you?"

Dante shrugs. "I didn't think about it. Why does he need to know?"

"BHU?" I ask stupidly.

"It was a last-minute decision," she says. "There's no place like home, and if I'm going to get a degree, I need to get started."

"You weren't going to college in Colorado?" I don't know why

I assumed she would.

She shakes her head. "Just working at Aunt Phyllis's service center."

"Right," I mumble.

She takes a deep breath. "Well, when you see your dad, tell him I said thank you again for the job. I can't wait to get started." She turns to her brother. "See you at home for dinner."

She waves to each of us before heading out the door, and I have to focus every bit of my willpower on keeping my eyes up when I want to drop them to the curve of her hips in those skintight jeans.

It's only when the door swings shut that her words register. "What job?"

"Your dad hired her to replace Mike. She'll handle the oil changes and basic maintenance shit."

"Oh." The single syllable is all I can say, because it's the only word that will fit around the lump forming in my throat. Alex is back in town, she's going to BHU, she's working at Dad's body shop, and unless someone's invented a time machine and erased my teenage mistakes, she's as forbidden as ever.

I. Am. Fucked.

CHAPTER 2
ALEXANDRA

It's not every day you get to lock eyes with the man who ruined you, but apparently today's going to be special in more ways than one.

Wake up in my childhood bedroom surrounded by memories of my twin sister? Check.

Register for my first college classes? Check.

Land sweet new gig working with cars? Check.

Look into the eyes of the first guy to break my heart and realize I'm not over it? Not even a little? And, oh yeah, learn that he'll be working by my side and going to the same college as I am? Checkity-check-check.

Sebastian Crowe is the kind of tattooed bad boy who likes classic cars and wild girls, who parties hard but is fiercely loyal to his family. He was the first guy to make me aware of my body and want to be *wanted*, through no fault of his own. And instead of grinning when he saw I was back in town, he stood three feet in front of me and stared at me as if he'd seen a ghost.

Even after two years, the sight of Sebastian makes a mess of the thoughts in my head and tangles a knot low in my belly. He looked as gorgeous as ever in jeans and a Crowe's Automotive T-shirt that stretched too tight around his biceps and across his broad chest. He's the same in so many ways—still wears the neatly trimmed beard he grew our senior year and has that aura of quiet strength about him. He's broader than before and he's gotten a few more tattoos, but he's still every bit the guy I lost my naïve heart to.

As soon as my sneakers hit the gravel in the back lot of Crowe's Automotive, I remember Dante is my ride home. I can't make myself go back in there and face Sebastian yet, not when I just found out that he'll be living and working right by me all year.

So what? I'll just walk. It can't be more than a couple of miles, and fresh air beats facing Sebastian again so soon. I keep my head up and smile at old neighbors as I pass. I don't let myself run, but walk with my hands tucked into my pockets, as if every cell inside me isn't shaking.

"Alexandra DeLuca, is that you?"

I turn at the sound of the familiar voice and see an old friend coming out of the Pretty Kitty. "Bailey?"

Her grin is so wide that it takes up half her face. "Come hug me, you twerp! You've been gone forever!" Before I can reach her, she rushes over to me and wraps me in a hug, trapping my arms at my sides and rocking me left and right. "How long are you staying?"

"I moved back." Her smile in response to this news is so much better than Sebastian's horror-glazed eyes that I have to grin in return. "I start BHU next week."

"And tonight, you drink with me," she announces. When my eyes shift to the Pretty Kitty neon sign, she must sense my hesitation, because she laughs. "Not at the strip club. At a party. Come on, what do you say? I just collected my last paycheck from this meat market. I want to celebrate my freedom, but my bestie is working all night."

"Okay," I say carefully. Bailey and I never shared a social circle. In fact, we didn't even go to the same schools in Blackhawk Valley. Instead, life threw us together in one of those experiences that's so painful and awkward that you immediately bond with anyone else who's a part of it. "What time?"

She looks at her watch. "How's seven sound?" She points a thumb over her shoulder. "I was only in there five minutes but still need to shower it off me."

"Seven's good."

"Should I pick you up at your parents'?"

"Yeah. I'm there for a couple more nights."

"I can't wait," she says, pulling me into another hug. "I've missed you."

"I've missed you too." We separate and wave goodbye.

There's a bounce in my step the rest of my walk home. I've been really nervous about coming back here, and maybe

Sebastian's reaction to my return was disappointing, but at least *someone* is glad to see me.

When I step through the front door of my childhood home, I draw in a deep breath, close my eyes, and remind myself I need to chill the fuck out about Sebastian. I catch the scent of the pumpkin candle Mom burns in the kitchen and the faint smell of pipe tobacco that lingers under everything else, even though Mom hasn't let Dad smoke in the house for ten years.

When I graduated from high school, I didn't know what I was going to do with myself. I knew I couldn't stay in Blackhawk Valley, but after two years living with my aunt and working on cars in Colorado, I learned you can't run from ghosts. If I'm going to be haunted by mine, I want to do it somewhere closer to the people I love.

The truth is, even though my four brothers are frustrating, bossy, and sometimes chauvinistic pigs, I missed them. I missed Sunday dinners at Mom's big oak dining table. I missed the sound of the screen door slamming and my brothers arguing over football. And I missed Sebastian, too. His deep brown eyes. The crooked tilt of his mouth when he's trying not to smile. The way his lips part and his nostrils flare as he studies a new project in the body shop.

But I made a promise to myself. I'm not going to fall back into old habits. It's just that "don't pine over Sebastian" seemed like a much more reasonable plan when I thought he was still at Purdue and would only be home on holidays.

I might always love Sebastian from afar, but I'm done letting unrequited love rule my life. So even though I stand here and want to close my eyes and indulge in a fantasy of a different kind of greeting from Sebastian, the fantasy of how his fingers would feel sliding up my neck and into my hair, I won't let myself.

I cut off the fantasy only to be left with the memory of the night before I left. How many times have I mentally replayed the moment he spun me into my room? How many moments have I wasted remembering the rough pads of his fingers as he cupped my jaw in his hands or the heat in his eyes when he looked at my mouth?

Usually when people look at my mouth, I assume they're looking at the scar that covers the corner of my lips and the side of my chin. It's the only part of my scarring I can't cover inconspicuously, and I've been self-conscious about it for as long as I've had it. I feel like people either look at it, wondering how disgusting the worst of the scarring looks, or they stare at it, trying to wish it away. But that night two years ago, I knew Sebastian wasn't wishing away my scars or pondering how much of me they cover. He *wanted* me—if only in that moment—and it felt so fucking amazing.

I left for Colorado the next morning, and I've spent the last two years mentally rewriting the end of that night. What he should have done. What *I* should have done.

I tried to tell myself that he stopped because he was leaving. That he didn't let his lips touch mine because he didn't want me to wait around for him. But the truth is, Sebastian Crowe had three years before that night to make me his if that was what he'd wanted. If you want someone badly enough, you don't give a shit about all the other stuff—family, college plans, overly protective older brothers. But he's never been interested.

We shared one moment, and in that moment I got to see heat in his eyes directed at me. I got to watch his pulse thrum at the base of his neck and feel what it was like to have his fingers start their slow slide into my hair. All it took was thirty seconds of having his attention one hundred percent on me, and I was ruined.

I'm done fantasizing about a night that never happened. Which is why, instead of hiding in my room all night, I'm going to go out with an old friend and pretend I'm like every other red-blooded college female in the world. I strip out of my clothes, slide into my robe, and go across the hall to the bathroom, where I step under the hot spray of the shower. There, I try out a new fantasy—one where I'm not growing old and waiting for Sebastian Crowe.

CHAPTER 3
SEBASTIAN

I flip the sign at the front of the shop to *closed* and twist the deadbolt on the front door. It was a quiet day, and Dante's already gone. I could have left an hour ago, but I stayed to sweep the service bay and organize new inventory. I was hoping the mindless work might clear my head after seeing Alex. It didn't. If anything, my thoughts are even more scrambled now than they were before.

"Don't set the alarm," Dad says, coming out from his little office behind the front counter. "I'll get it when I go. I'm finishing up some paperwork."

"No problem. Need any help?"

He shakes his head. "I got it."

"You hired Alex?" I ask. I can't stop fucking thinking about her bent under that hood and how much I'd have liked our reunion to have taken a different turn. I *have to* get that idea out of my mind. Alex is off-limits.

"Alex?" His brow wrinkles. "Who?"

"Alex DeLuca."

His eyes widen in recognition. "Oh, Alexandra. Yes, of course I hired her." He gives me a hard look. "She needed a job, and I needed a service tech. She has experience. What would you have had me do?"

I turn away. When Dad hired Dante, I tried to explain that I wanted to keep my distance from the DeLucas, that it just didn't feel right bringing them into our lives. But Dad insisted that hiring Dante was the right thing to do, and I'm sure his reasons for hiring Alex are the same. What would he do if he knew I'd told Dante the truth about our ugly past? Would he feel the same? Would he be bringing the DeLucas closer if he knew one of them knew our darkest secrets?

"Son." He waits for me to look him in the eye before he continues. I wish I had pride when I looked at my dad. I wish I was one of those people who believed his father could do no wrong, but Dad and I have never had that kind of relationship. He points to me now, a stern frown creasing his brow. "Don't dredge up the past."

How can I not when he just brought the past right to my door? "I care about her."

He folds his arms and holds my gaze. "All the more reason to keep your relationship professional. We talked about this before."

"Of course." I want to argue that if he's so set on me keeping my distance from Alex, he shouldn't have hired her, but I know he's right. Giving Alex a job is the right thing to do. And hell, she is great with cars. When other kids were hanging out at high school parties and going to football games, Alex was in the garage with her brothers, learning to rebuild an engine. Her passion and experience are paired with a dynamite intuition. We're lucky to have her. I just have to figure out how to keep my thoughts in check when she's standing close. "Of course I will. I'll see you tomorrow."

He grunts his goodbye, and I'm heading to the back door when I hear the deep "Crowe" Dad uses when he answers his phone.

I stop, listening as hard as I can. I only make out pieces of his side of the conversation. "Sure… Why?… I gave you the money… Consequences…"

I shake my head. The snippets give me a bad sense of déjà vu, but it's ridiculous that my mind wants to jump to the worst possible conclusion from so few words. I leave, not letting myself listen any more.

As I'm unlocking my truck, my phone buzzes. It's a group text from Chris Montgomery, the Blackhawks quarterback, to a small group of us from the team. Even as I read his message, the replies start rolling in.

> ***Chris:*** *I just dropped Grace off at the airport. Need a beer and a distraction. There's a party at Trent's house tonight. Who's in?*
> ***Mason:*** *Fuck yes. I just found out I passed A&P.*

Time to celebrate.

Keegan: *I might need something stronger than beer, but I'm in.*

Arrow: *Enjoy your freedom, assholes. Drink one for me.*

I hesitate, my thumb hovering over the screen. I should go to my apartment and clean, because my roommate is a complete slob who'd rather live in a cockroach-infested sty than wash a dish, but I'm still reeling about Alex. Seeing her is like waking up under ice-cold water and having no idea which way is up—which might be a reasonable analogy if seeing her only turned me upside down and inside out, but the cold water analogy is all wrong for the other ways her presence affects me.

And now I'm going to see her at work all the time.

I type a quick reply, letting the guys know I'll meet them there. Half of Chi Omega attends Trent's parties, and a pretty sorority girl and half a case of beer might just get my mind off one gorgeous, off-limits brunette.

ALEXANDRA

"You're sure I look okay?" I fidget with my scarf as Bailey surveys me. We're parked along the street in front of a house just off campus.

"It's adorable that you don't know how hot you are. Stop fidgeting. It's just a party, not a job interview. We're here for the free booze and, if we're lucky, a few dances with some cute boys."

"Right," I mutter, as if I have *any* experience dancing with cute boys.

"You don't have to hide, you know." Her gaze dips to my mouth and the scar that begins there and continues down my neck. "It's really not that bad."

"That's easy for you to say. You haven't seen me without a shirt."

"*Yet*," she says, waggling her eyebrows. "But maybe if I play my cards right tonight…"

I roll my eyes. "You're a dork."

"You missed me," she says, grinning.

"You have *no idea* how much." When I say it, I realize how true it is. Bailey and I met at a support group for family members of addicts. Even though we only got together outside of that setting on a couple of occasions, we slipped into a friendship back then that I'm easily falling into again. It's odd how much easier it is to bond with someone when they understand the kind of demons you're up against.

Taking a breath, I pull down the visor to look in the mirror. I frown at my reflection. I don't want to have to meet a bunch of new people who are going to ask questions about my scars, or worse, not ask questions, but wait to whisper and get their answers from the rumor mill.

Is this what Sebastian saw when he looked at me today? A

plain girl who could have passed for pretty before the fire?

"What are you thinking so hard about?"

I draw in a shaky breath. "I need a favor."

"What do you have in mind?"

I wrinkle my nose. I was hoping my time in Boulder would help me find some self-confidence and maybe my own sense of style. I know I'll never be gorgeous like Bailey, since these scars aren't going anywhere, but I'd like to be a little more comfortable in my own skin. "Have you ever given someone a makeover? Because I know it's too late for tonight, but I need one. Like, ASAP."

A slow, mischievous smile curls her lips. "Well, you've asked the right girl."

"Seriously? You'll do it?" I'm not sure if I'm more giddy or relieved. I've never had a clue when it comes to fashion and makeup.

"Makeover lesson number one?" She reaches over and flips up my visor so I can't see the mirror. "*You. Are. Beautiful.* We'll take on the rest another time."

"I definitely missed you." I climb out of the car before I can psych myself out, and Bailey follows, punching the button on her key fob to lock the doors.

She slides her arm through mine, and we walk through the damp grass toward the front door. "Is this your first college party?"

"Yep." I take a deep breath. "I assume it's like everything I've seen in the movies and I'll be swept off my feet by my soulmate before the end of the night?"

She winks as she knocks on the door. "Absolutely."

The door opens, and we're swept into the party in a flurry of greetings and movement. Bailey keeps me close as we're pulled through the crowd to a table by the television. Bottles of alcohol sit lined up alongside various two-liter bottles of soda.

"Here's the strategy." Bailey speaks into my ear as she positions two plastic cups in front of her. "Always start with diet soda. Everyone will assume it's rum and Coke or something anyway. Then, if the party is lame, your buzz isn't lying to you and telling you to stay. And if the party is good, you can decide if you want to drink. But always mix your own, drink less than you think you can handle, and if you want to keep the buzz to a minimum, stick to the cheapest beer on hand—lower alcohol content combined with the taste of piss will keep you from overindulging."

I arch a brow. "Spoken like a pro."

"Don't look so surprised. I've had *years* to perfect this strategy." She shoves a cup of diet soda in my hand then takes me by the wrist to lead me down the stairs.

The music echoes off the walls, and my skin seems to vibrate with the beat, but the lights are low, and no one who looks at me will be able to see how awkward I feel. Bailey and I dance to a few songs, and I'm feeling much more relaxed, even a little buzzed on the energy of the room.

"What do you think?" Bailey asks, raising her empty soda glass. "Liquor or beer?"

"I'm good with diet," I shout. I wrinkle my nose. "Is that okay with you?"

"Of course! You do *you*."

A short guy taps Bailey on the shoulder and whispers something in her ear. She nods at him before turning back to me. "A friend of mine is outside looking for me. Do you want to come?"

I shake my head. "You go. I'll get a refill."

"Don't take drinks from anyone, and text me if you need anything," she says. "Otherwise, I'll meet you back here in ten."

It isn't until Bailey's gone that I realize how much her carefree energy was putting me at ease. Maybe a little rum in my Coke wouldn't be a bad idea after all.

I head upstairs to find the beverage table, and the first thing I see is Sebastian Crowe.

CHAPTER 4
ALEXANDRA

My heart stutters an awkward little dance step before hammering heavily.

Sebastian's sitting on the couch in the front room with a redhead straddling his waist. People mill all around, but my eyes are drawn to him and I can't look away.

The redhead combs her hands through his hair and whispers something in his ear. When she pulls back to look at him, he grins before kissing her. He has one hand in her hair, the other curved around her hip. The girl is perfect. Smooth ivory skin, long red hair that flows down her back and curls at the ends, cut-off shorts, and a crop top.

I'm still staring when he breaks the kiss and whispers something in her ear. Is he suggesting they go find a room? Maybe offering to take her home with him? Is she his girlfriend, or does he pick up a different girl at every party, a college football star notching his bedpost like a bad stereotype?

Once, Martina warned me to stay away from Sebastian. She said he was bad news. But he's the only guy who's ever made my heart pound and my skin feel all tingly. After the fire, he was the only guy who looked at me as if he didn't see my scars.

My gut twists with a confusing mix of jealousy and disgust. Some days, I hated the way he made me feel. I hated that he was the only one who understood my love of classic cars and that one of his smiles had the power to put me in a good mood all day. I hated that he almost kissed me two years ago and didn't. But right now, more than anything, I hate that he's touching someone other than me. I hate the way girls throw themselves at him. And I hate that I've never had the courage to do it myself.

As if he can sense me staring at him, he meets my eyes over the redhead's shoulder and blinks in confusion.

My cheeks heat. I feel like a voyeur caught looking in someone's bedroom window.

I shouldn't have come to this party. The stench of beer fills the air and makes me sick to my stomach, and my eardrums ache from the loud music in the basement. It's sweet of Bailey to include me, but I'm not a party girl. I never have been. That was my sister, Martina—the loud to my quiet, the sexy to my plain, the vibrant color to my black and white. I guess I felt a little of my sister in my blood tonight, because until this moment, this was where I wanted to be. I didn't come for the beer or the weed or the possible hookup like Martina would have. I came here because I wanted to spend my first full night back in Blackhawk Valley acting like a girl who's going to live her life instead of hiding from it.

I shouldn't have come. He's going to wonder why I'm staring at him, and how can I explain it? He whispers something in the redhead's ear, and I bow my head and walk away.

The kitchen is crowded with a mix of strange and familiar faces. I went to high school with some of these people, but I always kept to myself. With the exception of Bailey, I never knew how to talk to perfectly put-together girls who liked boys better than books and parties and fashion more than Netflix marathons and pajamas.

I grab a red plastic cup from the counter and turn on the faucet to fill it.

"Why are you wearing a scarf?" a girl with short black hair asks. "It's, like, ninety degrees outside." Her eyeliner is thick and as dark as her inky-black hair. Judging by her strapless top and short shorts, she wouldn't know the first thing about being afraid to show her skin.

The blonde next to her chuckles and reaches for my scarf, pulling it off my neck with a single tug. "Because she's hiding Freddy Krueger skin under there. Don't you remember her from high school?"

Instinctively, my hands fly to my neck and collarbone to cover the puckered skin. I should yank the scarf back from her, but I'm frozen in horror, picturing her holding it above her head and taunting me when I can't reach it.

A tall guy with broad shoulders and glazed eyes steadies

himself with the edge of the counter as he takes in my scars. "What'd you do? Run into a burning building to rescue orphans or something?"

"Who invited you here anyway, Krueger?" the blonde asks. I'm so embarrassed I feel like I could puke.

"I did." All eyes swing to Sebastian as he steps into the kitchen and snags my scarf from the blonde. "Learn some fucking manners, Mandy." Stepping close to me, he slides the thin cotton scarf behind my neck and loops it around loosely. He meets my eyes and swallows hard. "You okay?"

I lift my chin. "I'm fine." It's not the first time I've been mocked for my burns, and it won't be the last. I should tell him that I didn't need him to come to my rescue, but I can't put the words together when he's standing so close and I'm feeling so vulnerable.

He slides his hand down my arm, his fingertips grazing my skin. I squeeze my eyes shut, willing the riot in my belly to calm and the electric shiver to go away. He takes my hand and interlaces his fingers with mine.

"Why would you be with her? Doesn't her skin gross you out? Why not be with someone pretty?" the blonde asks. "Someone who looks good naked. Like me."

"Mandy!" The inky-haired girl smacks her friend on the arm. "Jesus. You're such a mean fucking drunk."

Sebastian cuts his eyes to Mandy. His jaw is hard, and there's so much anger in his eyes that I almost feel sorry for her. "Pretty like *you*?" he asks. "In the last sixty seconds, you've shown everyone in this room just how ugly you are."

"Ooh! Burn!" the drunk guy from earlier says. His eyes go wide as he seems to register his word choice. He turns to me. "I mean, fuck, not *burn* burn." He doubles over with laughter.

"Wanna get out of here?" Sebastian asks.

I nod weakly. I don't know where he wants to go, but he could ask me to go to Jupiter with him right now and I'd agree.

Outside, the moon is bright and round. The frogs and cicadas sing their nighttime songs. It's still hot even though the sun set hours ago, and the promise of rain weighs heavy in the air. I reach for my scarf, flapping it so my skin can breathe. Tonight, Bailey said my scars aren't that bad, but the truth is I could ditch the scarf and the worst of them still wouldn't show. Mandy's not the first mean girl to cut me down because of them, and she won't be the last. When it happens, I remind myself I was lucky, considering how bad it could have been. Lucky it wasn't worse. Lucky most of my face was spared. Lucky to be alive. Some days I believe that, and others it's harder.

I'm not sure if Sebastian and I are walking to somewhere or just away from the house, but we move along the sidewalk side by side.

"Thanks for coming to my rescue." I pull my phone from my pocket and text Bailey.

> **Me:** *I'm just going to walk home. Will you be okay?*
> **Bailey:** *Are you sure you want to leave? I'll drive you. I haven't had anything to drink yet.*

> *Me: No. It's not far. I want some fresh air anyway.*
> *Bailey: Where are you? I don't want you walking alone.*

I'm too embarrassed to face Bailey right now. I don't want to rehash what happened in the kitchen or have her try to talk me into remaining at a party I suddenly feel ridiculous for attending in the first place.

> *Me: I'm not alone. I found an old friend.*
> *Bailey: Oooh. Then why didn't you say so? ;) Text me when you get home. And use protection. Condoms in my glove box if you need one.*

I feel guilty for lying to Bailey. Well, I didn't lie. I did find an old friend. But I made it sound as if he's walking me home, and I'm not about to ask him to do that.

Sebastian leans against a peeling beech tree in front of the house, his dark eyes lazily assessing me. He looks so freaking edible, from his neat beard to his tight shirt and tattoos to the way his jeans hang on his narrow hips. He's out of my league, and I'm embarrassed that I dragged him away from his perfect girlfriend/date/hookup.

"I'm taking off," I say, motioning to the house. "Go back to your girlfriend."

"My girlfriend?" His brow wrinkles, and judging by the glazed look in his eyes, I'm pretty sure he owes his confusion in part to intoxication.

"The redhead who had her tongue down your throat?"

The corner of his mouth quirks up in a grin. "Ah, yeah. Lacey. She's not my girlfriend."

"Your date. Whatever."

"She wasn't my date either. Just a girl at a party." He pushes off the tree and steps toward me. "Were you texting your boyfriend? Is that why you're so anxious to get away from me?"

I laugh. "No. I'm just letting my friend know where I am. I don't have a boyfriend." As soon as I say it, I wish I could snatch the words from the air. Why did I tell him that? Did I think I needed to make that clear so he could make his move? "I'm going home."

As I turn away, he falls into step alongside me. "I'll walk you."

"You don't have to."

"I *want* to." His arm brushes mine as we walk. "I'm sorry about those assholes back there."

I shake my head. "No, I'm sorry you had to come to my rescue."

"Mandy's a bitch." The words slur together and come out sounding more like one—*Mandeezabitch*—telling me my suspicions were right and he's not sober.

"I didn't mean to ruin your night."

He releases a puff of air. "Are you kidding me? Seeing you is the best part of my whole day." His voice is low and rough, but his words curl at the edges. "I knew I missed you, but until I saw you this afternoon I didn't realize how much."

"Are you high?" I don't mean to sound so judgmental, but the question comes out too sharp to hide my feelings. It's one thing if he's had a few drinks, but I detest the idea of him doing more, and I'm having trouble imagining him saying something like that without some serious drugs in his system.

He flinches, then shakes his head. "I had a few beers." He reaches into his jeans, pulling out a handful of bottle caps. "More than a few, I guess."

"Why do you save the caps?" I ask.

"Easier to keep tabs on how much I've had." He spreads them out on his palm and winces. There have to be six or seven there. He tucks them back into his pocket and waits for me to meet his eyes before he continues. "Just beer. I don't do that other shit anymore. You know that, right?"

I take a deep breath. I didn't know that. I don't know anything about Sebastian or his hobbies or his life since I left, and I've spent the last two years making a concentrated effort not to care. To be fair, in high school I never knew for sure that he did more than drink. Martina told me he did, but I didn't want to believe it. The word *anymore* tells me she was right.

We walk in silence down three blocks and cut through the park before rounding the corner to my parents' house. With each step, I remind myself not to give too much weight to his words, not to get too excited about him saying that seeing me was the best part of his day. He's been drinking, and the thousands of what-ifs running amuck in my brain won't change *what is*.

The porch light casts a soft green glow on the lawn, and I can see through the front windows that Mom left a living room lamp on for me.

"Thanks for walking me home," I say as we climb the front steps. Of course, it didn't occur to me until this minute that we've been walking in the opposite direction of his parents' house. "How will you get home?"

He looks over his shoulder toward the street. "I have an apartment now. It's only three blocks north. I think I can handle the walk on my own."

Folding my arms over my chest, I nod. Standing here with him now, I can't help but think of the last time he was on my porch. The last time we were alone in the dark. The memory makes my hands shake. "I don't want you to think you need to do this now that I'm back."

He steps forward, close enough that I can feel his heat. "Do what?"

"Spend time with me. Come to my rescue. Make sure I make it home safely." I wave a hand. "All of it. You don't owe me anything."

"You think I'm here out of a sense of obligation?" He laughs. "Fuck, that's insane."

"Is it? Can we just talk about the elephant in the room?" I ask him.

He's staring at me, and it takes a few beats for him to process that I've spoken. I'd laugh if seeing him drunk didn't also unsettle something deep inside me, some old part of me that still wants Sebastian to be my rock. But I'm not the girl recovering in the hospital anymore. I'm not the girl crying at her sister's grave. Those experiences are part of who I am now, but I'm more, too. I'm stronger. I don't need Sebastian's strength to hold me steady. Or I shouldn't.

I tuck my hands into my pockets. "Two years ago, the night before I left for Colorado…" He goes still, and I can't make myself finish the sentence.

"I crossed a line," he says.

I snort. God, the problem isn't that he crossed a line—it's that he didn't. "Are you serious right now?"

He cuts his eyes to me again, the muscle ticking in his jaw. "It was a mistake, and you're obviously still angry with me about it."

I step away from him and wrap my hands around the porch rail. If I let myself look at him, I'll overanalyze every expression that crosses his face. I realize I'm holding my breath and exhale. "It was a shitty thing for you to do."

He's silent for several heavy beats of my heart. When I can't stand the silence anymore, I release the railing and turn to face him. "Let me make sure I understand," he says. "Since I almost kissed you two years ago, I can't walk you home anymore?"

"I don't want…" I take a breath as I search for the words to explain how this makes me feel. "I don't want a pity friendship."

"What the fuck is a *pity friendship*?"

"It's when you spend time with someone because you don't want them to be alone."

"You're an expert on what I want now?"

"I think you made it perfectly clear what you do and don't want from me two years ago."

He takes half a step forward, and his gaze drops to my mouth. Can you *feel* someone looking at your lips? Because his gaze is so intense on my mouth right now that I'm sure I could close my eyes and still feel it as distinctly as a touch. "Dammit, Alex, if I'd have known you'd hold such a grudge for thirty seconds of weakness, I *would* have kissed you that night. Fuck my better judgment. At least then I'd know how you taste."

I swallow hard and tell my pounding heart not to make more of this than it is. "You're drunk, Sebastian."

Stepping back, he drags a hand over his face. "Yeah." He takes another step back. "Good night, Alex."

I unlock the door and go inside, shutting it behind me without looking at him again. Slowly, I take the stairs up to my old room, close the door behind me, and lean against it. Only then do I allow myself to squeeze my eyes shut and take a long, deep breath to calm my racing heart.

His words replay in my head, making the muscles in my stomach grow tight. Just once I'd like Sebastian Crowe to make good on one of the fantasies he inspires. Just once I'd like him to follow me into this room and lock the door before pushing me against it and lowering his mouth to mine. I'd like to feel those rough hands slide under my shirt to unbutton my jeans...

I pull out my phone and text Bailey, letting her know I made it home okay. Then, without washing my face or changing my clothes, I fall into bed, close my eyes, and break a promise to myself by fantasizing about Sebastian Crowe.

"At least then I'd know how you taste."

CHAPTER 5
SEBASTIAN

Alex didn't work today, thank God. I'm going to have to face her eventually, but if we're going to talk about the things I said last night, I'd rather not do it at the shop. Or in front of Dante.

Last night, I set out to get my mind off Alex, but ended up on her porch looking at her mouth and thinking about how much I wanted to kiss her. *At least then I'd know how you taste.*

Jesus. I don't think I meant to say it out loud. Or maybe I did. Maybe part of my mind wanted the excuse of the buzz to allow me to speak the truth. Maybe I want her to push me away.

I'm not sure I can handle being her friend. I'm not some Neanderthal who doesn't believe guys and girls can be friends. I was her friend throughout high school, as best I could be, but back then my reasons for not asking for more were fresher, my mistakes so close their bitter taste lingered on my tongue.

Friendship requires a certain amount of contentment in the relationship, and with Alex I can't imagine ever not wanting more.

In sober retrospect, I know I said too much. And clearly Alex agrees. I'll just text her and apologize. I try to imagine what that text would look like.

Sorry I said I wish I'd kissed you. To be honest, I'm sure knowing how you taste would only make me want you more.

Right. That's not going to work, but I'll figure out something.

I expect the back lot to be empty except for my car and Dad's, so I'm surprised to see Dante still here. He's standing by his beat-up Jeep and frowning into his wallet.

"Is everything okay?" I ask.

He shakes his head, folds his wallet shut, and slides it into his back pocket. "Nothing. It's all good." He's such a shitty liar.

"Do you need money?"

"Nah. I was just making sure I had enough to get gas. I've got it covered."

I start to reach for my wallet before I remember I used the last of my own cash to gas up the truck this morning. "Good thing today's payday, right?" I say, but he shifts his eyes away. *Fuck.* "Tell me Dad paid you today."

"Sebastian, it's no big deal."

"It fucking *is* a big deal. You worked like anybody else, and you should be paid." This is why I came back here over a year ago. Before I left for my freshman year at Purdue, we found out Mom's cancer was back. Between all her appointments and Dad spending more time with her, the business we'd worked so hard to make viable and *honest* was falling apart. Dante would go sometimes a couple of months without a paycheck. People think that when you're a small business owner, you rake in the cash, but the opposite is often true. When times are tough, the owner is the last one to draw a check, and in the case of Crowe's Automotive circa "the breast cancer years," Dad and Dante both took the hit.

I came home to save the business and be closer to Mom. Dad was so tied up in his grief over her illness that he didn't give a damn about anything else. I knew Mom would beat it and he'd be glad the body shop was still around to support the family. And I was right. She fought and beat that evil shit, and Crowe's Automotive still stands and people get paid what they're owed. Or they did.

"Sebastian," Dante says. "I'm fine. I have savings. I'll just dip into that until your dad has the cash to pay me."

I set my jaw and grit my teeth so I won't say more than I should. Business has been steady. The money should be there. And Dante's no fool. He knows that. Fuck, he's responsible for well over half of our accounted billable hours.

"Don't do that," he says.

"Do what?"

He arches a brow. "Don't assume the worst. It's one paycheck."

"I'm going to figure this out," I tell him, and the gnawing in my gut demands that I do it soon.

"It's fine." Dante combs his jaw-length hair out of his face and draws in a deep breath. "Actually, I do need a favor."

"Anything."

"It's Alex."

Anything but that.

"She's nervous about starting at BHU. I was hoping you could introduce her to your friends. You know, some nice girls she could study with or something."

I want to tell Dante that I don't have a lot of friends outside of the guys on the team, but that's not entirely true. I could introduce Alex to Bailey and Mia—I have no doubt they'd love her. The problem with that plan is that then I wouldn't just be seeing Alex at work and possibly on campus—she'd be around my friends off campus, too. Hell, even without introducing her to any of my friends, I ran into her at that party last night.

But I can't tell Dante that I'd prefer to keep my distance from his little sister because I can't stop fantasizing about her. I don't think he—or any of her three other brothers, for that matter—would appreciate that very much.

I have no doubt that Alex could hold her own against any unwanted advances, but with four older brothers playing guard dog, she's never had to. The DeLuca boys have one rule for their friends when it comes to their baby sister, and it's a simple one: Alex is off-limits. You don't check her out. You don't come on to her. And you sure as fuck don't touch her. I think it's always been that way, but when her twin died four years ago, the DeLuca brother protectiveness kicked up a few notches.

If a few hotheaded brothers were all that stood between us now, I'd happily take a few punches. Hell, if I met Alex today,

I'd only need one word to describe her: *mine*. But I didn't meet her today. I met her five years ago when I was a different person, and the choices I made are unforgiveable. So she can't be mine. I forfeited that right before I had any idea what I was losing.

"I'm not asking you to move her in with them," Dante says, mistaking my silence for hesitation. "Just include her every once in a while. For me?"

I nod. "You've got it."

He grins. "But tell the guys to keep their distance, will ya? She's..." He grimaces, looking for the word, and I think *innocent*. "She's not like other girls her age."

"I know," I assure him. "I'll watch out for her."

We both climb into our cars, and I head to my apartment, where I'm greeted with a pile of dirty dishes and a coffee table covered in pizza boxes and empty cans of beer. I just cleaned this place up yesterday, and it already looks as if it's been ransacked.

"I'm not cleaning up his mess this time," I mutter to myself. Suddenly I'm exhausted, so I head to the kitchen for some caffeine.

When I move aside a stack of papers so I can get to the coffee pot, something catches my eye. The copy of our new lease that I gave my roommate two weeks ago is still sitting on the counter unsigned.

"Doug!" I call. I shove the coffee pot under the faucet and turn on the tap. "Don't forget to sign this lease before you head out today. They need it by this weekend."

Doug comes out of his room as I'm measuring the coffee

grounds. "Didn't we talk about that?" he asks. His eyes are only half opened and his hair is sleep-mussed. It's five fucking thirty at night.

I press the brew button on the coffee pot. "Didn't we talk about what?"

"About the lease." He yawns. "Change of plans, man."

My stomach sinks, because I know that look on his face. Doug is four years older than me and should, by all conventional standards, already have his shit together. I moved in with him last year when I started at BHU and didn't want to pay for dorm living but couldn't handle living with my parents. "What do you mean, *change of plans*?"

"Moving back in with my folks. I need to take some time to find myself, ya know? Don't worry about me. I'll move out, and you can have one of your college buddies move in here with you."

"You're kidding, right?"

"Nah, man. I'm serious. I gotta do me, but you'll be fine."

"That's fucking presumptuous of you, Doug." I want to throw something. Even if a small fraction of my brain is relieved that I won't have to live in his filth anymore, the rest of my brain understands that no Doug means no apartment. All of my friends have their living arrangements in place for the semester, and the week and a half left in our lease doesn't give me enough time to vet strangers as potential roommates. "Thanks for the notice."

"Oh, you're welcome, bro," he says, completely missing my sarcasm. He grabs a mug from the cabinet and fills it with coffee from my fresh pot. "Thanks for the brew."

ALEXANDRA

Martina's bed is piled with boxes of Mom's scrapbooking supplies. Every time I look in that direction, I have to push down the knee-jerk reaction to clear them away so Martina can just climb under her covers when she gets home. I used to do that when we were in high school. She'd go out with her friends, and I'd be stuck at home looking at her laundry-covered bed. I'd put it away for her so she wouldn't have to do it when she got back... and so Mom wouldn't know Martina had blown off her chores *again*.

But she's not coming home, and sleeping in this room we shared for so many years makes my chest ache. I can't wait to move tomorrow. I planned on spending my evening packing my bags, but since I've only been home two nights, it turns out that task only took me fifteen minutes.

"Looks like it's time for another night hanging with Mom," I mutter, but then, as if on cue, my phone buzzes, and it's a text from Sebastian.

Sebastian: *Are you free tonight?*

I scan the words three times before I'm convinced that I'm not misreading them. First, I'm surprised he still has my number.

But then, he's still programmed into my phone. Second, he's asking me about my plans. Why does my heart do this? It's as if it decided years ago that Sebastian was my one and only, and my brain's opinion doesn't count. His words from last night are *definitely* not helping the situation.

> **Me:** *No plans.*
> **Sebastian:** *My friends are having an end-of-summer cookout. Want to come? I thought you might want to meet some people from BHU.*

His friends are having a party and he wants me to go with him? Like, *with him* with him, or just as the buddy tagging along? It would be awesome if I could just say yes without analyzing every word, but I'm not built that way.

> **Sebastian:** *It's okay if you don't want to.*
> **Me:** *No, it sounds good. Thanks for the invitation.*
> **Sebastian:** *I'll pick you up at seven.*

My eyes go wide as I look at the clock. Seven past six. He's going to pick me up in less than an hour.

Let the panicking commence.

CHAPTER 6
ALEXANDRA

Fifty minutes later, I'm staring into the mirror and wishing I'd declined his invitation. I'd like to say I didn't change my outfit fifteen times and that I didn't spend extra time on my makeup, but that would be a big fat lie. I'd have changed my clothes another five times if I thought it would make Sebastian look at me tonight the way he did in that one moment two years ago.

And for a minute last night.

But he was drunk, so that doesn't count. Does it?

Obviously, Operation Forget About Sebastian Crowe is going just great.

I stare at myself in the full-length mirror on the back of my closet door and try to focus on the good things. I look kind of fashionable. I settled on a pair of jeans Aunt Phyllis bought me, some black ballet flats, and an off-the-shoulder shirt that was also a gift from my aunt. The shoes are comfortable but cute, and the jeans say I'm not trying too hard.

My problem is with the shirt. My hand settles on the puckered skin that marks the left side of my neck and collarbone. This shirt shows way more of my scar than I'm comfortable with, so even though I'm trying to push myself to embrace my body and its scars for what they are, I grab a scarf at the last minute and wrap it around my neck. After putting on some hoop earrings and a light coat of lip gloss, I feel almost pretty.

I spent my last two years of high school in high-necked shirts and scarves, but there was no hiding the scarring on my face. People would stare and ask questions I didn't want to answer. It's been almost four years since the fire, so you'd think I'd be getting to the point where I'm comfortable with both the scars and the questions, but I'm not that Zen.

I tear myself from my critical self-inspection in front of the mirror and go down to the kitchen. Mom's cooking chicken at the stove, and Dante is setting the table. My brothers are all good about making sure they come home for dinner at least once a week, though they rarely manage to make it on the same night.

"Mr. Patterson dropped off the keys and security code while you were in the shower," Mom says. She sprinkles some crushed red pepper on the chicken. "Are you sure you're going to be okay staying alone in that big house?"

"I'll be fine, Mom." Mom's old boss owns a gorgeous house in the historic district by campus, and while he spends the next nine months in Europe, I'm going to housesit for him. In other words,

I'm going to live in a gorgeous home rent-free instead of trying to spread my wings from the confines of my childhood bedroom. The arrangement doesn't suck.

"Well, you tell me if you get lonely. I'll stay with you if you need."

"I'm twenty-one," I remind her. I celebrated my birthday before I left Boulder, and in truth I was glad to do it there—away from the memories and the hollow ache of thinking about how Martina and I should have celebrated turning twenty-one together.

Mom looks at the calendar on the fridge and points to the date. "But you shouldn't be twenty-one for another six weeks."

I shake my head. Martina and I were born almost eight weeks premature, and Mom always insists that I'm not as old as I think because I shouldn't have been born so soon. She did that with Martina, too. "Either way," I say, "I think I can handle housesitting half a mile away, but I promise I'll invite you for a sleepover if I get too lonely."

"Or I could come by for a *Murder, She Wrote* marathon."

"Okay," I promise. "It's a plan."

"Are you joining us for dinner?"

I shake my head. "No. I'm going out."

She looks me over and gives a wolf whistle. "You look hot, sweetie. Do you have a date?"

I shake my head. "Sebastian's picking me up to introduce me to some of his friends."

"That's nice," Mom says. "I've always liked Sebastian. Are you going as friends or"—she waggles her brows—"*something more?*"

That's the million-dollar question. "Friends, Mom. Seriously."

Dante scowls as he pulls a stack of plates from the cupboard. "Better be. When I asked him to introduce you to his friends, I wasn't suggesting that he take advantage of my little sister."

The excitement that's bubbled in my blood since getting Sebastian's text simmers down to cold sludge. "You asked him to do this?" My smile falters despite my best efforts.

Dante is oblivious. "Sure. He hangs out with guys from the team and their girlfriends all the time. You were always so shy in school. I thought he could help you fit in."

Before I can reply—though really, what would I say?—the doorbell rings.

Grinning, Mom turns down the heat on the stove, wipes her hands on a towel, and rushes past me toward the door.

"I can get it, Mom."

"I want to see Sebastian," she calls over her shoulder.

I feel helpless as I follow her. I was nervous before, wondering if maybe it would be better to stay home than to be awkward in front of new people, but after what Dante just revealed, I don't want to go at all.

"Mrs. DeLuca," Sebastian says when Mom opens the door. He's dressed in jeans and a T-shirt that's fitted around his biceps, his tattoos peeking out under the tight sleeves. "You look beautiful, as usual," he tells Mom.

She hugs him and chuckles. "Call me Elaine. Please."

"Whatever you say, Mrs. DeLuca," he says.

Mom steps away, and when Sebastian's smile turns to me, I fully understand what Martina used to say about bearded guys.

There's something about a bearded man with a cocky smile that will make me imagine his face between my legs. Every. Single. Time.

No kidding, sis. No kidding.

"Are you ready, Alex?" Sebastian asks.

"Sure." I force a smile for Mom's benefit and grab my purse off the front table before following Sebastian outside. When he opens the passenger door of his brown pickup truck for me, I arch a brow. "Seriously?"

He shifts his eyes from side to side, as if looking to see if I'm talking to someone else. "What?"

"Why are you opening the door for me? Did Dante say you had to?"

"It's called manners, Alex. It's not a marriage proposal."

I swallow hard and climb into the truck. He closes the door behind me, and I buckle my seatbelt as he comes around the front to his side. He cuts a glance at me from the corner of his eyes, but he slides his key into the ignition. The truck comes to life with a rattling growl, as if it's as cranky about being here as I am.

He pulls out on to the road and is heading out of town without either one of us uttering another word. His silence only adds to my irritation. If he doesn't even have anything to say to me on a short drive, why did he invite me?

We pull up to the house, and I'm so preoccupied with my anger that I barely register the enormity of the brick home.

He pulls the keys from the ignition and takes a deep breath

before facing me. "So you *are* mad about last night?"

I blink at him. "What?"

"I said I wished I'd kissed you." His gaze dips to my mouth, but it's brief, nothing like last night's lingering, tingle-inspiring mouth ogle. "I said it, and now things are weird between us, and I'm sorry."

"I'm not mad about what you said."

He frowns. "Then what's wrong?"

"Dante told me you only invited me tonight because he asked you to."

"Does it matter?"

I gape at him. Surely he's not this clueless. "I told you last night that I don't want your pity friendship, and this was what I was talking about. I don't want to be included out of some sense of duty or honor or because you're doing my brother a favor." I turn away. It's a beautiful night, and the sun spreads low across the horizon like it's stretching out in bed. "Contrary to what my entire family seems to think, I didn't move home because I need special assistance to live my life. I'm capable of making my own friends."

He sighs, and his fingers brush my shoulder before falling away. "I'm sorry I made you feel that way, but— Would you please just look at me?" When I turn in my seat, his eyes meet mine. His irises are dark brown and he has the thickest eyelashes. "I wouldn't have invited you if I didn't want you here."

He's really trying to kill me, isn't he? Each moment of his sweetness is like a melon baller to my heart, scooping out what

I've spent the last two years painstakingly reclaiming. Two weeks from now, I fear there will be nothing left.

"I'll take you home if you want," he says, studying me, "but I hope you'll stay. My sister's here, and I've never had the chance to introduce you two. I think you'll like her. Plus, when I told Mia I was bringing you, she was really excited. Please stay."

I made it through high school knowing Sebastian wasn't interested in me, and even if it hurt, I never held it against him. But he changed everything that night two years ago when he almost kissed me.

I'm going to have to get over it. Sebastian's part of my life. Thanks to his dad's body shop, our families are close, and I'm going to work with him and go to school with him. Maybe getting over him won't be easy, but it's what I need to do.

"I'll stay," I say. "But next time, if you don't think of inviting me somewhere without my brother mentioning it, please don't invite me at all."

"I would have thought of it." His brow wrinkles as he studies me. "I might not have acted on it without your brother's suggestion, but I would have thought of it."

I'm not sure what to make of that, but instead of letting myself analyze it, I climb out of the truck. Sebastian points to the gate at the side of the house, and we walk around back, where half a dozen people are scattered between the pool area and a fire. A couple of girls lounge on rafts in the pool, one guy flips burgers on the grill as a girl hangs on his arm, and a couple of other guys poke at a smoking pile of logs in the fire pit.

"I didn't bring my suit," I whisper to Sebastian.

"Neither did I," he says. "I wasn't planning on swimming so I didn't think about it. Do you want to go back to the house and grab one?"

I shake my head. I'd be even more self-conscious in a swimsuit than I am in this shirt. Truth be told, I'm glad I didn't know. It gives me the perfect excuse to stay covered. "I'm fine."

"Come on, let me introduce you to Arrow." He points to the tall, broad-shouldered guy at the grill. "This is his place. We hang out here a lot because he's not allowed to leave."

I arch a brow. "Not allowed? Like, his mom won't let him or..."

"House arrest," Sebastian says. "He got mixed up in drugs for a while and got caught." When I don't move forward, Sebastian squeezes my arm. "He's not into that anymore. I wouldn't have brought you here otherwise. He was going through some bad stuff, but he got through it." He waves to the group. "We all got through it *together*."

I swallow hard. I wish Martina had had friends to get her through her "bad stuff." Instead, she only had people happy to offer her the chemical escape she craved.

My thoughts must be all over my face, because Sebastian drags in a ragged breath. He takes my hand and squeezes my fingertips. "Will you be okay?"

"I'm fine." I give what I hope is a reassuring smile, but I'm disappointed when he drops my hand. I follow him over to the grill.

"This is my friend, Alex," Sebastian announces to the couple.

The girl on Arrow's arm steps back and smiles when she sees us coming. She's beautiful, with long, soft brown hair and light brown skin. She extends a hand. "I'm Mia. This is my boyfriend, Arrow."

I shake her hand. "It's nice to meet you." Arrow turns away from the grill, and my eyes go wide because—*wow*. He's as gorgeous as Sebastian. How do girls handle them both in the same space at the same time? "Thanks for letting me crash your party," I tell him.

"Any friend of Sebastian is a friend of ours," Arrow says. "Dinner will be ready in a few minutes."

"Sebastian, why don't you introduce Alex to everyone?" Mia suggests.

I'm so out of my league with these people, it's not funny. It's as if Arrow's having a gathering of all the beautiful people but no one has the balls to tell Sebastian he shouldn't have brought me. I have a fleeting thought that Martina would fit in here much better than me, but I push it away, lift my chin, and paste my smile in place.

Sebastian leads me around the pool to a stone fire pit and points to a curvy blonde with short shorts and hair that's longer than her T-shirt. I'm stepping toward her with a smile even as he says, "This is Bailey."

Bailey hops up, her jaw dropping. "Oh my God! What a small world!"

We hug, and Sebastian clears his throat. "So you two know

each other. That's…great?" He doesn't sound too sure. Sebastian points to the brunette who was sitting beside Bailey before she jumped up to hug me. "Alex, this is my sister, Olivia. I don't think you've met before. Olivia, this is my friend, Alex."

Olivia has one of those sweet and innocent faces. She could play the part of "girl next door" without missing a beat, but she arches a brow, and some of her sweetness leaves her face as she studies me. "*Friend?* You don't say." She gives me a once-over, and even though I put a lot of thought into my outfit, I feel a little frumpy. It's not that there's anything cruel or hateful in the way she looks at me—her gaze is more curious than critical—it's just that she's so put together in her beaded brown tank dress and matching sandals that I feel awkward and unfashionable.

"Alex and I graduated together." Sebastian either ignores the implication in her tone or he's missed it entirely. "She's going to be running service for Dad part-time, and she's starting at BHU next week."

Olivia points across the pool to where we just came from. "Mia's a transfer student too."

My cheeks heat. "No, I'll be a freshman. I took some time off after high school."

"She's been in Boulder, working with family," Sebastian says.

"Lucky," Olivia says. "Think you could hook me up with a job? I'd love to get out of this town."

I laugh. "I mean, I guess if you know how to do oil changes and check brake pads, go for it. It wasn't exactly glamorous."

"But at the end of the day, you were still in Boulder," she says.

"True. I can't deny that was pretty cool. It's beautiful out there."

A tall guy with messy brown hair comes to stand next to Sebastian and offers me his hand. "I'm Chris Montgomery," he says, and I catch a hint of a Southern accent in those three words.

"Nice to meet you." I shake his hand and can't help but return his smile when he flashes me the cutest damn pair of dimples I've ever seen.

"Mind if I steal Sebastian away for a minute?" he asks.

I shrug. "I don't own him."

"You'll be okay?" Sebastian asks.

"She's fine," Bailey says, shooing them away.

The guys head to the back of the house. Chris points at a television that's mounted in the covered cabana area.

"They have to talk football," Bailey says. "Chris's girlfriend just went back to New York, so he's pretty much eating, breathing, and sleeping football to keep his mind off how miserable he is without her."

"Poor guy."

"More like poor *us*," Mia says, joining us by the fire. "Since Arrow's on house arrest, he can't even play until midseason, but he's spending all his free time watching film and analyzing all they can about every team they're up against, even the ones he won't be playing."

"They're obsessed," Olivia adds. "Every one of them."

Another guy joins us by the fire. "The word you're looking for is *dedicated*." He offers a hand, and I take it. "I'm Mason. It's nice to meet you."

"Alexandra," I say. Mason's as drop-dead gorgeous as the others. He's tall and broad-shouldered, but it's the contrast of his dark brown skin and bright green eyes that makes him gorgeous in that I'd-like-to-just-sit-and-look-at-you-for-a-while way. "You must play football too."

He grins right at me, and my cheeks heat. "Number eighty-eight. Wide receiver. Are you a fan?"

"Um—"

"She will be," Bailey says, saving me from an awkward explanation of how I've never really been into sports. "She doesn't have a choice if she's going to hang with us."

"It's true," Mia says. "Prepare yourself to learn the playbook like you're part of the team."

"If Chris keeps running them this hard, they're not even going to have the energy for sex," Bailey says.

"Wanna bet?" Mason runs his gaze over her, from her crop top all the way down to her bare feet. With this one look, he achieves what I would have thought was impossible, and makes her blush.

She clears her throat. "Anyway, I hope you didn't want to spend too much quality time with your boy Sebastian."

"Oh, no." I shake my head. This whole conversation makes me uncomfortable, from having to be introduced to Sebastian's friends like a backward child who needs the teacher to tell the class to be nice to her, to having to explain that my relationship with Sebastian is entirely platonic. "Sebastian and I aren't *together*.

He's best friends with my brother Dante, and Dante asked him to introduce me to people."

Bailey grins. "Your brother is Dante DeLuca? How did I never put that together?"

"Uh-oh." Dante runs through girls faster than bottles of his favorite whiskey. "You know him?"

She shrugs. "I knew him from my old job. He was a good tipper."

The humor drains from Mason's face, and he turns on his heel and leaves the conversation.

"Is he okay?" I ask, watching him go.

"He's in love with Bailey," Mia says quietly.

Bailey waves away the explanation. "Mason doesn't like to be reminded that I showed other men my tits for tips. It seems irrational to me, since I'm happy to show them to him for free."

I grimace, not even sure where to start with all that information. "So you know my brother from the strip club? Where you worked, and he was…a patron?"

"Yep."

"I can't decide if I want to apologize or puke a little."

Bailey lifts her arms out wide, her palms up. "I'm a big girl, and I made my own choices. I earned the money I needed for school, and *I'm* not sorry, so you certainly don't need to be."

"But that must have been weird for your boyfriend." I look to Mason, who's joined the guys by the television.

"He's not my boyfriend." She sighs. "He was my excellent booty call for a while, but he cut me off."

I'm curious, but I'm not sure if it's my place to ask her to explain. Before I can figure out a way to ask, Olivia's changed the subject back to me and Sebastian.

"So you're not with my brother." Olivia surveys me critically. "Do you have a boyfriend?"

Bailey arches a brow. "Are you hitting on her? Because I saw her first."

Olivia laughs. "If only my love life were that simple. But sadly, I'm all about the D."

I bite back a laugh at her bluntness and shake my head. "Too bad for us both." I lower my voice. "Though it's been so long since I've had any quality D time, I'm not even sure I'd remember what to do with it."

Bailey guffaws, and the guys turn away from the television and stare at us. She makes two fists and holds them to either side—one for me and one for Olivia. "Sexually deprived chicks unite."

"May our common bond be short-lived," Olivia mutters.

I bump Bailey's fist as Sebastian returns to stand by my side.

Bailey says, "May we have a reason to spread our legs very soon," and Sebastian turns on his heel and walks away.

CHAPTER 7
ALEXANDRA

Sebastian's friends are awesome. I'm not sure what I expected. Maybe a group of guys standing around, drinking cheap beer and belching the alphabet? Or girls rubbing themselves all over the nearest jock? What I got was a full dinner under the setting sun and lots of laughs.

As much as I objected to Dante thinking I needed help making friends, I have to admit that I've never had a group of friends like this. They tease and compliment each other in equal measure, and they seem more interested in talking than in getting wasted. This isn't like the party Bailey took me to last night. This is quieter, calmer, and all-around *better*.

After the burgers and brats were devoured and Bailey's bottles of sweet red wine were empty, we all helped clean up. Olivia said she was tired and went home, but everyone else has returned to the patio. The reflection of the fire dances in the pool, and the moon creeps higher into the sky.

I settle into the seat beside Bailey, my belly full and my cheeks warm from wine. "I'm glad you're here. I was really nervous about meeting Sebastian's friends. I don't want anyone letting me into their circle out of obligation."

She arches a brow. "Trust me when I say we don't do that," she says. "Life is too short to share with people who don't make you happy. But I already like you, which is lucky for me, and lucky for you, too, because we're the best friends you could make."

"She's right," Mia says from the chair on the other side of her. "Wanna sit in the hot tub for a while?"

"I didn't bring a suit," I say.

"It's cool," Bailey says. "I don't feel like changing into mine anyway. Let's just put our feet in." I shoot her a grateful smile, and she winks at me before toeing off her shoes and padding toward the hot tub. I follow her lead, rolling my jeans up to my knees.

The hot tub is set in stone and elevated from the rest of the pool area, and Mia and I climb the steps behind Bailey. Bailey taps the button to turn it on and then takes a seat on the edge. I sit beside her, and Mia takes a seat beside me.

The water is warm but not too hot, and the jets feel amazing on my calves. It feels so good that I wish I weren't such a freak about showing my body. With the sun down and the temperature dropping, I can imagine how awesome it would feel to sit in the water and relax with a drink while talking to the girls.

"So this will be your first semester in college?" Mia asks.

I nod. "I don't even have a major, though. I have no idea what

I want to do."

"I thought you liked cars," Bailey says.

I shrug. "I do. If I had buckets of money, I'd have a bunch of them. But I've worked as a service technician for the last two years. I got my certifications and I know what that life is like. I don't think it's what I want to do forever."

"You'll figure it out," Mia says. "Are you living with your parents or in the dorms?"

"Neither, actually. My mom works for a man who's going to be out of the country for the next nine months, and I'm going to live at his house and take care of his cats and pool and stuff until he returns."

"You'll have a pool?" Bailey asks. "So maybe I don't have to interrupt the lovebirds out here every time I want to swim?"

I smile. "You're welcome to come over, but they're coming out to close the pool for the season at the end of September, so there's not much time."

Mason heads over to us and sets a couple of glasses full of red slushy mixture on the edge of the hot tub. "Someone requested strawberry margaritas?"

"You're my hero!" Mia says, grabbing one.

"Thank you," I say.

Bailey takes hers and winks at Mason. "You're not so bad."

"How's the water?" he asks.

"So good." I wiggle my toes under the surface.

"Next time you'll have to bring your suit," Mia says.

"You can bring your brother, too." Bailey waggles her

eyebrows, and Mason's jaw goes hard.

"Enjoy the margaritas," he says before walking away.

"Why do you do that to him?" Mia asks Bailey.

I lower my gaze to my lap but keep my attention on their conversation. I'm curious about Bailey and Mason's relationship and want to know more without asking.

"I don't know," Bailey says. "He's shutting me out, and I guess I'm just pissed that he's decided to be all or nothing about our relationship."

Mia stares at her for a long, tense minute. She must decide to drop it, because she turns to me. "If you want to get in, I can go grab one of my suits for you."

I shake my head and turn to study all the people at this party. "I don't wear swimsuits much. I'm pretty self-conscious." Loosening my scarf, I casually wave toward my mouth and face and try to pretend it's no big deal. I like Mia, and I like this group, and I want to get the awkward and inevitable explanations out of the way.

"What happened?" Mia asks.

"I was in a fire when I was seventeen." The words alone are enough to make my chest tighten. I exhale slowly and circle my feet in the water to distract me from the horrible panic I feel talking about that night.

"I'm so sorry," Mia says. "That must have been so painful."

"I'm lucky, actually. It could have been much worse." I skim my fingers over my neck and down to the top of my shirt. "My sister didn't make it."

Bailey reaches over and squeezes my knee, and when I lift my eyes to hers, I see tears there.

Mia gasps. "I remember that. Holy crap. You were the girl who ran into the burning house to save her sister."

I flinch. "Not real smart, huh?"

"It was brave." The sound of Sebastian's voice makes my heart squeeze and grow bigger all at once. He climbs the steps and sits on the landing by the hot tub, looking at me. The sadness in his dark eyes slingshots me back in time to days I don't like to think about. "Are you ready to head out?"

I'm not. I want this night to last longer. I'm afraid tonight was a fluke and that the next time I see this group, I won't fit in. But common sense tells me it's time to go. Tomorrow I get settled at Mr. Patterson's house, and the day after that is my first class at Blackhawk Hills University.

I look to Bailey then Mia. "Thank you so much for tonight. You two are great."

Mia grins. "You're welcome to come over anytime you want."

"Maybe I'll see you on campus." I turn to climb out of the hot tub.

"You're coming to the game next weekend, right?" Mia asks. "It's the season kickoff, and it's a home game. You've gotta come."

I look to Sebastian. "Um…"

"It would be cool if you were there," he says softly. "I'd like that."

Scoop. Another chunk of my heart gone. "I'd love to."

SEBASTIAN

Alex is quiet on the drive home.

I liked having her there tonight. Maybe I liked it too much. It was just so good to see her smile and laugh with the other girls. Fuck, it was more than that. It was good to have her close. Period.

The guys gave me plenty of curious looks, and I know they're wondering what she is to me. I've never brought a girl over to Arrow's. I've never wanted to. Bringing Alex seemed significant, and maybe it was, but I'm glad they didn't ask for details, because I didn't feel up to giving the "we're just friends" speech and having them call my bluff.

The closest I came to having to explain was when we were cleaning up after dinner. Arrow pulled me aside. "If you and Alex want to hang out and drink, you can crash in the guestroom."

I exhaled heavily and shook my head. "Not tonight, man," I said, but my imagination had already run away with the idea. Alex's cheeks were flushed from wine, and it was too damn easy to imagine keeping her slightly buzzed and pulling her into bed with me at the end of the night, sliding that shirt off her shoulder and kissing my way down—

"Your sister's sweet," Alex says, pulling me from my thoughts. "She did seem really tired, though. Is she okay?"

I slow as I turn into her parents' neighborhood and try to

refocus my thoughts. "She's pregnant, and it's really wearing her out, but she's okay."

"She's pregnant?"

"Yeah." I grip the steering wheel and bite back the rant that rushes onto my tongue every time I think about my little sister being sexually active. And with my fucking teammates at that. Sure, she's an adult, but she's still my little sister. "She is. Trust me when I say I was horrified when I found out." I was more than horrified. I was pissed and took it out on my quarterback, since Liv led me to believe he was the father.

"Wow. Who's the father?" She throws her hand over her mouth. "I'm sorry. Is that rude? I'm not trying to be rude. It's just that tonight she gave me the impression that she's single."

"She is. The dad's named Keegan. He wasn't there this time, but you'll meet him. I have to give the guy credit. He's trying his best to be there for her even when my sister's done everything she can to push him away."

"She's gotta be confused. I can't imagine getting pregnant now, and I'm two years older than her. Her whole life is about to change."

"No kidding. She knows that, but at the same time I don't think she has any concept of how different everything will be. Thanks for being nice to her. She had a rough start with that group, and she could use some friends."

"I wonder if the girls are planning on throwing her a shower. I'll ask Bailey if I can help. That would be fun."

I pull up in front of her house and throw the truck into park.

I wish I'd taken the long way home. I don't want to let her go in yet. I want a few more minutes to talk to her and watch the wine-flush of her cheeks. She's so pretty it makes me itch to grab my camera, to capture the crystal-clear blue of her eyes and the pink in her cheeks, to put in print the evidence of how beautiful she is. "How do you know Bailey?"

The question seems to catch her off guard, and she hesitates before answering. "She and I went to the same support group."

"Support group?"

"For family members of addicts." She bites her lip. "I hope she'd be okay with me telling you that."

"I didn't know you went to a support group."

She nods. "Just that summer before..." She pulls her purse into her lap and toys with the strap. "I thought maybe I needed to meet other people going through the same thing so I could help her." She shakes her head. "It didn't make a difference, obviously, and when she came home from rehab, she wasn't the same. It wasn't just about addiction. Then she ran away, and I kept going to the support group because I needed it more than ever."

My throat goes thick with too much I've never said. "Your sister…"

She swings around to look at me. "Can we not talk about her? I've had such a nice night. I don't want to feel sad right now."

I don't want you to feel sad either. Ever again. But that's not the way life works. Not for anyone. And especially not for a girl who watched her sister die in a fire, not for a girl who almost died herself. "Let me walk you to your door."

She arches a brow. "Don't you remember how that ended last night?"

I clear my throat. "Good point."

She returns my smile, and the silence stretches between us—not tight and uncomfortable, but soft and easy.

"I'll see you at the shop this week?"

"Yeah." She looks up at me through her lashes, and those blue eyes tear right through me. "Thanks for tonight, Sebastian. It was a lot of fun."

She climbs out of the truck, and I watch her walk up the front steps. And the warmth in my chest from a great fucking night is met with the ache of wanting something I know I can't have.

Martina's Journal

I met the cutest guy last night.

It's not every day in this town when I meet a guy who doesn't bore me out of my mind. I mean, all the guys here are the same. They want to take you to the movies, maybe buy you dinner before they feel you up in the back seat of their car.

That was fun for a while, but I'm ready to pull my hair out. Guys all have the same moves and the same lines.

But this guy I met? His friends call him Crowe, and I met him at this college party just off campus.

(And, yes, the girls at school think I'm crazy for going to college parties, but I think they're crazy for settling for the boredom of high school parties, where the most interesting thing that happens is some bitch losing her virginity in someone's parents' king-size bed.)

So, yeah, I prefer college parties. Nobody questions whether or not I should be there. I've always been able to pass for a little older than I am—one of the many reasons I'm glad God blessed me with great tits.

So this guy, Crowe. He caught my eye. He knows how to look at a girl and make her feel alive. I finally got his attention—no easy task, since he was a little stoned and ambivalent to what was going down around him—but once I had it, he looked me over all the way from my head down to my toes, not missing an inch in between. His eyes lingered in this way that said he liked what he saw. It was the way a guy looks at a girl when he knows what to do with her.

Anyway, he was there with this friend who lives in the house, and initially his friend was putting on the moves, and I think that's why Crowe wouldn't give me the time of day. But I can be pretty persuasive. We did snakebites with the salt, lime, and tequila. When I put the salt on my stomach for his shot, his tongue circled my navel before dipping under the waistband of my jeans. Before the end of the night, we were trashed and making out in the corner.

I didn't sleep with him. I thought about it, but we didn't have an opportunity. He said he'd see me around, so maybe next time. If I see him again...

CHAPTER 8
SEBASTIAN

"Women's studies?" Mason says from behind me.

I fold my schedule and shove it into my back pocket before turning to face him. The locker room bustles with the energy of the first day of classes. We're all ready to get back to it, because back to class means that our first game is coming, and after a summer of beating each other up on the field, we're more than ready to pound an opposing team. "Do you make a habit of reading over people's shoulders?"

"Women's studies at nine with Scheck?" Keegan asks.

"Yeah." Why are these guys suddenly so interested in my schedule? Jesus. I don't want to take the fucking class, but it fulfills my multicultural elective, and I'm trying to stay on track to graduate on time—not an easy task as a transfer student.

"Me too," Keegan says with an approving nod in my direction.

He finishes tying his shoes before pointing at me. "Great way to pick up chicks."

"That is not why I'm taking the class, and it had better not be why *you're* fucking taking it."

Keegan just grins. He has a baby-daddy thing going on with my sister, but his days of being scared that I'll kick his ass are behind us. Mostly because Olivia handled the whole pregnancy thing terribly, trying to convince everyone that the baby was Chris's before she revealed the truth. "If you're wondering when I'm going to make an honest woman of your sister, you need to ask her that."

I sigh. I'm well aware of how ridiculous Olivia is being about this whole situation, and honestly, I feel for Keegan. "Just take it easy on the whole 'picking up chicks' thing until my niece or nephew is born, okay?"

"It's an elective." Keegan punches me in the arm.

"Picking up chicks is an elective?" Mason asks. "I thought it was your major."

"Women's studies is an elective, asshole," Keegan says with a grin. "Maybe it was *once* my major, but I've changed my ways."

"It's an elective for me too," I say. "The multicultural contemporary art class I was supposed to take at the same time was canceled for low enrollment."

Keegan slings his backpack over his shoulder. "I heard that Scheck gives an easy A to any guy who calls himself a feminist on the first day."

Mason arches a brow at Keegan. "You're a feminist? *You?*"

Keegan puts his hand on his heart. "Women are very important to me, from their pretty heads to their toes to everything in between."

"Women's *rights,* not their parts, idiot," I mutter. I grab my bag and head for the door.

Mason follows me. "So, your friend's nice. Quiet but sweet. She and Bailey sure are close."

It takes me a minute to figure out who he's talking about—not because Alex isn't on my mind all the fucking time, but because as special as she is to me, I spent the whole morning and all of last night thinking of her in every way except *friend.* "She and Bailey knew each other in high school, I guess."

"Yeah. They're going shopping later or something."

This surprises me. I don't know why. Bailey is nice enough, but she's kind of over the top, which is exactly the opposite of Alex. Bailey can be loud and brash and...

And a whole lot like Martina.

"So you and Alex?" Mason asks.

"Friends," I say, contradicting my own thought from minutes before.

"Mm-hmm," Mason says. He's not buying it, but it'll be clear soon enough. If Alex were mine, I wouldn't hide it. Hell, I'd keep her so close, no one would have to ask what we were to each other. "You enjoy that women's studies class. I'll see you at practice tonight."

ALEXANDRA

"Welcome to Introduction to Women's Studies," the woman at the front of the class says. "My name is Dr. Scheck, and I'll be your guide through this course." She surveys the class, and I like her already. Her loose, silky top and scarf are paired with skinny jeans and heels, and she has an easy smile. "As this is an introductory class," she says, "you'll find that the course requirements aren't terribly stringent. Above all else, I want you to keep an open mind to the concepts we'll cover over the semester, show up to class regularly and on time, and participate in the discussion. I'll admit I have a bit of a pet peeve about tardiness, and being punctual is the best way to stay on my good side."

As if on cue, the door at the front of the room opens to a duo of tardy students.

I'd like to pretend that I'm mature and enlightened enough that I wouldn't be surprised to see anyone walk into an introductory women's studies seminar. But apparently I'm neither enlightened nor mature, because when I see Sebastian come through the doorway with one of his too-broad-for-his-T-shirt football buddies in tow, I burst into a giggle-snort that comes out way louder than I expect, and Dr. Scheck levels her stern gaze on me before turning to the guys.

"I was just telling the class how important punctuality is to me," she says.

"I apologize," Sebastian says. He exchanges a glance with his buddy. "We were looking at the room on Keegan's schedule and didn't realize it had been changed."

"I'm a feminist," the other guy—Keegan—announces, flashing a grin that is so charming I can feel its full wattage three rows back.

Dr. Scheck arches a brow. "Good to know." She motions to the empty chairs on either side of the aisle, and one is next to mine. "We saved you seats, gentlemen."

Sebastian spots me on his way to the seats, and when Keegan turns to take the desk beside me, Sebastian puts a hand on his shoulder and turns him toward the opposite side of the aisle. Keegan looks from me to Sebastian, and his eyes go wide in understanding—though of what, I'm not sure.

"Right." He smirks at Sebastian and speaks low. "Of course you'd want to sit by your *friend*."

The implication in his voice embarrasses me so much that I pretend to study my notebook while Sebastian slides his backpack off and takes his seat.

I try to keep my focus on the professor, but Sebastian must have just showered, because his hair's a little wet at the base of his neck and he smells so damn good I want to lean closer. Dr. Scheck goes over the course syllabus, her policies, and the major tests and projects for the semester. Next to me, Sebastian leans back in his chair, his legs spread so wide his knee brushes mine when I shift.

Seriously, is he planning to sit next to me every day? How am I going to make it through an entire semester with him so close?

I curl my fingers around the top of my notebook, and when I sneak a glance at him, he catches me and winks.

Holy hell. I'm done for. Doesn't he know I'm trying to move on? To get over him?

No. Of course he doesn't, because that would involve him knowing how I feel about him to begin with.

CHAPTER 9
SEBASTIAN

Alex smiles up at me after Dr. Scheck dismisses the class. "Women's studies, huh?"

"Don't start. It's one of those semesters where I just have to knock out my liberal arts requirements."

She hums and bites back a smile. "You're sure you're not doing it to pick up chicks?"

Fuck Keegan and every immature little boy like him. "I swear to you, I'm not taking women's studies to pick up chicks."

I could beat myself up for sitting next to Alex when I need to keep my distance, but what was I supposed to do? Let Keegan sit next to her and flash her that "I'm a charming doofus" smile the girls seem to go mad for? Hell no.

I can sit by her without crossing any lines. I'm just being a good friend—to Dante, who's worried about his little sister fitting in at BHU, and to Alex, who's always a little nervous in social situations. I can be her friend without hurting her, and I will be for as long as she needs me. I owe her so much more than that.

We file out of the lecture hall and into the bright, sunny day, where humidity smacks me in the face. I can't wait for the cooler temps of autumn to come around.

"Where are you headed after this?" I ask Alex.

"I have a short break, actually. What about you?"

"Same. Want to grab a drink?" I mentally kick myself as soon as I ask, because grabbing coffee with Alex is *not* in the plans.

"Did someone just suggest alcohol?" someone says. I turn my head to see Bailey sidestepping her way through the throng of students to get closer to us. "The bar around the corner from the College of Business opens in fifteen."

I grunt. "I was thinking coffee or a bottle of water."

Bailey throws her arm around Alex's shoulders, and Alex grins. It's good to see her so comfortable with my friends. And maybe a little dangerous, too.

"My breakfast hasn't fully digested yet and I have class in an hour," Alex says. "So maybe I'll stick with Sebastian's suggestion."

"Pfft." Bailey waves a hand. "First rule of college: It's never too early for alcohol."

"That bad already?" I ask her.

Bailey nods. "Fucking terrible. The idiot adjunct teaching my chem lab used to frequent the Pretty Kitty, so of course he's already formed an opinion of my abilities." She turns to Alex. "You know those chauvinist men who assume your intelligence is conversely related to your hotness, and so they discount everything that comes out of your brain just because you're a babe?"

Alex clears her throat. "Can't say I've ever had that problem."

Bailey looks to me and arches a brow. "She doesn't have a clue that she's smoking hot, does she?"

"Not the slightest," I agree, enjoying the way Alex's cheeks turn pink and her lips curl into a delicate smile. Fuck all the complications of her being back in my life—seeing that smile on a daily basis isn't gonna suck.

Alex tugs on her scarf, and Bailey sighs. "Just take it off, girl."

It's hot as fuck out here. Summer seems determined to hang on for dear life and blast us with everything it's got. Alex is wearing short sleeves, but she has to be hot with that cloth wrapped around her neck.

I nod. "You should."

"It's not just the way people look at me." She fans herself with the sheer material. "It's the questions."

"You don't owe anyone explanations."

She meets my eyes and pauses for a beat before unlooping it from her neck and pulling it off.

Bailey hoots and holds up her fist for me to bump in victory.

Alex lifts her hand to her neck then drops it.

"You look beautiful," I say.

Alex keeps her eyes averted and murmurs a soft "thanks," but Bailey looks right at me, and her smirk tells me she sees far more than I want her to.

But then her smirk falls away and she whispers, "Incoming!"

I turn just in time to see the redhead from Friday night

rushing toward me before she wraps her arms around my neck and kisses me on the mouth.

ALEXANDRA

I hold up the black dress Bailey brought me and look at her skeptically. "This?"

Bailey climbs onto a stool by the service counter and nods. "Oh, yeah."

The dress is simple, a stretchy black cotton number without embellishment. That part is great. Totally my style. The only problem is, there's not much to it. Bailey's shorter than me, and I can't imagine the skirt even hits her mid-thigh, and let's just say the cut of the top means a full-coverage bra is out of the question.

"You're joking, right?"

She looks offended. "I never joke about fashion."

"It's going to show…everything."

She smirks. "Not everything. Just enough." Her gaze narrows in on my neck, and I realize I'm holding my hand over my scar. Well, part of it. "Stop worrying about that. You're hot. You have scars, but they do nothing to take away from your foxiness. In fact, they might just add to it."

"Yeah, right."

"*Trust. Me.* You're hot. Quit hiding. You wear this dress to the Cavern and there will be male eyes on you for all the right reasons."

"Can't we take baby steps?"

"I'm a believer in full immersion." She puts a pair of high-heeled red Mary Janes on the counter next to a pair of black, strappy wedge sandals. "As for shoes, the choice is yours."

I groan, but her attention has left me and settled on the glass doors at the front of the shop. I follow her gaze to the guy pushing into the waiting room. Tall and lean, with dark hair and a thick shadow of stubble across his strong jaw, he has a young Hugh Jackman vibe going on. He's wearing crisp black slacks, a button-up shirt and tie, and a pair of dark sunglasses that he slides off as he approaches the counter.

He smiles at Bailey. "Hey, girl."

A hot guy walks into the shop, and Bailey knows him. Why am I not surprised?

She returns his smile, but it's not the usual happy-go-lucky Bailey smile. "Hi, Logan. Long time no see." She points to me. "This is my friend, Alexandra. This is Logan Lucas, an old friend. What are you doing in town, Logan?"

"I moved back," he says. "My brother and I are opening a new bar."

"Seriously? Where?"

"We bought the building by the Cavern."

"*You're* the one opening The Lemon Rind? That's awesome. I'm excited about that place." She skims her eyes over him, but the gesture is more assessing than sexual. "It's really good to know you're doing so well."

He nods, and I wonder what it is they're not saying, what shared history they have that's made the mood in the room go from fun and easy, when we were talking about the dress, to somber, when Logan walked in the door.

They don't say anything else to give me any hints, but the moment ends when Logan turns his smile to me. "I got a call that my car was ready. Logan Lucas, the white Shelby."

I gape at him. Hot guy drives an even hotter car. "She's yours? Crazy sweet ride."

"The sweetest." He grins. "I don't typically have a temper, but you should have seen me when that asshole hit it. How hard is it to back out of a parking space? He rammed right into it with me standing there. Not one of my finer moments." He shakes his head and looks out the window to where the car is parked. "Anyway, it's good to see her back to her old self."

"She's good as new. I hope you don't mind I checked out her engine. She must be one hell of a ride."

His grin grows wide. "You like cars?"

"I like cars like yours." I turn to grab his keys off the wall, and when I turn back to him, I catch him staring at me. At my ass, actually. Which is…unexpected.

He lifts his eyes to meet mine. "You should take her for a drive sometime."

As much as I love the idea of getting behind the wheel of a '65 Shelby, I'm pretty sure he's only saying that to be nice. I mean, like *ninety-percent sure*, but his eyes definitely make me wonder. My cheeks warm as I hand over the keys. "Mr. Crowe said there was no charge."

"No, let me pay. I want to."

I turn my palms up. "I couldn't charge you if I wanted to. I don't have an invoice."

He shakes his head. "I should have known he'd pull something like this. I'll make it up to him somehow." Pocketing his keys, he studies me for another beat before pulling a business card from his pocket and placing it on the counter. "So you know where to find me in case you want to take me up on my offer." He waves goodbye to Bailey and backs toward the front door with his eyes on me. He stops before pushing outside and points to the shoes still resting on the counter. "I'd go with the red ones."

Then he pushes outside, leaving me with hot cheeks and that nervous, fidgety feeling in my stomach.

"Tell me you're going to tap that."

I swing around to Bailey, who innocently twirls a lock of blond hair around her finger. "You didn't just say that."

"It's adorable that you think I need to give you a makeover so guys notice you. Logan noticed you the second he set eyes on you, and let's not even start with the way Sebastian looks at you."

My warm cheeks kick up a notch closer to *inferno* at the mention of Sebastian. Yesterday he called me beautiful, and seconds later, a gorgeous girl had her tongue down his throat. It was almost like the universe was trying to remind me where I stood.

I change the subject. "Logan seems nice." I'm not completely naïve. I know guys find me attractive, but when they don't see much of my scarring, I always feel as if I'm misleading them. It's like I can't trust that anyone thinks I'm pretty until after they see the whole not-so-pretty picture, and to date, no one but my doctors have. "Is he?"

"What?"

"Is he nice? You seemed to know each other."

She shrugs. "Honestly, I never knew him that well, but he was tight with Nic Mendez."

"Mendez?" I frown, trying to place the name. "Mia's brother?"

She nods and picks at her nails. "Yeah. He died last year." That explains the somber tone when they talked to each other. She lifts her gaze to mine, and I recognize the sadness there. It's the kind of sadness you feel when you lose part of yourself. I recognize it because I've experienced it. I wouldn't wish that feeling on anyone.

"I'm sorry, Bailey. I had no idea."

She hops off the stool. "Me too. But I'm starting to figure out that life isn't fucking fair, and this is no different." She slings her purse over her shoulder. "I'll see you at the game Saturday, then we'll get ready for the party together?"

I nod and watch as she heads out the door. "Bailey," I say, stopping her. "Thanks for doing this. It's really nice of you."

"It's fun," she says, and it's good to see her smile after watching sadness fill her eyes when she talked about Nic. "I'd much rather focus on your problems than my own, anyway."

CHAPTER 10
SEBASTIAN

I have a beautiful, blue-eyed brunette who won't get off my mind, a redhead who thinks making out at Trent's last weekend was some sort of marriage proposal, and a father who may or may not be using company funds for illegal activities. Usually, it's a couple of weeks into the semester before I feel stressed, but this semester is going to be special.

After my last class on Monday, I head over to Mom and Dad's. I texted Dante this morning, and he still hasn't been paid. He said it's no big deal, but his reassurances do nothing for this anxiety gnawing at my gut every time I think about it.

Dad hasn't spent much time at the shop lately. He's been handing over more responsibility to Dante and only coming in to take care of the books. I don't have any problem with him delegating more and working less, but I hate not knowing what he's up to—as if he's my wayward child whom I need to keep in line. He's not the kind of guy to laze around the house, so I know he's filling his time somehow, and the whole money situation is far too fucking familiar for comfort.

When I walk in the front door, I'm relieved to find Dad in the living room with Mom. They're curled together on the couch, watching an old movie. She's wrapped in an afghan and has her head tucked under his arm. The sight makes me stop and take a breath. I don't know what I expected to see—I'd rather not analyze that—but I'm grateful for moments like these. I'm grateful for all evidence that the dark days are behind us.

I clear my throat so they know I'm in the room.

Mom looks up first. "Bash, you're home. Don't you have practice tonight?"

I do. In fact, I need to make this quick with Dad so I can get back to campus and be on the field by six. "I just need to talk to Dad for a minute." Her brow wrinkles, and I give her my best reassuring smile. "Just work stuff, Mom."

She pulls out of Dad's embrace, and he grumbles something I can't make out as he climbs off the couch. I nod to the back doors and head to the deck, since I want to be able to talk without Mom overhearing.

Dad follows me and closes the door behind himself.

"Dante didn't get paid on Friday," I say. As if he can see my ugly fears, Dad stiffens. *Fuck.* I take a deep breath and recite my prepared speech. "I think it's time to look at the budget, Dad. We should be able to pay everyone. Business is steady."

"Everything costs more these days. Never mind all the

government disposal regulations and fees," he grumbles.

I clench my fists and look up at the watercolor evening sky. Soon the leaves on the trees will match the yellows and reds of the sunset. The evidence that life goes on isn't as comforting tonight as usual. Instead of the view making me itch to grab my camera, it makes me wonder if everything really does come back around—the sun, the seasons, our worst mistakes. "I know, but we should still be able to pay what we owe."

"We *will*, Sebastian. Dante knows this is temporary."

"I want to pay everyone what they're owed *when they're owed it*. That's the kind of business we run."

"Dante was very understanding when I told him money was tight this month."

"Yes. Because he's like family. But that doesn't mean we should take advantage of it." I have two more years of school left here, and the truth is, I've always been afraid the business might fall apart when I leave. Even if I don't get to play pro ball, I'll need to get a job, and I can't see sticking around Blackhawk Valley. The truth is, I don't have the time to hold the business together over the next two years. Football keeps me busier than a part-time job, then there are study tables, and my classes, which are going to be more challenging than ever this year. I'm irrationally frustrated that Dad hasn't figured out a better way to manage cash flow, and I'm frustrated with myself for imagining the worst. "I just want to take a look at some of the new vendors. Maybe switching brands can save the business on expenses here and there." *I want to make sure you're not skimming money off the books. I* need *to know you haven't fallen into trouble again.*

His chest puffs out and he tilts up his chin. "You planning on buying the business off me and running it yourself?"

I flinch. This is an old fight, and instead of addressing the problem at hand, he's going to pick at a scab. "You know that's not my plan," I say softly.

"Then back off. It's my business, and I have it under control."

I open my mouth but decide not to fight. He's made up his mind, and at the end of the day, if cash flow is a problem and he can't pay Dante, seeing that for myself in the numbers isn't going to change anything. And if this sick feeling in my stomach means Dad's taking money from the business to get something else going…

I can't think about it. Going straight after years of meddling in the dark side was a battle, and I don't know if my dad could survive it again. Unless I have a reason to believe he's dealing, I need to trust him—for the sake of our relationship and my sanity.

"Just let me know if I can help," I say, shoving my hands into my pockets.

"You can, actually. I'm running to Chicago on Friday and I want you to check on your sister."

"A day trip to Chicago?" So much for putting my suspicions to rest. "Why?" It's not a short drive.

"There's a musical Mom wants to see. That *Hamilton* all the kids are talking about."

"*You* are driving to Chicago to see *Hamilton*?" It doesn't surprise me that Mom's interested. I guess I'm just surprised that

Dad's willing to humor her—never mind spend the money on the tickets.

"Happy wife, happy life," he says.

"I'll check on Liv," I say. I want to ask where he got money for the tickets if he can't afford to pay Dante for his work. I want to demand that he promise me he doesn't have any other business in Chicago.

I want to go back in time and tell my father that no matter how bad things are, it's not worth it.

"She's taking her pregnancy pretty hard," Dad says. "What do you think about the father?"

"Keegan?" Wincing at the way I unintentionally made it a question, I scratch my head. I don't want to get involved. Olivia's pregnancy and the way Keegan handled it made me respect Keegan off the field for the first time since I met him. My sister's an idiot, and Keegan has every right to walk away after her lies and manipulations. Instead, he's doing his best to stick around, even as Liv tries to push him away. "He's fine. He'll do right by her if she'll let him."

"Poor guy's trapped," Dad says, shaking his head. "She shouldn't have fucking gotten pregnant."

That is so quintessentially my father. Even when it comes to his own daughter, the pregnancy is entirely the woman's fault. "I think Liv feels pretty trapped right now too."

"She'll be fine," Dad says. "I'll take care of her."

My stomach twists. If the business falls apart, he won't be in a position to take care of Liv. I study Dad's face and wish I could ask the question I need to ask. *Are you dealing again?* But I can't. I'm too afraid of the answer.

Chris closes his laptop and takes a deep breath. "We should have this."

"We do. Absolutely." I bump his shoulder with my fist. I wish he weren't so stressed about making this a winning season, but I also know that the team gets its strength from Chris's calm leadership and high expectations.

"You're going to destroy them," Bailey says from Chris's kitchen. I'm pretty sure she spends most of her free time hanging out with Mason, who shares this apartment with Chris.

It's Wednesday, three days until BHU will play its first game of the season. Chris and I spent the last two hours watching our opponents' games from last year, identifying their weaknesses and strategizing ways to tackle their strengths. We did it with the team and the new head coach last week, but when Chris asked me if I'd come review them again with him tonight, I saw it as the perfect opportunity to put off packing my bags and telling my parents I had to move home by the end of the month.

"Sorry for keeping you so late," Chris says, looking at his watch. "Fuck. You probably wanted to see Alex tonight."

Bailey snorts. "I'm *sure* he did."

"She's just a friend," I explain to Chris.

His eyes go wide in surprise. "Sorry. I thought…"

"That's what everyone thinks," Bailey tells Chris.

I groan. "Why is it so surprising I have a female friend?"

Chris and Bailey exchange a look, and Chris bites back a grin. "Nah, it's not surprising. I just misunderstood."

"We like her, Bash," Bailey says. "She's really sweet. Now that Grace is back to New York and Mia's so busy playing house with Arrow, I've decided I'm adopting Alex."

Chris's phone rings, and he grins down at it. "Speak of the devil." He swipes his screen. "Hey, gorgeous."

"Hi, Grace!" Bailey shouts in Chris's direction before filling her wine glass.

Chris stands and covers the receiver. "She says hi, but I'm going to take this in my room. Night, Sebastian. I'll see you in the morning."

I follow his lead and stand from the couch. "Sleep well."

Chris heads down the hall to his bedroom, and Bailey holds up her wine glass. "You want some?"

"I need to get out of here anyway." I toss my beer bottle in the recycling bin under the counter. "I should start packing so I don't have to do it all on Sunday."

"Packing?" Bailey says. "Where are you going?"

"Fuck. Home, I guess." Not that I want to. I already work for my dad; having him looking over my shoulder all the time would be worse. "My roommate totally flaked on the lease, and now I don't have anywhere to stay. If he'd given me some notice, I might have been able to find a new roommate or an apartment I could afford on my own, but it turns out he's not just a lazy slob, he's also an inconsiderate asshole. I've asked around, and no one needs a roommate, and I don't really have time to find one."

Bailey studies me for a minute, thoughtful, and I'm convinced she's going to suggest a potential roommate when she says, "You can move in with me."

"You're serious?"

"Um, yeah. I quit shaking my ass for money. I need all the help I can get. I have a second bedroom, and I hate most girls too much to live with them." Topping off her wine, she grins. "I mean, you have to walk around shirtless all the time and bring me coffee in bed." When I arch a brow, she rolls her eyes. "I'm joking about the coffee in bed. But yes, I'm serious about you moving in with me."

"Why?"

She ticks reasons off on her fingers. "I know you. You're normal. You have good personal hygiene. You're not going to come on to me. You're responsible, and you're no drama llama. Oh, and you're nice to look at. In other words, you're my ideal roommate."

I fold my arms and rock back on my heels. "Why do you assume I'm not going to come on to you?"

She takes a long pull of her wine and hums, avoiding my gaze. "I just know."

"How, exactly?" She's right, after all, but I find her confidence in the matter surprising. Bailey's hot in the most obvious way. Long blond hair, curves, and a wicked sense of humor. And though she's right not to worry about me hitting on her, because I just don't see her that way, I'm curious why she would be so sure. "Bailey?"

She swirls her wine in her glass before lifting her eyes to meet mine. "Because, Sebastian Crowe, you're in love with someone else."

I frown, and in the back of my mind I hear the warning blare of distant sirens. "Where did you get that idea?"

Sighing, she walks around the island and gives my cheek a light smack. "If you don't want everyone to know, you should probably stop looking at her like she's half angel sent from heaven, half walking wet dream."

Martina's Journal

I went to that house again, looking for Crowe. I tried to play it cool, but his friend laughed at me and shook his head when I asked about him. He laughed, said Crowe was busy, and that a little girl like me shouldn't mess with a guy like him.

Seriously? Challenge accepted.

CHAPTER 11
SEBASTIAN

When I walk into the Commons on Thursday afternoon, my eyes immediately land on Alex. I swear we could be in a crowded room with thousands of people, and if she were within a hundred yards of me, I'd spot her. Women's studies is on Monday, Wednesday, and Friday, so I don't get to spend time with her on Tuesday and Thursday unless we run into each other at the shop. Seeing her now feels so damn good it's almost like relief.

I walk over to her. She's scribbling in a notebook and biting her bottom lip, as if she's thinking hard. A lock of hair falls in her face, and I have to tuck my hands into my pockets to keep myself from tucking it behind her ear.

"Can I interrupt?" I pull out the chair across from her and nod to her notebook. "What were you working on?"

She worries her bottom lip between her teeth. "I'm trying to keep a journal. It's something I started when I moved to Colorado, and trust me when I say I had plenty of time for journaling." She laughs. "Anyway, it's been good for me. It's helped me start to work through…" Her eyes flash to me and back down.

"The fire," I say.

She nods. "Yeah, and everything else."

"Well, I think that's cool. Keeping a journal, I mean. It's something you can look back on later."

She toys with her pen. "Martina was religious about it. Well…" She shifts. "She had periods where she wasn't as good about it, but before…she made it a priority. She was a great writer."

All the warmth I felt in my gut when I spotted her turns to cold stone. "Really?" I try to sound intrigued rather than panicked.

"She was a fanatic. When we were in middle school, she'd write in it twice a day. Less once we hit high school, and then more sporadically once she got wrapped up in…everything." She shakes her head. "She was so private about it, and sometimes I wonder if I'd have been able to help her change course if I'd sneaked a peek. Maybe I could have gotten her help sooner? Maybe everything would have been different?"

Her questions make my chest ache. "Don't do that to yourself."

"Don't worry." She shrugs. "I can't feel bad about not reading them. Those books were her space. We shared everything—a room, clothes, friends, even our car when we turned sixteen. She insisted that our diaries were our space and no one else's. We made a pinky promise that we'd never read the other's, and that we'd never let anyone else read them either."

I can't think about what might or might not be in Martina's journal. "You kept one too?"

"I wasn't very good about it. I have one partially filled book that covers six years, whereas she filled so many she has a full shelf in our bedroom lined with hers."

Not all of them. The rock in the pit of my stomach crumbles and digs into my gut like gravel embedded in a flesh wound.

"I'll read them someday. Maybe." She shakes her head as if to clear away the thoughts. "Sorry. I didn't mean to bring you down."

"You don't need to apologize for talking about your sister." *Even if it ties me in knots. Even if it makes me want to choke on guilt and regret.*

"Yeah. I know. But I'm trying to move on—not leave her behind, just move forward." She lifts her palms up and pastes on a smile. "And that's why I'm here having the real college experience."

I laugh. "The real college experience is living in a one-bedroom apartment with three other people who get on your nerves and one bathroom that always smells like shit. A million-dollar mansion on the swanky side of town doesn't compare." Bailey told me about Alex's housesitting arrangement, and as much as I hate the idea of her living in that big house alone, I understand why she took the opportunity to live away from home.

"Ah, but a girl can dream, can't she? I'm sure I'll get my turn at the stinky apartment too."

"God willing." I take a breath, glad for the change of subject. "Are you working tonight?"

She shakes her head. "Nope. I have the night off."

"I'm hanging out at Chris and Mason's after practice. Do you want to come?"

She folds her arms. "Why do you assume I'm available? Maybe I have a date."

I flinch at that slap to the face. I don't like thinking of Alex dating anyone, because dates lead to kissing and kissing leads to touching. And touching leads to... *Shit.* "Anyone I know?"

"I said *maybe* I have a date."

I frown. "So you don't?"

She shrugs. "You've been awesome, Sebastian, but I don't want you feeling like you have to hang out with me."

"Are you going to give me that *pity friendship* line again?"

"Come on. Did we ever hang out in high school? Other than doing projects for class, did we ever go to the movies or have mutual friends? You were my friend. I considered you a *good* friend, but I had no idea who you were when you weren't in class. I still don't." She shakes her head. "It's fine. I appreciate you introducing me to Mia and your sister and the guys, but I don't need you to babysit me."

I want to object. I want to tell her how much *I* want her around, how much I love just being close to her. But I keep my mouth shut.

When the girl you need to keep your distance from pushes you away, let her.

∽

Fuck. Fuck. Fuck.

The game should have been in the bag, and we almost lost it. Mason has better ball control than every other wide receiver on this team—better than ninety percent of the guys in the Big Ten, honestly—so his first fumble was completely out of character. The second was unheard of. I'm just glad I was there to land on it before the other team could get the turnover.

Mason's fuming in the locker room at halftime. I walk over to him and tap him on the shoulder. "Shake it off."

"Fuck you." Standing, he puffs out his chest and takes a step toward me, his jaw hard. He's been giving me the cold shoulder all day, but I figured he was just stressed about school or something. Suddenly, I'm realizing this isn't just Mason having a bad day. I've pissed him off somehow, and maybe if I didn't have so much of my own shit going on, I'd feel bad about that. But as it is, I don't have time or the energy for his bullshit.

"Mason," Chris says, warning in his tone.

I hold up my hands. "Whoa. What's the problem?"

Keegan snorts from his seat in front of the lockers. "Jesus, Crowe, you're not really that clueless."

I look at the anger in Mason's eyes, to the sympathy in Chris's, to the amusement in Keegan's. Something's going on, and apparently every-fucking-body but me knows about it.

Chris shifts his eyes to meet mine and holds my gaze for a

beat before he says, "Bailey."

I'm confused for a minute—what about her?—but then I see the hurt on Mason's face, and instead of being irritated at his moodiness, it clicks, and I feel like a complete dick. "This is about me moving in with Bailey?"

Mason doesn't answer, but he doesn't look at me, and I can see the truth in the set of his jaw.

"Well, fuck." I shake my head. "I didn't even think about it, but Mase, I swear it's not like that. I'm renting a room from her. There's nothing between us."

"Whatever." Mason gives me his back and throws his towel into his locker. "It doesn't fucking matter anyway."

Chris is still staring at me, his eyes delivering his message loud and clear: *Make this right.*

If we're going to win this game, we need Mason to have his head on straight, it's true. But for Chris, it's more than that. Mason's his roommate and one of his best friends. This isn't just about football. It's personal.

I lean against the lockers next to where Mason's standing, and fold my arms. "It's better this way," I say softly. "Any other guy might have gone in there and tried to hook up with her, but you know me. That's not what I'm about. I respect Bailey, and I respect you. I'm not going to come between you two because I'm not interested in her that way."

Without looking at me, Mason slams his locker shut and leans his head against the red metal door. "I have no right to be jealous or territorial. I fucking know that."

"Five minutes!" Coach calls from the other side of the locker room.

Mason's got it bad for Bailey, and she won't commit to him. Last spring, he told her he didn't want to mess around anymore. He wanted her to be his girlfriend or nothing. He got nothing. No one knows what's keeping Bailey from giving him a chance. They're still great friends, and as far as we can tell she's not sleeping with anyone else—even if she likes to pretend she gets around.

"Mason," I say, waiting for him to look at me.

When Mason turns around, the anger in his face has faded. "Not right now, okay?"

"Are you good?" Chris asks him, and Mason nods. "Then let's go win this game."

CHAPTER 12
ALEXANDRA

"Fuck this," Bailey mutters. She chews on her nails and stares down to where the BHU marching band is making their way onto the field. "Mason never fumbles. Something's up with him."

My stomach is in knots. For someone who's never cared much about football or sports of any kind, my visceral reaction to this game surprises me. Judging by the look on Bailey's face, and the way she's holding her stomach, I'm not alone.

"Maybe he's just having an off day," Mia says from the other side of me.

"Yeah." Bailey shakes her head as if to clear out the worry. "Yeah, he'll be fine after halftime."

"Alexandra? Is that you?" I look up to see Logan Lucas, owner of the super-hot '65 Shelby, standing on the bleacher stairs. He steps into the empty row in front of us to face me. "It's great to see you here."

I'm immediately aware of my exposed scars, and I lift my hand to cover the skin at the base of my throat. "Hi. How are you?"

Grinning, he takes my hand from my neck and kisses my knuckles. "Better now." Maybe from any other guy, this move paired with that line would be awkward or over the top, but Logan's smooth enough to pull it off somehow. "You never called."

I turn to look at Bailey, whose raised eyebrow and pursed lips communicate her *I told you so* as clearly as if she said it out loud.

"Sorry." Logan pulls my attention back to him. He sighs heavily and squeezes my fingertips once before releasing my hand. "I have a weakness for beautiful women who know their cars."

"No, it's fine. I've just been busy."

He arches a brow, and I know he doesn't believe that's the reason I haven't been in touch, but he lets it go and waves to Bailey. "You having an okay night?"

She looks at the scoreboard. "Could be better."

"They'll get it together for the second half," Mia says, but she doesn't look convinced.

"I have faith in these guys." Logan looks out at the field before turning his gaze back to me. "Alexandra, my offer stands." With a wink, he walks away, and my stomach does a soft little flutter. That's gotta be a good sign, right? Sebastian's been the only guy capable of eliciting that reaction in me since I was sixteen years old, but here's this sweet guy with fabulous taste in cars who not only seems to genuinely like me, but he makes me *feel* something. Maybe I'm not ruined after all.

Mia leans over Bailey's lap and gives me a wide-eyed stare. "What was *that*?"

Bailey answers before I can. "Logan Lucas wants to wine, dine, and make sweet love to her, and she's not interested."

I gape. "Bailey!"

"And you're not interested, because…?" Mia asks.

Bailey smirks. "I don't blame you, chica. I personally prefer *fucking* to *making love*, so I can see why you might hold out for someone a little more…" She clears her throat, pausing as the crowd erupts into cheers. She shifts her gaze to the sideline, where the Blackhawks are filing back onto the field. "Dominant."

Sebastian turns toward the bleachers and looks right at us. His helmet's in his hand by his side so we can see the smile on his face.

"Oh," Mia says. "I *see*."

Sebastian lifts his empty hand to wave.

"See what?" I ask, not bothering to pull my gaze from Sebastian. Because *damn*. Tight pants and shoulder pads have never looked so good, and having all that beautiful male attention coming at me makes me all gushy inside.

I have to remember what I promised myself: No pining after Sebastian Crowe. I'm home, but I'm moving on. *Remember the redhead.*

"I don't want Sebastian." Maybe if I say it enough, it will be true. "I might call Logan."

"I like the way Logan calls you *Alexandra*," Mia says. "Both times he said it, I kind of expected your clothes to magically fall off."

"It is pretty hot. But then again, so is the way Sebastian looks at you." Bailey grins. "Seriously, this is like choosing between the triple-fudge brownie sundae and the apple crisp a la mode. There's no wrong answer."

There is if the triple brownie sundae doesn't want me back.

"Are you Martina DeLuca's sister?"

All three of us turn to the painfully thin girl who steadies her critical gaze on me.

I swallow. "Yeah."

She screws up her face in disgust as she stares at my neck. "I'd heard you'd come back, but I didn't want to believe it. A word of advice? Leave before God punishes you worse than he punished your sister. This town doesn't need your drugs."

The crowd erupts into cheers as the team lines up for kickoff, and I can only stare at the girl. She wipes her hands on her jeans and wanders away as if she didn't just stab me in the heart with her nastiness.

"What the *fuck*?" Bailey says, standing.

I grab her arm before she can go after her. "Don't."

"Someone needs to set her straight." Indignation colors her face, and I hold her tighter. She might be small, but right now all five feet, two inches of her is boiling with rage. "People said shit like that to Mia about Nic." She yanks her hand from my grip. "The *bitch*."

"We can't control what people think," Mia says, and even though her voice is fighting for calm, I can hear that she's shaken. "We can only control what we do."

"Don't worry about it," I say. "I'm fine." I fold my hands in my lap, hoping to hide the shaking.

There's so much I don't know about Martina's life in the year before the fire, and sometimes I'm not sure I ever want to find out.

Martina's Journal

I found Crowe. There's this old warehouse on the south end of town, and I heard rumors that there are big parties there sometimes. I figured, what better place to find a bad boy than in the thick of trouble?

Sure enough, there he was, and he tensed when he saw me. Someone must have told him how young I am, because he tried to shrug me off. But I'm persistent, and I managed to play it cool and hang near him all night, and when the party turned up a notch and he was stoned, I put my mouth on his ear and whispered exactly what I wanted to do to him.

He gave me that slow stoner grin and asked me if I liked to party. When I said yes, he told me to open my mouth. He put this little pill on my tongue that melted and made me feel alive. Like every cell in my body was waking up for the first time.

Dancing wasn't just dancing anymore. It was an experience. And when he kissed my neck, I could feel it everywhere. His hands were in my hair and under my clothes, and it was fucking bliss...until he got called away.

I'm grounded now because Mom knows I missed curfew. Alex usually covers for me, but she went to a friend's house, so she wasn't around to make the usual excuses. Fuck it. It was worth it.

CHAPTER 13
SEBASTIAN

She's drunk. Sweet, innocent, ultimate good girl Alex DeLuca is drunk and dancing on a table.

I wasn't going to go out tonight. Even though we pulled out the win, the game left me drained instead of energized, and tomorrow I need to finish packing for a move that suddenly seems foolish and impulsive. I'm pissed at myself for never considering Mason's feelings when I agreed to move in with Bailey. I was so fixated on finding a solution to my living situation that it honestly never crossed my mind.

I declined when Trent invited me to his house to party. I went back to the apartment, where I halfheartedly packed my car with boxes.

At half past ten, I was unpacking at Bailey's place when I got a text from Chris. *I know she's just a friend, but I thought you should know Alex is here at Trent's. It might not be a bad idea to come by and check on her.*

I expected to walk in the door and find Alex playing wallflower. Instead, she's easy to spot. Because there she is, standing in the middle of the pool table and swinging her hips to the music. Guys circle the table, talking and laughing, and a few are even shouting out suggestions that she "take it off."

She's wearing a silky tank top that I'm guessing was a layer beneath the BHU jersey she wore to the game. One strap is slipping off her shoulder. Part of me wants to stand here and just give myself a minute to take her in—the flush of her cheeks, the sensual sway of her hips, the curve of her rarely exposed neck, and the soft tendrils of hair that have escaped her long braid. The other part of me wants to stride across the room, scoop her off that table, and throw her over my shoulder to get her out of here.

"Glad you could make it," Chris says, clapping a hand on my back and nodding toward Alex. "I was worried about her."

"Whatever asshole thought it would be a good idea to bring her to this party and get her drunk is gonna get a piece of my mind," I mutter.

He clears his throat. "That would be me." My eyes go wide as I spin on him, and he throws up his hands. "She was walking by, and I invited her in. I was trying to be a good friend. I didn't expect…this."

Before I can decide what to do, Alex spots me across the sea of people, and her face lights up. That's what gets me—the way her half-mast eyes widen and the drunken smile turns big, all because she sees me.

"Sebastian!" She hops off the table and stumbles as she lands. A guy in a white ball cap steadies her, then takes his fucking time removing his hands once she's standing. She grins at him before stumbling in my direction. She's so toasted that her movements remind me of her sister, and the memory makes my chest ache. "What are you doing here?" she asks when she reaches me.

I open my mouth to tell her I'm here to take her home, but then I think better of it and shrug. I'm here now. She's safe. That's all that matters.

"I'll leave you alone now," Chris says before walking away.

"You look angry." Alex takes another step closer and lifts her face so she can study mine. "What's wrong?"

"You're drunk."

She lifts her arms and turns her palms up. "I'm in college. This is what you do in college."

"No, Alex. This is what *they* do, but not you."

"I can be like them."

"Why would you want to be?" I look around the party—drunk girls hanging on each other, guys slamming beers, a game of flippy cup in the corner. "You don't need this shit."

"Why do you always call me that?"

"What?" I don't remember calling her anything, but then again, she's trashed.

"*Alex.*"

I frown, my attention only half on her drunken rambles as I search the crowd for Bailey. I might have come here to take Alex home, but now I'm wondering how wise that is. She's so damn tempting and I'm not sure I trust myself. "That's your name."

"It's a boy's name, and it's fine, but I've never heard you call me *Alexandra*. It makes me wonder if you think of me as one of the guys."

That's so absurd that I actually laugh, when nothing about this night or this moment is funny.

"I don't want to be one of the guys to you, Bash."

That shuts me right up. I'm not laughing anymore, and I'm not scanning the faces in the crowd. I'm just looking at her. Wishing for more. "You're not." My voice is rough and hard.

"I don't believe you." Her hand settles on my chest, and her gaze settles on my mouth. Is that Alex or the alcohol? "Do you know what it was like to be her sister?"

The air leaves my lungs in a rush, as if I've just been tackled by a lineman who's been running at me for fifty yards. She doesn't have to say who *she* is, but I don't want to talk about Martina while Alex is touching me. Her hands skim over my chest to my shoulders, and her eyes focus intently on my mouth.

"I was always in her shadow. The plain to her gorgeous, the tomboy to her princess." Something crosses over her face, taking the joy of her buzz with it. "And now she's gone, and I'm not even allowed to resent her for it."

"Alex…"

The music changes, and she turns toward the sound. As if someone flipped a switch, all the sadness from seconds ago leaves her face and is replaced with a wide grin. "I *love* this song." Without warning, she steps closer, loops her arms behind my neck, and swings her hips.

I squeeze my eyes shut and fist my hands at my sides. She's so close and smells so good, and her breasts brush against me as she sways. I'm holding on by a thread here, doing all I can not to touch her.

She rises onto her toes and puts her mouth against my ear. "Do a drunk girl a favor and pretend this isn't a chore for you. Dance with me the way you'd dance with a beautiful girl."

"You *are* beautiful." It's a punch in the gut that she doesn't believe it, and a kick in the nuts that I might be responsible for her inability to see the truth.

Her fingers trail down my arms and wrap around each wrist. She moves my hands, positioning them on her hips. "I didn't say lie to me. I said dance with me. Or were you expecting your not-quite-a-kiss from two years ago to hold me over until I'm an old woman?"

She always avoids my eyes when we talk about that night, and now is no different, but I can see the bravado in her voice is at odds with the flush in her cheeks. The soft pink makes her skin glow, and I want it to be for me.

"There's something I can't figure out." I brush my thumbs over her hipbones because *damn,* they're *right there.*

"What's that?"

"The night before you left for Colorado…were you angry with me afterwards because I almost kissed you or because I didn't?" I'm trying to push her. To scare her away. To shock this drunk, touchy, so-close-it-hurts Alex into realizing I'm the trouble she doesn't need in her life.

But she surprises me by meeting my eyes. "Because you didn't." She drags a hand down my chest and holds my gaze. "Are you happy? I was mad because that night screwed with my head. You confused me and then you walked away, and it made me feel like I wasn't good enough."

My stomach twists. She has no idea how wrong she is, no idea how hard it was to walk away. "I'm sorry." I swallow the words I know I can't say. "For what it's worth. I'm sorry I made you feel that way."

Her gaze drops to my mouth. "Then make it up to me."

"Alex, you've been drinking, and—"

She puts her finger against my lips. "Tomorrow, I'll be back to worrying what people think about me and thinking I should stay far away from you and all the things you make me feel. Tomorrow, I'll be sober, and I won't have the courage to ask for what I want. *Please*, Sebastian?"

Swallowing hard, I let my fingers curl into her hips, and I pull her closer, sliding one hand up over her tank until I'm cupping the back of her neck.

Her lips part and she stills for a breath before speaking. "Was that so hard?"

"Touching you is never difficult. The hard part is letting go."

She blinks at me, confusion flashing in her eyes. I slide my thumb over her jaw, landing on the scar at the corner of her mouth. Her scars make her more beautiful somehow. They're a reminder of her bravery and the night that haunts us both. I trace the rough skin, following it over her chin and brushing across her neck. She flinches and pulls away.

That's where it is. All her insecurities are in those scars, but to me, they tell a story. A dark night and flames licking the clear, moonlit sky. She knew her sister was inside. She tried to save her and almost lost her own life in the process.

"Hey, Alexandra," some guy calls from a few feet away. "Is this guy giving you a hard time?"

She blinks at me before turning to the guy. "He's fine. He's an old friend." She lifts her hand and drops it before backing away.

"Perfect," the guy says. "So you can come dance with me now." The asshole runs his eyes over her as if she's a steak dinner he's ready to devour.

I step forward and pull her back into my arms. "She's busy."

"Just friends," she repeats, as if she's trying to convince herself.

"That's not all," I whisper against her mouth. "That's never been all." And I'm tired of pretending it is. I'm tired of pretending I haven't wanted her since the beginning, tired of pretending I'm glad I walked away two years ago when I've never stopped thinking about what would have happened if I hadn't.

When I touch my mouth to hers, I'm not sure who's more shocked. She gasps, and then she loops her arms behind my neck. Her lips are warm and sweet, and I've wanted to do this for so long that the logical part of my brain shuts down and I skim my tongue along the seam of her mouth. She moans softly as she parts her lips.

If a kiss could last forever, I'd want this one to. Because even though she's drunk and probably won't remember it, and even though we're surrounded by people and this isn't how I imagined it, I know this isn't just the first kiss we've shared. It has to be the last.

CHAPTER 14
ALEXANDRA

I wake up with a pounding head, a dry mouth, and a vague sense of self-loathing. I roll over in bed and reach for my cell phone on my nightstand so I can see what time it is.

But there's no nightstand, and I'm not in my room at home or the master bedroom at Mr. Patterson's.

I squint against the morning sun coming in the window. Where am I? I'm in a twin bed with a dark blue afghan on top of me—the kind my mom likes to crochet. There's a BHU poster on the wall and a stack of boxes in the corner. The closet is empty, but beside the bed there are three laundry baskets stacked full of neatly folded clothes.

I climb out of bed slowly so my head won't protest too much. I slept in my clothes. Well, that's a relief, at least. Waking up hung over in a strange place is bad enough. I'm glad I don't have to add *naked* to the description. When I open the door, I immediately recognize Bailey's living room.

Did she come to the party last night?

I hung out at the stadium talking to Mia after the game, but my heart was only half in it, so when Bailey and Mia said they were going to the Cavern to do karaoke, I begged off. I remember walking back to Mr. Patterson's, and I saw Chris on the front porch of that party house where I saw Sebastian last week. Chris said hi and invited me in. Maybe I was hoping to see Sebastian in there, or maybe I just wanted to grab a drink. The ugly words from the woman at the stadium felt like a dirty film on my skin, and I just wanted to wash them away.

But Sebastian wasn't there and neither was the redhead, and I kept thinking about how maybe they were together and how maybe he was kissing her. After a few glasses of that delicious red punch, I didn't care that I didn't know what Sebastian was doing. That was before I climbed onto the table to dance.

I drop my face into my hands.

I danced. *On a table.*

The memory isn't complete—more like the shards of glass left in a broken window. Sharp, sticking out at odd angles and clearly missing pieces. Did Bailey meet me at the party and bring me here?

"How are you feeling?"

At the sound of Sebastian's deep voice, I snap my head up. He's coming out of the bathroom. He has wet hair and is shirtless, a pair of athletic shorts slung low across his hips. He's still a little wet from his shower, and his skin looks so warm that I'm surprised the beads of water along his chest and shoulders don't dissolve instantly. I should look away, but…*shirtless Sebastian*. Of course. Because this isn't just Bailey's living room. It's Sebastian's. Because Sebastian lives here…or will soon. Which means the bed I slept in belongs to Sebastian.

That revelation sends liquid warmth pooling low in my stomach, but that warmth turns to horror when I get another flash from last night. Sebastian at the party. Sebastian holding his hands at his sides as I threw myself at him. Then Sebastian… kissing me?

When I lift my eyes to meet his, he's studying me, worry all over his face.

Oh my God, oh my God, oh my God. I threw myself at Sebastian and kissed him. Or did he kiss me? The memory is fractured, but I feel like he kissed me. Did I ask him to? Did I beg? I catch snippets of our conversation before they can fade from my mind.

"Tomorrow, I'll be sober, and I won't have the courage to ask for what I want."

Yeah, that's pretty damn close to begging. Ice-cold mortification snakes through my blood and I want to turn around, close the door, and climb right back into bed.

Sebastian's bed.

Oh hell, this is bad.

Swallowing hard, I scan the room and see the blankets on the couch, still rumpled. Of course he didn't sleep with me. "Last night…" I begin. I'm so embarrassed that I'm not sure what to say.

"I'm sorry. I didn't mean… I shouldn't…" My words are stolen from me by the memory of his hand in my hair and the way he slanted his mouth over mine, the way his hand gripped my hip. If it was a pity kiss, it certainly didn't feel like one.

"You scared the shit out of me," he says. He goes to the kitchen and fills a glass with water, then walks toward me. He's all bare skin and tattoos, coming my way. He has a sexy morning voice that's still laced with sleep and makes me imagine being tangled in his sheets, his thick arms holding me close as he whispers dirty words to wake me up.

He hands me the glass of water, and I take it, but dear God, I'm struggling to get my eyes off his body. It's not that I haven't seen his bare chest before, but somehow it feels more intimate this morning. The memory of his kiss swirls around my brain the way the scent of his cologne stays in the room after he leaves.

"You can't do that," he says.

"Sorry?" I lift my eyes to his. He grabs a shirt off the back of the couch and tugs it on over his head. It's both a relief and a tragedy, to be honest. I mean, all that gorgeous muscle was making it pretty hard to focus on a conversation, so it's best that he covered it up. On the other hand, how often do I get to be that close to him half naked? *He kissed me last night.* "Do what?"

"You can't go to a party alone and drink like that. Christ, Alex, don't you watch the news? Drunk girls get taken advantage of at parties. And worse." He heads back to the kitchen and pours himself a cup of coffee, and my head reels. He kissed me, but he wants to talk about how guys could have taken advantage of me?

I comb through my mind, looking for the rest of last night—what happened after the kiss? How did we get back here? Did he say anything about the kiss? Was he taking advantage of a drunk girl?

"Thank God Chris texted me and told me where you were." He shakes his head. "Jesus. You were literally dancing on the table when I got there."

"You kissed me," I blurt, and he freezes with his mug halfway to his lips.

He swallows hard and slowly sets it on the counter. "Yeah."

I stare at him, waiting for more—an apology, an explanation, a heartbreaking chuckle, *anything*—but he just studies his coffee and avoids my eyes. I wish he'd look at me, because every second he doesn't, I feel smaller and dumber. "*Yeah*? I was drunk, and you kissed me, and all you can say about it is *yeah*?"

Lifting his chin, he meets my eyes. His jaw is hard, as if he's pissed that we're having this conversation. "What do you want me to say, Alex?"

I gape at him. "Anything. I want you to say *anything*. But don't just stand there and give me a lecture about the buddy system and pretend you didn't stick your tongue down my throat."

His nostrils flare and somehow his jaw goes harder. "Do you want me to explain that I'm no better than the rest of the assholes at that party? Or maybe I need to confess that I'm worse? Because, fuck, I thought you already knew that. Do you want me to apologize? *I'm sorry.* It was a shitty decision and shittier timing. Do you want me to tell you I won't do it again? That I won't touch you again? You have my word."

It's like he carved out my insides and now he's staring at me, wondering why I'm not thanking him for freeing me of the burden of those pesky organs. "I have your *word*?"

"I like you. I... *Fuck.*" He turns away and drags a hand through his hair. He looks out the window over the kitchen sink as he speaks. "You work for my dad, and your brother is my friend, and I kissed you, but it was a mistake because I don't want to screw up our friendship." He turns around slowly and meets my eyes. "I promise I won't do it again."

I don't want anything to do with that promise, but I'm not given a choice. "I'll get out of here. Thanks for taking care of me last night." I find my purse on the floor in his bedroom and sling it over my shoulder as I head out the door.

"Alex," Sebastian calls after me. "Shit. Can we talk about this?"

"You said your piece." I pull the door open. "And I don't have anything to say."

He swallows. "Let me drive you home?"

I pause and take a slow, deliberate breath. He couldn't possibly know that his kiss was something I've dreamed about for five long years. He couldn't know that his apology and his promise to never do it again are the last things I wanted to hear this morning. "I need the walk to clear my head, but thanks for the offer."

I leave the apartment and close the door behind me. I don't stop walking until I get back to Mr. Patterson's house, where I sink onto the porch and fish Logan's card from my purse. I stare at it. He's so damn nice and good-looking. If Sebastian weren't in the picture, I probably would have called Logan the day I met him at the shop.

Sebastian isn't *in the picture, idiot. He just made that painfully clear.*

I take a deep breath and grab my phone from my purse. I decide against a call and go for a text message. I type, *This is Alexandra DeLuca. It was good to see you at the game yesterday. Maybe we should go out for a drink sometime so we can really talk.*

My thumb hovers over the "send" key as my mind plays Sebastian's kiss on repeat in my head.

"Do you want me to tell you I won't do it again? That I won't touch you again? You have my word."

I have to figure out a way to let go of Sebastian, no matter how hard it is.

Martina's Journal

O.M.G. I am dying.

Crowe, the boy I partied with last weekend? He's no college boy at all. In fact, he goes to my high school. And his first name isn't Crowe, it's Sebastian. He definitely looks older than he is, so I guess we have that in common, but here's what's hilarious: My twin sister has a crush on him.

This is one for the history books for sure. Alex and I have never liked the same guys, and she's certainly never gone for the bad boys. Apparently, she has no clue who he really is. Sebastian sits next to Alex in English and is her fucking lab partner in chemistry. What are the chances? I wish he sat next to me in class. Those big tables in chemistry? He could totally slide his hand up my skirt, and no one would ever know. Unfortunately, Alex gets all the luck, which is sad in this case because she wouldn't even appreciate the beauty of getting off in the middle of class.

Back to Alexandra's crush. I don't have the heart to tell her that he parties. She'd want to know how I know and has no tolerance for my recreational choices. If she knew just how much I indulge, she'd probably have Mom and Dad institutionalize me. So I didn't tell her the truth about Sebastian. I didn't even tell her that I know him. I let her go on a little about her new crush and his dreamy brown eyes and adorable grin. I'm not worried she'll get anywhere with him. Alexandra is painfully shy. It's like by the time God got done making me, there wasn't room for any more outgoing in Mom's womb.

After I learned about Alex's little crush, I promptly tracked down "Sebastian" (way less of a badass name than Crowe, but whatever). I cornered him in the boys' restroom after school and told him to stay away from her. You should have seen his face when I told him we were twins. Really, two girls couldn't be any more different. We were born on the same day, and we have the same parents, but that's where our similarities end. Alexandra's so quiet, and I'm loud. She's the good girl, the well-behaved one. And we don't look anything alike, either. She has brown hair and blue eyes, and my hair is a lighter brown that I keep highlighted enough that I can almost pass for blond, and my eyes are as dark as her hair.

He likes her. I could tell by the look in his eyes. But I could also tell that he's smart enough to know when he needs to stay away. Look how much convincing it took him to hang with me—and I'm not the innocent my sister is. Yeah, under that bad-boy persona is a guy who wants to do the right thing. It's kind of adorable, actually.

Then, after explaining that he needs to keep his distance from her, I unbuttoned his jeans, dropped to my knees, and went down on him. I know people think I'm a slut, but life's too short to be bored, and there's nothing boring about knowing that at any minute, someone might walk in and catch you.

After, I made him promise he wouldn't tell my sister we were fucking.

"Why would I tell her that when we haven't fucked?" he asked.

I laughed and pressed my index finger to his lips.

"Yet."

I think maybe he's not sure what to make of me. He should join the club. He wouldn't be alone.

CHAPTER 15
SEBASTIAN

My chest aches as I watch Alex walk away. I totally fucked this up. Last night. This morning. All of it.

Sometimes I like to torture myself by imagining what my life would be like if I'd met Alex before Martina. I imagine it would have gone something like this: I'd have walked into English class and sat next to the brunette with the sweet smile and blue eyes. When I felt that first tug toward her, that need to know more, maybe that was when I'd have cleaned up my life—turned it around *for her*.

I'd have told her that I was a screw-up and had done things I wasn't proud of, but that I really fucking wanted to be with her. To be worthy of her. Maybe she'd have laughed in my face, but I like to imagine she'd have given me a chance.

Over time, she'd have helped me forgive myself for my

mistakes, and we'd have done normal teenager things—gone to movies, made out in the back seat of my car, held hands while we walked through the county fair. I'd have bought her flowers. Maybe we'd have gone to prom together.

I wasn't the type to go to prom, but when I'm feeling a little masochistic, I like to imagine Alex in a red dress—something modest, because that was who she was even before the fire. I'd have held her in my arms while the other kids from our high school surrounded us. I'd have taken her somewhere after, somewhere we could be alone so I could show her just how beautiful she is to me in the best way I know how.

We'd have both gone to BHU from the start to stay close to our families, and we'd become one of those obnoxious young couples who, at twenty-one, has already been together for five years and has their whole future planned.

Fuck, but I was drawn to Alex from that first day, to her sweet smile and her kindness, to her quirky sense of humor. I knew instinctively that I needed to keep my distance, but I didn't want to. Because suddenly there was someone who interested me more than my next high, someone who gave me a bigger thrill, and she smelled like vanilla and sat next to me in English. She was my partner in chem lab.

Could it have changed everything? Alex made me want to be better, but by the time I met her I'd been partying with her twin, and Martina's biggest worry was that I might tell Alex about our extracurricular activities.

"She's innocent," Martina said to me about her sister. "Like a legit sweet girl who wouldn't understand that I'm just trying to let loose."

I've never stopped regretting what I did with Martina, and if I could go back in time, I'd undo it. I'd ignore her bold advances and tell her to go home. Because the night I put that X on Martina's tongue was the beginning of a domino effect I didn't have the power to stop.

I go to my new bedroom and squat beside a box of books. I run my hands along the old textbooks and stop on the well-worn spine of the old journal. She left it at my house before she died, and when I texted her about it, she said she'd get it from me next week.

Next week never came—not for Martina. And I've spent four years holding on to a dead girl's journal. Too afraid of my past to read what's inside. Too protective of my future to give it back to her family. And yet last night, when I tucked Alex into bed beside the box with Martina's journal, I imagined her waking up and finding it. I imagined with equal parts relief and terror what would happen if she knew I had the journal and then read it. Part of me wishes I could just tell her everything, but I would be breaking a promise to my father. Besides, a confession won't change the past.

If I'd met Alex first, neither sister would have had to endure the horror of that fire. Alex wouldn't have a third of her body covered in scars. And Martina would still be alive.

ALEXANDRA

"Oh, I don't know about this." I stare into the giant mirror over Mr. Patterson's bathroom vanity and frown at my reflection. I'm wearing Bailey's little black dress, emphasis on *little*, and I'm getting ready to go meet Logan for dinner. It's Friday, and it's been almost a week since Sebastian kissed me. Six days, to be exact. Five days since he told me what a big mistake it was. So tonight I'm going out with Logan.

Bailey rolls her eyes and shakes her head. "Why are you so nervous?"

I shrug. "I don't really *know* him. He seems like a nice guy."

She narrows her eyes at me. "Have you never dated before?"

"I've been on a date!" *Sort of. Kind of.* I had a boyfriend my sophomore year of high school. We met through the academic honors society. He was sweet, and I really liked him—enough to stay with him for seven months and give him my virginity—but he never made my heart race or my stomach dance just because he walked in the room. By the end of the year, I decided I wanted more.

My senior year, I went to prom with a boy from my calculus class. His hands shook so hard that dancing with him was beyond awkward. I never figured out if he was nervous because he liked me or nervous because the girls mocked him for asking "Freddy

Krueger." We danced a couple of times at the beginning of prom, but then he ditched me and I spent the rest of the night wishing I hadn't gone.

Then there was the date the summer before I left for Colorado. The guy took me to a frat party that was so wild and loud that I ended up leaving without him after half an hour.

"I don't have much experience," I tell Bailey. "I just don't want to look like an idiot."

She smirks and gives me a once-over. "All you have to do is show up. You're gorgeous."

I huff. "Yeah, right."

She cocks a brow. "You think those old burns mean that boys don't drool when you walk into the room?" She chuckles. "Oh, girl, you're precious. Even Sebastian can't keep his eyes off you, and you know his whole 'sisters' rule."

"Sebastian?" I ask, and my voice pitches on his name, but I think Bailey misses it, luckily. "What's Sebastian's sisters rule?"

"A friend's sister is off-limits as far as Sebastian's concerned. I mean, he ranted about it like crazy when Olivia got pregnant." Bailey takes a long lock of my hair and wraps it around her curling iron. "I can only assume that's why he's steering clear of you when he likes you so much."

"He kissed me last weekend."

She releases the curling iron, and my hair bounces into a ringlet. She sets the iron on the counter. "I'm sorry. Say that again?" She already knows that I got drunk at Trent's after the game and that Sebastian brought me back to her place to sleep it off.

"Saturday night, Sebastian kissed me."

"Was that before or after he tucked you into his bed?"

"Before, but then the next morning he told me it was a mistake and he wouldn't do it again."

She leans back on the counter and studies me. "And how are you feeling about all this?"

I bite my lip, probably messing up the pretty red lipstick Bailey convinced me to wear. "I don't know how I feel. Kind of rejected, honestly." I shake my head. "I just want to give Logan a chance and stop trying to figure out Sebastian."

She takes a deep breath and picks up the curling iron. "Let's do it, then."

I watch her in the mirror as she curls the rest of my hair. "You're really nice."

"Don't tell anyone," she says. "You'll ruin my street cred."

Thirty minutes later, I'm heading into the Cavern to meet my date. On Bailey's recommendation, I drive myself rather than letting him pick me up.

"I can vouch for Logan," she said. "He'd get you home safely and all that, but driving yourself is a power move. You can leave any time you want."

I spot Logan as soon as I walk in the door. He greets me with a wide grin and stands as I approach the booth. He's wearing a black polo shirt and tailored dress pants, and looks absolutely delicious.

"You look amazing." His gaze skims over the simple black

dress I'm wearing. He gets bonus points for not lingering too long on my exposed collarbone. If I give this a chance, will I ever get the same thrill from his eyes on me as when Sebastian looks at me?

Stop thinking about Sebastian.

I take my seat. "Thank you. So do you."

"I was really glad to get your text." He props his forearms on the table and leans forward. "You made my day."

"Don't get too excited," I say. "I might just be in this for the hot car."

He laughs. "You're here, aren't you?"

When the waitress comes to our table, we order food and drinks—a pilsner for him and a glass of the house white wine for me—and while we wait for our meals, he tells me about getting ready for the grand opening of his new bar.

I manage to make it through dinner without spilling food on myself or saying something embarrassing. After the server clears our plates, I excuse myself to the restroom, where I hide in the stall and get my phone. There's a text waiting from Bailey.

> **Bailey:** *So, how's it going?*
> **Me:** *Good. I don't think I've made a fool of myself yet.*

Her response comes immediately.

> **Bailey:** *What do you think of Logan?*

Me: *He's sweet. I think I like him.*
Bailey: *Perfect. You can let him kiss you. On the lips if you want, but no tongue.*

I cover my mouth, but laughter slips out anyway.

I take care of business, wash my hands, and push out of the restroom to return to our table. I'm starting to think that maybe I can handle this dating thing, but all my confidence fizzles away when I get to the table and find Logan chatting with Sebastian.

CHAPTER 16
SEBASTIAN

Alex walks toward me in a black dress that hits her right in the middle of her soft thighs. Her hair is down, hanging past her shoulders and curled at the ends, and her lips are painted a bold red that sends my imagination into overdrive.

Did she know I was coming here tonight? Did she dress like this to torture me?

"Sebastian," Logan says, snapping my attention back to him. "I'm sure you know my date, Alexandra. She works for your dad."

Alex stops by the table and smiles at Logan before sliding into her seat. His *date*?

I blink at Alex. "I didn't realize you were seeing anyone." It feels like a betrayal. As if I've been punched in my heart by the only person who has access to it.

Alex meets my gaze and holds it for a beat. I wish I could read her thoughts, because I can't read her expression. Is she nervous? Is she worried I'll tell Logan we kissed?

"This is our first date," Logan says when the silence has stretched a bit too long. "But hopefully not our last."

"How do you two know each other?" Alex asks.

Logan and I exchange a glance before he turns his smile on her and says, "That's a story for another time."

Some days I'm glad to be back home in a town where I'll see a familiar face almost anywhere I go. Tonight, Blackhawk Valley feels so small that I'm suddenly claustrophobic. Seeing her with Logan is only one reminder of what it will mean to have Alex live here when I've promised to stay away.

"Sebastian!" Chris calls from a booth on the other side of the bar. "We're over here."

I swallow hard and nod to Logan. "I won't take any more of your time. Enjoy your date." The last word comes off my tongue like it has a bad taste, but I don't bother trying to cover it or allow myself to look into Alex's blue eyes for one more minute.

I head to the booth where Chris is waiting with a pitcher of beer and three glasses, and take a seat. I was glad when he called me. I spent all of my scant free time this week getting settled into my room at Bailey's. I needed to get out of the apartment and away from my thoughts before I did something stupid—like calling Alex and telling her I liked kissing her and I wanted to do it again.

Chris fills my glass.

"I might need something stronger tonight," I mutter.

He follows my gaze across the bar to where Logan is holding Alex's hand on top of the table. "Well, shit. Who's the guy?"

"His name is Logan Lucas. He grew up here, lived in Indy for a while, and just moved back to open that bar next door."

"Do you trust him with Alex?"

My knee-jerk reaction is to say *no,* but I don't know if that's because I wouldn't relish seeing Alex with anyone or because I have actual reservations about Logan. He's five years older than her, which seems like a lot, but she's not a kid anymore. Her twenty-one to his twenty-six isn't all that odd. The truth is that Logan's always seemed like a good guy, and he was a friend when I needed one the most and deserved one the least. But does that mean I trust him with Alex? "I don't know."

Chris fills his glass. "Either way, it blows."

Frowning, I point to the third glass. "Who else is here?"

"For fuck's sake, Chris," Mason says when he steps up to the table.

"Sit." Chris points to the spot next to him in the booth. "I can't have you filling my locker room with animosity."

Mason glares in my direction, not sitting. "You mean like *he* did when he thought you got his sister pregnant and took a swing at you?"

I flinch. I still feel bad about that, even if Chris was quick to forgive me.

Chris rubs the back of his neck. "Jesus, Mase. Just take a fucking seat."

Mason slides into the booth, but tension radiates off him. He stares at the table as he speaks. "There's nothing to talk about. I know Bailey isn't my girl, and I have no right to be pissed about her moving some other dude in with her." He lifts his gaze to meet mine. "But that doesn't mean you should have done it."

"There is nothing between me and Bailey," I say, knowing he needs to hear it again.

"But what happens after you two have been living together for a month? Three months? Does that change?"

Chris leans back, watching. It's as if he's designated himself the fucking referee for this conversation.

"It doesn't change," I say, keeping my voice low. "Because I wouldn't do that to you. I know something about wanting someone you can't have."

Mason's eyes are full of frustration and anguish. He's such a good guy, and I wish I could make it better. I'm not about to become some meddling female who's going to sit Bailey down and give her a come-to-Jesus talk. I figure she has her reasons—and drawing the line with Mason probably has more to do with her dead ex-boyfriend, Nic Mendez, than with Mason himself.

My gaze drifts across the bar to where Logan is helping Alex out of her seat.

"Alex?" Mason asks.

I don't think I've ever admitted my feelings for Alex to anyone, so it's not easy for me to do it now. I might be transparent to my friends, but there's a big difference between having people think you have feelings for someone and outright admitting it. Even so, acknowledging my internal torture with the slight lift of my chin feels like a weight off my shoulders.

"So why don't you go after her?" he asks.

"It's complicated."

"I know all about complicated." He offers me his fist, and I bump it with mine. It's a truce, and I'll take it.

When I turn to check on Alex and Logan again, they're already gone.

CHAPTER 17
ALEXANDRA

It's the quintessential Blackhawk Valley autumn night. Summer is finally relinquishing its hold on the temperature, and the air is cool and crisp. As Logan and I walk through downtown, the sounds of the high school drumline echo off the hills.

"May I buy you a scoop of ice cream?" Logan points to the shop on the corner.

If that can't make me appreciate this night, then nothing will. Logan is cute, and kind, and charming. Even so, when we study the menu, and he points to the fresh apple pie, I hear myself say, "I'm in the mood for a triple-fudge brownie sundae."

Logan steps up to the counter and orders two of my favorite childhood treat, and then we return to the sidewalk and wander toward the park while we eat.

"You're awfully quiet tonight," he says. "Is something on your mind?"

"I'm just tired. It's been a long week." I know my mood's changed since seeing Sebastian, and I hate that he affects me so much. I point to a bench nestled between two tall maple trees before sitting.

I take a small bite of my ice cream and silently curse Sebastian for showing up tonight. And for never straying far from my thoughts.

"I lost my twin sister four years ago."

He shifts forward, giving me his full attention. "I heard about that. And you got caught in the fire too. It's so terrible."

I bite the inside of my cheek. Four years later and talk about that night sometimes results in spontaneous tears. That's the last thing I want tonight. "It's just that I haven't really dated since," I admit. "I've been so tied up in trying to figure out who *I* am." I shrug and put my sundae down on the bench beside me. My appetite is nowhere to be found. "Truthfully, you've been so sweet, but I'm sitting here questioning whether or not I'm ready."

He swallows his bite and puts his bowl next to mine. "If you promise to call me when you are ready, I promise I'll take it as slowly as you need."

Martina's Journal

Since the day in the boys' bathroom four weeks ago, Sebastian's been avoiding me. It's ridiculous. It's as if when I said he needed to keep his distance from Alexandra he thought I meant from me too.

For a couple of weeks, I told myself I didn't care, that there were plenty of boys who were interested in me and I didn't need him. But it's kind of like when you go on a diet and tell yourself you can't have chocolate. Suddenly you want chocolate more than you've ever wanted anything in your whole life. I'm not talking a little baby craving that'll be gone by morning. I'm talking "I'd trade my right tit for some sweet cocoa plant goodness right now."

For the last month, I've been on a Sebastian Crowe diet, and now I want him more than I want anything. Maybe it makes it worse because Alex goes on about him. The way he made her laugh when they were studying John Donne in English class, the joke he cracked in chemistry.

My sister is awesome. She's fucking amazing, and anyone would be lucky to have her, but guys don't usually see that. So when I hear Sebastian Crowe seems to be going out of his way to make her smile, I feel like the green-eyed monster and I don't even have green fucking eyes. Yeah. I'm jealous of my twin sister, which is stupid, because I want her to have better things than I have. I want her to be happier than I am. I fucking love that goody-two-shoes buzzkill. And if Alexandra knew the kind of guy Sebastian is, she wouldn't be interested anyway. Jealousy isn't necessary here, but I have it anyway.

I tracked him down at the quarry. It was a beautiful autumn day. The wind was blowing and the leaves were falling off the trees. A group of people were sitting around the bonfire. Other than Sebastian, I didn't recognize anyone from school, which confirmed my suspicions that he hangs out with older kids mostly. Are they dropouts or college students? Who knows?

I tried to act like I wasn't looking for him, but he had that look in his eyes that said he's used to girls looking for him. I hate being that transparent.

There was a girl hanging on him and another staying close by between her shots of God-knows-what. This gathering just seemed so ordinary compared to the night I first met him. I waited until the girls were distracted greeting friends before I made my move.

I asked him if he wanted to get out of there, go somewhere and have some real fun. He arched a brow. "You think that just because I'm not with you, I'm not having fun?"

So here's the deal. I don't just have a thing for bad boys. I have a thing for assholes. I can't stand boys who hang on my every word and want to kiss the ground I walk on. It makes me feel like they're short a few circuits. So Sebastian's cold-shoulder treatment didn't exactly scare me away, and it wasn't helping my—yeah, I'll admit it—crush.

"Do you have anything so we can party?" I asked.

He nodded toward the cooler of beer. "Help yourself."

"That's not what I mean and you know it."

"I have no idea what you're talking about."

Stepping forward, I dropped into his lap and looped my arms around his neck. "Come on. Don't you want to play?" I trailed a hand down the front of his body, and his eyes went hot.

"You're trouble," he said.

I grinned. "You've got that right."

Next to him, his buddy drained his beer, crushed the can, and tossed it into a pile of other empties. "Come on, Crowe. Give the lady what she wants."

"She doesn't know what she wants," he said, not taking his gaze from mine.

I licked my lips. "But I do."

"See?" His buddy chuckled. "She wants to party."

He flashed a hard look to his friend. "I don't have anything."

"Right," the guy said. He chuckled again, as if this was hilarious. "Whatever you say."

"You sure are making an impression on my

sister," I said. I just wanted his attention at this point. I was sick of getting the brush-off. "You make her laugh. She tells me about it."

He arched a brow. "Is there a law against having a sense of humor?"

"No. It's cute. It's cute how much she likes you."

He drained his beer and added it to the pile. "Come on," he said. "You're sober. You can drive. Let's get out of here."

"I like the sound of that," I said, and followed him to his car.

We didn't go anywhere exciting. He said he needed to drop something off at a friend's house, so I took him to campus. I have my suspicions as to what he was delivering, but I kept my theories to myself.

When he got back in the car, I climbed over the stick shift and straddled his lap, guiding his hand up my shirt. His eyes were glazed, and I thought he probably took something in that house. He was a little drunk and maybe high, but not far enough gone to forget to stop me when I unzipped his pants.

At this rate, this boy is never going to let me seal the deal.

CHAPTER 18
ALEXANDRA

When I got to Mom and Dad's for Sunday dinner, there was a package waiting for me. It had a Blackhawk Valley postmark, but there was no return address, and no note—only a box with a tattered journal inside. I recognize the journal and know it belonged to Martina. The date on the first page is the day of our sixteenth birthday.

As soon as I spot the date, I close it fast and run it upstairs to put with the others. Who sent it? Why did they have it? Why did they address it to me and not my parents? And why wait until now to send it? My hands shake as I put it in place on the shelf.

Can you invade the privacy of a dead girl? Because looking in her journals seems wrong. But maybe it's not just that. Maybe I'm not ready to read about life from her point of view. I haven't even had the courage to read her diary entries from middle school, but the idea of reading what she wrote in her last year? It leaves me sick to my stomach.

My twin sister's gravestone has a circle of fairies etched into it because when she was nine years old, she was mildly obsessed with them, and my parents thought it would be a good way to remember her. That's what we do when people die. We revise their story. Maybe we change some of the details and maybe we don't, but we all mentally smooth out the rough edges. We camouflage their bad choices by highlighting their goodness. We cut down the hard-to-love parts and beef up the easy ones.

I'm no better than my parents in this way. When I think of Martina, I think of a childhood playing Barbies and hide-and-seek. I think of late nights when we'd sneak down to the basement to watch movies after bedtime, of giggling so much our stomachs hurt. I think of the way she held my hand through haunted houses—because I hated them as much as she loved them. Those moments are the keystones of the safe space where I keep my memories of her.

But sometimes, when it's dark and I'm tired and sleep is an elusive stranger, I think of the girl I tried to save from the fire. She wasn't like the addicts you see in movies, the painfully thin girls with acne, greasy hair, and track marks. She was still beautiful and funny, if thinner and quicker to anger than the girl I'd grown up alongside. Her ability to appear "normal" meant everything to her, but in truth, she was like the stereotypical addict in the only way that mattered: She was controlled by an addiction so much bigger than herself and so much stronger than her willpower. Sometimes the darkness of that night grabs me by the throat and I have no choice but to relive it—horrified panic that made me run into a burning building, the heat, the searing pain of fire licking skin, the horrible smell, and the terror.

I know the answers I want won't be in her journal. I can't imagine she sat down the night she died and wrote an explanation of why she was going into that meth lab. Hell, until today, I wasn't even sure she kept a journal at all during that last year. She wasn't like herself.

I sit on my childhood bed and stare at the journal in the bookcase as if it's a scary toy I'm afraid might come to life.

Martina's Journal

Guess who came to the house tonight? Sebastian fucking Crowe.

Alexandra's been home sick, and she sent him a text asking him to bring her their chem study guide.

I answered the door, which threw him off, but I could tell he was uncomfortable being there anyway.

"Her room's this way," I said, waving him into the house.

He held out a packet of papers. "You can just give these to her. I don't need to come in."

"She'll want to see you." I intentionally walked away without taking the papers, and he took the bait and followed me in the house. "Mom," I called out

as we passed the living room. "This is Sebastian, the boy Alexandra talks about so much."

Mom hopped up off the couch so fast you'd think I'd just announced that the queen of England stopped in for a visit. "Sebastian!" She held out a hand. "I'm so glad to meet you!" She glanced over her shoulder, presumably to make sure Alex wasn't around, and lowered her voice before she added, "Alex thinks very highly of you."

Sebastian cut his eyes to me, and his Adam's apple bobbed as he swallowed. "Nice to meet you too, Mrs. DeLuca. I'm just here to drop off some paperwork for Alex."

"Alex said you like classic cars," Mom said, totally missing Sebastian's attempts to dodge this "meet the mom" moment. "She's just wild about them. She's been working on cars with her brothers since she was old enough to hold a screwdriver. And your dad owns Crowe's Automotive, right?"

Sebastian was practically squirming, so ready to get out from under her inspection, but Mom persisted.

"I had some work done there a couple of years ago. Silly me, I backed into my garage door. I wasn't even paying attention. You know how it goes, late for work, mind not on the task at hand, and crash! Your dad thought he might be closing for business back then. Really glad he didn't have to do that. Do you want to stay for dinner? I have plenty."

"Mom!"

It was Alex who stopped Mom's diarrhea of the mouth. Poor girl looked awful. She was in a pair of black yoga pants and a tank top and her nose was bright red, her cheeks flushed from her fever, but the way Sebastian's eyes fell on her, you'd think she was dressed in a ball gown with a slit up to there.

No. The way Sebastian looked at her was more predatory than that. It was as if he was suddenly famished for the dinner Mom offered, and it was right in front of him.

Remember when I said I've never been jealous of my sister? Maybe I've never had reason to be. Maybe she's never had something I wanted. Right in that moment, I wanted Sebastian Crowe to look at me the way he was looking at her. There wasn't a single buzz or high I would take over that.

"Thanks for bringing these over," Alex said.

He stepped forward and handed her the stack of papers, and when their fingers brushed I could practically see the electricity popping between them. "I have to get going," he said, apology in his voice. He looked at Mom. "Thank you for the invitation for dinner. I'm sure it'll be delicious, but I can't stay."

Mom was all smiles when he left. "He is such a

nice boy."

"Not really," I said.

Alex frowned at me. "Why would you say that?"

I shrugged. I didn't want to have that conversation in front of Mom, but I had to do something. I don't want Alex giving her heart to a guy who wouldn't have the first clue how to protect it.

Does that make me a hypocrite? Maybe. But I'm not going to get my heart broken by Sebastian Crowe because I'm not planning to give him my heart at all. I've never been looking for a guy to sweep me off my feet. I just want to have a good time...and maybe a little sizzle.

Alex excused herself to do her homework, and I followed her into our bedroom, and I'm sure this was one of many moments she wished we didn't share. With us and our four older brothers, this house is bursting at the seams. Two kids to a room. It's what you do when you have a big family but not a million dollars to spend on a seven-bedroom home.

"I didn't mean to upset you," I told her, and she glared at me, knowing full well I did. "I just know how much you like him and I don't want you to get hurt."

"Why do you assume I'm going to get hurt? He's just a friend. It's not like he's even interested in me."

It's like she can't even see the way he looks at her.

"He parties, Alex," I said. I tried to be gentle, but she didn't even look fazed. "Like, he parties hard."

She snapped her head up and her eyes narrowed. "Sebastian?"

"Yeah." I bit the inside of my cheek. "You know what I mean, right?"

She shook her head. "He's on the football team. Don't they do drug testing?"

I shrugged. "I don't know about that. I just know he parties."

"And how exactly do you know that?"

I rolled my eyes. "Kill me for listening when people talk."

"Don't lie to me, Martina. I know you look for trouble. I just don't understand why."

"Don't make this about me. Sebastian isn't the good guy you deserve. Got it?"

"Yeah. Message received." She looked down to her open textbook. "Now go away so I can study. Some of us aren't natural brainiacs."

CHAPTER 19
SEBASTIAN

When I get to women's studies on Monday morning, Alex is ready for class with a pen in her hand and her notebook in front of her.

She smiles up at me when I take my seat. "Good morning."

"Morning." My voice comes out a little rough, as if I just woke up, when in reality I've been up for four hours already. I wonder if she got the journal I shipped to her parents' house. Judging by her grin, I'm guessing she hasn't read it.

"Congratulations on the W Saturday," she says. "It was good to see the Blackhawks deliver such a beat-down as the underdogs."

I draw back, impressed. Saturday's game was in Ohio against a big-name team, and it didn't cross my mind that Alex might watch it. "Thanks. It was a tough win."

She cocks her head. "You didn't make it look tough."

Last week, after I kissed her and our awkward morning

after, she barely spoke to me. I'm relieved she's over it. Maybe she's decided our friendship is important to her too. I draw in a deep breath. "What about you? Did you have a good night with Logan?" I can't believe I don't choke on the words.

"I did. He's really nice." That smile on her face when she talks about him? Yeah, that's a special kind of torture. "He took me for ice cream."

Did you let him kiss you? Did he take you home? "I'm glad you had a good time." I open my mouth to ask her if she plans to see him again, but Alex has turned her attention to the front of the room.

"Good morning," Dr. Scheck calls from behind the podium. "I hope you all had a great weekend. Today I'm going to give you a brief overview of the history of feminism, and then I'll introduce your first group project."

I pull out my notebook and a pen as Dr. Scheck dives into an explanation of first-wave feminism. Sitting next to Alex while trying to absorb a fifty-minute lecture is equal parts heaven and hell. Her hair's swept over one shoulder into a low ponytail, and she fiddles with it through the whole lecture. Every once in a while she cuts her gaze to me and smiles.

This isn't anything new. We sat next to each other in classes in high school, and I always found it hard to focus on the class material when Alex was nearby. But I managed then. I'll manage now.

In the middle of the lecture, she pulls a page out of the back of her notebook, scribbles something on it, and passes it to me. I love how her handwriting slants to the right and she left a smudge of ink on the paper from writing with her left hand.

The blonde on the other side of you can't stop staring at you.

I turn, and sure enough, there's a petite blonde right next to me. When I meet her gaze, she grins at me and shifts in her seat so her foot is against mine. I've been so focused on Alex, I honestly didn't realize there was a pretty girl anywhere in the vicinity, let alone one who was trying to play footsie with me.

I shift my foot away and poise my pen to write a response. *I'm pretty sure she's staring at you, actually. You look amazing today. I like your hair like that.*

I slide the note onto her desk before I think better of it. Her cheeks blossom into a pretty pink that matches her lips. She's dating Logan, right, so what does it hurt if I give her a compliment now and then? And anyway, "I like your hair like that" is pretty tame when I want to tell her how it makes me think of wrapping it around my fist while I…

The blonde puts a piece of paper in front of me, and I reluctantly pull my gaze off Alex to read it. The blonde's handwriting is a loopy cursive with hearts dotting her *i*'s.

Is that your girlfriend? She's pretty.

I stare at the note, not sure how to respond. If I say no, it opens a door I'm not interested in opening. Before I can answer, Alex puts her paper back on my desk.

She's looking at you, dork. Your redhead would be jealous.

My redhead? Oh, fuck. Yeah. Lacey, the girl from Trent's

party. She's pretty, but I thought we were both after the same thing that night. It turns out I was wrong. When I saw her on campus the first day of classes, she threw herself at me, told me she was looking forward to the football game, and promised to let me do some pretty dirty shit to her if I won. I let her down easy, but not before Alex walked away.

I take a deep breath and write a response to the blonde first. *Thanks. Yeah, she's gorgeous. I'm a lucky guy.*

She frowns as she reads it then lifts her palms in a gesture that says, *Can't blame me for trying.*

Now to let Alex in on it. *I told her you're my girlfriend. Be a pal and play along. I'm trying to spare the girl's feelings.*

When Alex reads the note, her jaw drops. She scowls at me. I just grin and scoot my desk a little closer to hers. Her pink cheeks turn a shade closer to red, and she keeps her eyes fixed on the front of the room. Being her *friend* might actually be a lot of fun.

"For your first group project, I'm putting you into groups randomly," Dr. Scheck says. She hands a basket to the first person in the front row. "Take a number from the basket, and that's your group number. Each group will research a local contemporary woman who I believe is making an impact in her field. Some of the women are based out of Blackhawk Valley, and some are a short drive away. The options will be posted on the online discussion board tonight at five p.m."

When the basket makes its way back to us, Alex pulls out a number and passes it to me. I grab my folded paper from the basket before passing it on to the blonde. The lecture hall erupts in chatter while everyone tries to find their groups.

"What's your number?" I ask Alex.

She holds up her paper to show me a seven. "What about you?"

I unfold mine. Four. That's disappointing.

The blonde nudges me. "Here," she says in a whisper. "Trade me."

"You're a peach." I grin at her and hold up my new number for Alex. "Lucky number seven."

"Cheater," she whispers, but those bubblegum-pink lips are smiling. *Fuck yes.*

"Did we hear number seven?" a guy asks, walking up the aisle toward us. He has a beanie and bloodshot eyes and smells like he's smoked weed for a week straight without showering.

"That's us," Alex says.

"Cool," the stoner says, pointing to his similarly attired stoner buddy. "Us too."

"They're boyfriend and girlfriend," the blonde says as she gathers her things. "Isn't that sweet?"

Cheech and Chong nod with something that almost passes for enthusiasm. "So sweet."

The blonde winks at Alex. "Nice catch."

Alex opens her mouth to reply, but the girl's already on her way to the front of the class, where the rest of group four is calling for their missing member. When the blonde is gone, Alex turns to me. "You're the *worst*."

ALEXANDRA

"You're a local contemporary woman," Sebastian says. "Why can't we do this project on you?"

I narrow my eyes at him. "You really think I want to do a presentation in front of the class *about myself*?" I extend a hand as if to shake his. "Maybe we haven't met before. My name's Alexandra."

He grins. "It would be my first college presentation where I wanted to study the subject matter as much as humanly possible."

My cheeks heat and I look away. I love and hate it when he says things like that. Love it because *oh my God, it feels so good.* And hate it because I'm a little embarrassed by how I can't take it for the casual flirting it is.

We're waiting in the Commons for the other members of our group to show, but we've been here fifteen minutes and sent a few unanswered texts. Clearly, our group members have decided to spend this time doing something else. If I got two guesses what, I'd probably get it right in one.

"Should we get started without them?" I ask Sebastian.

Sighing, he opens his laptop. "If it were up to me, we'd do the whole project without them. I swear they only make you do group projects in college because they want to prepare you for the deadweight coworkers you'll have to deal with in the real world."

"Paul said he'd pick the subject since he was going to be available when she put the topics on the discussion board." I scoot my chair closer to Sebastian's and watch as he pulls up the platform for BHU's classes.

"He never did it," he says, pointing to the screen. All the other groups have claimed a topic, but group seven still shows undecided.

I sigh. "Is there anything good left?"

"The other groups picked the stuff that's closest." He thrums his fingers against the tabletop. "Look at this. Maggie Thompson, New Hope, Indiana. That's not a bad drive. Maybe a little over two hours."

"New Hope? Why have I never heard of this place? Should I know where that is?"

He shrugs. "There's a college there that was trying to recruit me to play ball. Nice place about halfway between here and Lafayette."

"Why didn't you go there?"

"Their football team wasn't going anywhere." He shrugs. "Small school."

"Who is this lady? What will we be writing about?" I'm open-minded, but if Sebastian and I are going to do this project together, I'm really not up for writing about some obscure sex toy creator.

"Looks like she's an artist and curator. New Hope Art Gallery." He nods. "I stopped in there when I was visiting Sinclair."

"So we'd be presenting about art," I say. "I could do that."

"Me too. The owner of this gallery is pretty cool. He's a photographer. Amazing talent. I talked to him about…" He shakes his head and looks away. "Never mind."

I bite my lip and almost let it drop, but I decide I'm too curious. "Finish what you were going to say. I want to know. You're into photography?"

"It's an outlet more than anything," he says. "I don't know whether I'm any good at it, but it doesn't really matter. It's just something I do for fun."

"Have you taken any classes?"

"A couple. I'm in one now."

"Maybe we can do something cool with that when we get to the dreaded creative project part of this group work."

"Why, yes, I'll just take pictures of our stoner group members being useless and title it: *Millennials*. Subtitle: *Don't Worry, Gen X, Your Jobs Are Safe*."

I laugh. "Maybe Maggie Thompson can give us some ideas. I don't mind a road trip."

"I imagine our group members might, though."

I shake my head and groan. "You're right. We'd be better off if we didn't have to do this with them."

"A man can dream," he mutters.

"Well, they're not here and we are. I say we pick what works for us and make our plans. If the other guys can't come, too bad. They should have showed up today." I smile. "What do you say? Are you up for a road trip?"

"We'll take my truck so the guys will have to drive separately.

If they're in the same car as us for two hours, I don't know if I'd pass my next drug test."

I clap and do a little bounce in my seat. "It's a plan."

"Listen, about what happened at the party…" His gaze holds mine, and my stomach flips over. "I handled everything terribly—from kissing you at the party to the way I apologized the next morning. I don't want to screw this up."

He sounds so sincere, and it tugs on my heart. "I'm over it." I paste on a smile. "It's not like we'd be any good together anyway, right?"

He laughs, but it sounds as forced as my smile feels. "Right."

CHAPTER 20
SEBASTIAN

What kind of son follows his father? What kind of son thinks the worst of the man who raised him?

I turn my key in the ignition and start my truck. Dad said he wouldn't be at the shop today. Again. I want to believe he has good reasons, or hell, even *lazy* reasons, but it's not like he's going to spend the day golfing or chatting it up with the guys at the country club. That's not my dad.

Dante opens the passenger door and climbs into my truck. "Where are we going?" he asks, buckling.

Dad's old Jeep rattles down the street.

"What are you doing?" I ask.

Dante turns toward the road where Dad is stopped at a light before turning back to me. "Go ahead and follow him. It'll make you feel better."

"As if I didn't feel shitty enough about doing this, now I have an audience," I mutter.

"You have a *friend*," Dante says. "And I'm telling you, you're worried for no reason. Your dad is clean. Follow him. You'll see."

I let Dad get a block or so ahead before I pull out to follow.

Yesterday, when I walked into the shop and saw Alex standing at the counter, I had such a clear and sudden vision of her stuck in that fire. Panic filled my chest until there wasn't room for air. If Dad is dealing again, I want Alex as far away from it as possible.

Dad turns onto Center Street and parks in front of Tully's Tulips. He climbs out of the car and feeds the meter. I turn onto Fifth and park in a loading zone, where I see Dad walking into the shop.

Dante arches a brow. "Think Tully's is a front for a meth operation? Wait, no, maybe heroin."

I grunt. Tully is an old woman who wears loud clothes and likes to hand out meditation guides to all of her customers. "If Tully were in the drug business, I think she'd deal weed, not meth."

We both stare at the storefront, and in less than three minutes, Dad's climbing back into his Jeep with a bouquet of red roses—the kind he always gets Mom. I don't know if those are Mom's favorite or if Dad just isn't creative enough to get her anything else.

"Even if he just bought a joint from an old lady, you have bigger things to worry about," Dante says. "Do you want to tell me why you think your dad might be dealing again? *Other* than my paychecks?"

I rub the back of my neck. Dante and I didn't become close until after Martina died and Dad and I cleaned up, but Dad hired him when we were in the thick of the hardest change we've ever had to make. Dante got a front-row seat as we figured out how to run a clean business and did the sticky work of disentangling ourselves from the people in our old life. Maybe Dad wouldn't forgive me if he knew I'd confided in Dante, but I can't regret telling him—not despite the fact that he's Martina's brother, but *because*. His ability to accept what I did and how it impacted his sister was instrumental in helping me move on.

I shake my head. "Something's wrong. I don't know how to explain it, I just *know*. I can tell he's keeping something from me."

"Have you asked him?"

I slide him a look. "Seriously? *Hey, Dad, you dealing again? Why, yes, son. In fact, I am.*" I sigh. "If he is, he'll lie about it—if only to protect me. And if he's not... He'd be really fucking hurt to know that I even suspect anything."

"I guess you just have to decide if you can trust him."

But what if I can't?

Martina's Journal

I'm grounded. And it's stupid, too.
So what? I dropped out of cheer squad. Who wants to be a fucking cheerleader anyway?
Mom said I'm not grounded for leaving cheer.

I'm grounded because I need to think about my priorities. Then she proceeded to give me this long speech about how my choices now were going to affect the rest of my life, blah, blah, blah. I didn't point out that she's the one stuck at home without a life of her own after raising six kids.

Anyway, guess what I found out? Sweet little Alex has a boyfriend. Apparently she decided to listen to me for once, because she hasn't talked much about her crush on Sebastian since he dropped off her homework that day and I warned her he wasn't any good.

A boy from her academic honors society asked her out, and she said yes. (Side note: I should get bonus points for not laughing hysterically at the academic honors society meetup part of this story. But totally. It's like Tinder for nerds.) Fast forward a few weeks, and they've gone on a bunch of dates, "studied" in the basement together, and officially gotten to the point where he gets evil death glares from my brothers. I love it. And she seems happy. She's never been very interested in finding a boyfriend, despite my nudging, and she's really giving it a chance.

This all makes me feel a little less bad for what I did with Sebastian last weekend. I ran into him at a party. I mean, it was a legitimate coincidence.

I wasn't even trying to track him down this time. He was definitely high and his eyes had that glazed, faraway look that makes me want to demand he share the good shit. Alex can think whatever she wants about football players and drug testing, but Sebastian's getting around it somehow, because he doesn't let his position on the team slow him down.

"Where's your sister?" he asked.

I thought it was the most hilarious question, since Alex never goes to parties, but I just shrugged. "Probably fucking her boyfriend. Why do you care?"

He flinched, then set his jaw. "I just want to make sure she's not hanging around her evil twin."

"Evil, huh?" *I grabbed his shirt and dragged him into the nearest bedroom. He spun me around, pressed me against the wall, and kissed me hard. It didn't take much coaxing before his hands were sliding up my skirt and exploring everything underneath.*

I'll die before I admit it to anyone, but there's a small part of me that felt like maybe he was...God, I don't know...getting back at Alex for being with her boyfriend? That doesn't even make sense, since she wasn't there and doesn't know about us, but he just felt weirdly detached. Like he was going through the motions and was maybe more irritated than turned on.

After I got off on his hand, he stepped back and said, "Is that what you were after?" Then he turned on his heel and left the room, like he was mad at himself for what he'd just done.

I don't understand this guy.

CHAPTER 21
ALEXANDRA

I think my ovaries just exploded. Sebastian Crowe is barechested and holding a baby in the crook of his arm as if he's done it a thousand times. He grins down at her, swaying gently as he talks to Arrow.

"Psst," Bailey says beside me. "You've got a little drool—" She points to my open mouth, and I snap it closed before I realize she's teasing.

"Bitch," I mutter with a smile.

"It's a pretty picture," she says, nodding toward Sebastian and the baby.

"Is that Arrow's baby sister?" I ask.

"Yep. She's an adorable little thing, too. Come on, let's put this wine in the fridge."

I follow her into Arrow's house. Arrow invited everyone over for a Friday night cookout and an end-of-the-season swim. I got a ride with Bailey and intentionally left my suit at home. I might be leaving my beloved scarves behind now, but I'm not ready to model a swimsuit.

Before we make it back out to the patio, Mia comes in the French door with the baby in her arms. "It's Katie's bedtime," she says, snuggling the little one close. "Say good night."

"Good night, Katie," Bailey and I say in unison.

Bailey grabs a few wine glasses from the cabinet and fills two.

"How's the new roommate situation?" I ask as she hands me mine.

"Fine, I guess. He's never there. Between school, work, and football, he's always busy with something, so it's kind of like free money."

"I'm glad it worked out for you." I shift my gaze outside. "I don't get the impression that he and his dad get along really well, so I'm sure he's grateful that he didn't have to move home."

"What gives you that idea?" she asks as we head back outside and find seats around the fire.

"I don't know. They don't talk much, and when he and his dad are at the shop at the same time, it's always really tense, you know what I mean?"

She shrugs. "I don't get along with my old man, either. I think it's normal. Can I ask you something?" she asks, biting back a grin.

"Okay?"

"Do you think Mr. Crowe is kind of a hottie? I mean, for an old guy, he's still got it, am I right? And *those eyes*."

I shake my head at her. "I can honestly say the thought never crossed my mind."

"You're kidding! Why not?"

I enunciate carefully: "Because he's Sebastian's *dad*."

"Spoilsport," she says. "DILFs are a thing."

We dissolve into giggles, making all the guys turn to stare at us, and a couple of minutes later, Mia joins us. "What are you two up to?"

"The usual shenanigans," Bailey says, filling the third wine glass for Mia. "Bringing around the downfall of all good men."

"Of course," Mia mutters.

"The pool *is* heated if you want to swim," Arrow says, walking over to stand by Mia.

"No thanks," I say.

Bailey lifts her wine glass. "Priorities."

"Suit yourself," Arrow says. He stands behind Mia and rubs her shoulders.

Bailey scowls at him. "The girls need to catch up." She makes a shooing motion with her hand. "You get her all the time. Go be with your boys."

He grunts. "Yes, ma'am." He dips down and presses a kiss to the top of Mia's head before walking away.

My phone buzzes with a text, and I pull it out of my pocket to look at it.

> **Logan:** *I have dinner reservations at Oceanaire in Indianapolis tomorrow night. Any chance you*

want to keep me company?

"Oceanaire?" Bailey asks, staring at my screen. She looks at Mia. "Logan just invited her to dinner at Oceanaire."

Mia's eyes go wide. "Wow. That's such a nice restaurant. I take it this means your date last weekend went well? I want to hear all about it."

I shrug. "It was okay, I guess. He's really nice." *But I left the date more excited about his new bar than I am about the prospect of seeing him again.* I frown at the text. I thought I made it clear that I wasn't ready for this. "I told him I wasn't sure I was up for dating right now, though."

Bailey studies me. "I don't get it. Handsome man likes you, treats you right, and you seem to like him, so what's the problem? Is it the drug thing?"

I frown. "What drug thing?"

Bailey winces. "Shit. Sorry. It was a long time ago."

"Well, I didn't know, so obviously it's not that." But that information unsettles me more deeply than I admit. When someone you love loses their life to drugs—first metaphorically and then literally—the knee-jerk reaction is to despise them and anyone involved with them.

"What's the hold-up, then?" Bailey asks.

Mia rolls her eyes. "Don't mind her. She's totally aware of her hypocrisy as she asks this."

Bailey nods. "Oh, absolutely I am." She studies me while I type my reply to Logan, what I hope is a polite thanks-but-no-thanks. "So what is it?" she asks.

I pull my bottom lip between my teeth and look over my shoulder to make sure the guys are still otherwise occupied. "Sebastian."

"Sebastian?" Mia asks. Then her eyes light up and she bounces in her seat and smacks the back of Bailey's arm. "She said *Sebastian*!"

Bailey smirks. "Oh, I heard her."

I wave a hand, dismissing Mia's excitement. "He doesn't feel the same, so simmer down."

"The fuck he doesn't," Bailey says. "He can't keep his eyes off you."

My stomach flip-flops and my gaze settles on the man in question. Sebastian must have been in the pool before I got here, because his hair's wet and he has a towel slung around his shoulders.

A couple of years ago I would have laughed in her face, but things are different now. Not only did Sebastian kiss me at the party, I've caught him watching me. Sometimes he tries to hide it, but more and more, when I catch him, he just grins, unashamed. Like in women's studies, when he scribbled the note that said I looked *amazing*. "I don't understand what he wants," I admit. "One second, he's kissing me and tilting my whole world off balance, and the next he's backing away and telling me what a mistake it was to cross that line."

"Wanna sleep over and sneak into his room?" Bailey asks. "I think he just needs a solid shove across the line, and then he'll see it's not so bad."

That would be tempting if I weren't so mortified at the idea of him panicking after touching me. "He screws with my head. I think I've made peace with being his friend, and then he tells me how pretty I look with my hair down."

"You're his best friend's sister," Mia says. "He seems to think there are rules."

"That's what I told her," Bailey says.

I don't like that explanation. I've always believed that if you want someone badly enough, the rules don't matter. I'm not just some random girl who caught his eye. Sebastian knows me. "I'd just like to know how he really feels."

"You could ask him," Mia says.

Bailey rolls her eyes. "That would be a rookie mistake. Clearly this guy has spent five years trying to convince himself he shouldn't be with you, and yet he wants you enough that he kissed you anyway. Don't *ask* him, *seduce* him."

I gape at Bailey. "Yeah, right."

She chuckles and rubs her hands together. "I see whose idea catches your attention more."

"Because *yours* is ridiculous," I say.

"Why do you say that?" Mia asks. She cocks her head to the side. "Are you afraid he'd reject you or afraid it would change things between you?"

"Both."

"Who cares what you're afraid of?" Bailey says. "Do you want to hear my plan or not?"

My stomach is in knots, and I scowl at her. "Of course I want to hear it."

I should never ask Bailey for advice. She left the party early and without me so I'd have to get a ride home from Sebastian, and by the time he pulls his old truck into Mr. Patterson's driveway, the buzz of the wine has worn off enough that I'm not sure I can follow through with the plan.

"*This* is where you're living?" he asks as he throws the truck in park.

"Yep. It's ridiculous, isn't it?"

He lets out a low whistle and shakes his head. "Damn, Alex."

I grin. "Come in with me." Before he can answer, I pull my keys from my purse and climb out of the truck. I head to the front door, and when I turn back, Sebastian is standing by his truck, looking at me like he's trying to decide if following me is good idea. I'm not sure even I know the answer to that question, but I cling to the spontaneity that got me here, turn the key in the lock, and push into the house.

When I'm done disarming the alarm, Sebastian steps into the foyer. The empty house doesn't feel empty at all anymore. Everything about him makes me feel small. The breadth of his shoulders, the size of his hands. Even his voice seems big with the way it fills a room.

Sebastian scans the foyer, taking in the grand staircase, the marble floors, and the mounted deer heads before landing on me. "Jesus. I think this is what the other ninety-eight percent are pissed about."

Laughing, I grab his hand. "I want to show you something." With his warm hand in mine, I lead him through the house. "Come on."

We cut through the butler's pantry and into the sunporch that overlooks the pool area. Normally I take my time when walking through Mr. Patterson's house. It's beautiful. The kind of home I used to dream about buying for myself someday, and while Mr. P's choice of decor isn't necessarily my style (taxidermy much?), it's fun to daydream about having enough money to have and decorate a house this massive.

It's dark outside, but there's just enough light from the house and the moon that the pool is visible. I point to it as I spin around to him. "Are you up for it?"

"*You* want to *swim*?" Sebastian asks. He's standing just outside of the sunroom, hands tucked into his pockets.

"Yep."

"You hate swimming." He's confused, and it's cute.

"No, Bash. I hate people looking at me in a swimsuit. I actually love swimming."

His tongue darts out to wet his bottom lip and his chest rises with a deep breath. "Do you have a suit with you?"

I find the panel by the back door that controls the lights for the pool area. I click on the lights inside the pool but leave the others off. "Do I need one?"

CHAPTER 22
SEBASTIAN

Alex toes off her shoes then opens the door and steps out onto the dark patio. My gaze drops to the swing of her hips, the curve of her ass in those jeans, and my chest feels tight with everything I want but told myself I can't have. She stops in front of the pool, and all I can see is her silhouette in the moonlight. I'm hypnotized as she unbuttons her flannel shirt and lets it fall off her arms. She unbuttons her jeans and shimmies them off her hips before stepping free of them. She rises onto her toes and stretches her arms above her head, and I can't take my eyes off her.

When she turns to face me, I have to tamp down the impulse to reach over and hit all these switches until I find the one that turns on the patio lights. She's in a thin tank top and panties. I think the tank is white, but it's hard to tell. I want to see it all—the hard pebble of her nipples in the cool air, the hollow of her hipbones, the line of sensitive flesh just above her panties and below the hem of her tank. My heart races as if I've run the length of the field, and I'm just standing here, watching her, itching to touch, to take, to claim what I can't have. I want to follow the scar down her neck and over her breast and examine the juncture of smooth, unmarred ivory skin and textured scar. I want to brush my fingers over that space where demons I know too well reached beyond their boundaries and caught an innocent.

"Are you coming or not?" She turns away from me, and in one swift, graceful motion, she arches her back and dives into the pool.

I rush outside without letting myself think about what I'm doing. I can't be expected to be an arm's reach from Alexandra DeLuca in her panties and keep my hands to myself, but I'm not going to sit back and let her swim alone in the dark. I don't care if she's a good swimmer and I don't care if she sobered up on the drive here. She's buzzed enough to strip in front of me, so she's too buzzed to swim alone.

I stand at the edge of the pool, staring down into the glowing water and turned on as fuck. Because she's so beautiful it hurts. *Literally*, it hurts—a knee in the junk and a fist around my heart all at the same time. Every minute I spend with her is only confirmation of what I already knew—that hers is a beauty that starts at her very core.

When she surfaces, she props her elbows at my feet and smiles up at me. She slicks her hair back and pulls it over her shoulder, making rivulets of water stream down her chest and into her cleavage. The tank is white and low cut, and her bra beneath it is black and lace.

Fuck me.

"Are you getting in?" She grabs my jeans and tugs. "Come on, Bash. Strip."

I swallow hard. "I can't go skinny-dipping with you, beautiful."

"But I'm not naked. It's only skinny-dipping if you're naked. Isn't this the same as wearing a swimsuit? I have a shirt on. And underwear."

You wouldn't for long if I got in there with you. I step back, out of her grasp, and her hand settles on her chest and her smile falters. I'm trying real hard to be a saint here, and instead I'm hurting her feelings.

"Fuck." I yank my shirt over my head and unbutton my jeans, letting them fall to the ground before stepping out of them.

I can't tell for sure, but I think she's looking at my boxer briefs. I doubt the moonlight allows her to see how much blood my brain is directing to regions south of my waistband, but the idea of her looking doesn't do much to relieve my discomfort. I've had fantasies that start like that, and there's no reason to give my brain any ideas.

Tonight is no different than every other day with Alex. Two friends hanging out.

In their underwear.

She follows my every move as I lower myself into the pool. The water is warm, and sinking into it releases tension I didn't realize I was holding.

"Crazy things Alex DeLuca makes me do," she says, her voice low in an attempt to imitate me. "Swim in my underwear after dark."

"Crazy things Alex DeLuca makes me do," I say, swimming toward her. "Act out Juliet's lines in the balcony scene for a tenth-grade English project. After that, I'd say swimming in my underwear is pretty tame."

She giggles. "We got an A, didn't we?"

"I could have done without the dress."

I can't see her face, but judging from the scoffing sound she makes, I'm guessing she's rolling her eyes. "The girls *loved* you in the dress."

"I wouldn't have done that for anyone else."

She swims forward and loops her arms around my neck. "Well, tenth-grade me appreciated it." She looks up at me through wet lashes.

My breath catches.

How can you be so beautiful?

I keep waiting for her to back away and let me go, but her arms are still around my neck, her body nearly pressed against mine. I could have my hands all over her in the next breath. Does she know what she's doing to me?

I swallow hard, but the words I shouldn't say roll right off my tongue. "Having you this close puts ideas in my head."

"Anything good?" she asks.

My gaze drops to her mouth, to the delicate ridges of her collarbone, to the swell of her breasts in her wet tank. "Good but dangerous."

"Because we're friends?" she whispers.

"Because you're too precious to me."

"Precious things are for boxes and safes." She wriggles closer, the front of her body rubbing against mine. "They're locked away, hidden. I've spent more of the last four years hiding than I have living. If that's what it means to be precious, then I want to be cheap. Common."

"But there's nothing common about you."

"I want to live. I want to *feel*." She presses her lips together and drops her gaze to my chest. "I could swear I catch you looking at me, and I could swear that sometimes what I see in your eyes is a reflection of how I feel when I look at you. I'm here and I'm sober, and I'm asking. Please. Kiss me. Touch me." She brings her gaze back up to meet mine and tilts her head to the side as she studies me. "We can be friends again tomorrow, but don't make me stay in that box tonight."

"I'm sorry." I hate those words. They always sound too thin. Maybe it's because when we really mean them, they carry the weight of so much that's left unsaid that it's a wonder they can make it off our tongues at all. When the apology is sincere and necessary, there's too much weight for three syllables, too much burden. I don't know if she could ever forgive me for my secrets, but do know I'll break a million times before letting her shatter. "I can't."

She drops her arms to her sides and backs away, and I grab her wrist before she can get too far. I can't take it anymore. I can't take my guts being twisted with how much I want her. I can't take the way she's looking at me like I've broken her heart. But mostly, I can't take another second wondering if she really tastes as sweet as I remember.

I slide my arm around her waist and pull her back against me as the other hand threads through her hair. And it's stupid and foolish and selfish, but I kiss her. I lower my mouth to hers and sweep my tongue across her lips until she opens beneath me. I cup her face in my hands and kiss her for all I'm worth. I kiss her the way a man kisses a woman he's wanted for five years. I kiss her the way a guy kisses a girl when he needs her to know she's beautiful. If a kiss would speak, this one would say she's everything and I'm nothing. If a kiss were constructed with words, this one would be stacks of *beautiful,* glass windows of *precious,* and stone pillars of *too fucking good for me.*

Because this kiss isn't just a bad idea. It's a broken promise.

ALEXANDRA

Sebastian's mouth is magic on mine. It's like a fantasy but better, because this is real, and I never could have imagined the full heat of him or how small I'd feel when his big hands cup my face, or the way his breath is choppy and desperate—as if this is equal parts exhilarating and terrifying.

His mouth skims across my jaw and down my neck, then

back up to nip at my earlobe. "Is this what you want?" His voice is low, more breath than sound. "You want me to make you feel good?"

Before I can reply, he's kissing his way down my neck again, mouth sucking, teeth scraping. His hands find my ass and then he's shifting our positions in the water, pressing my back to the side of the pool and lifting my legs to wrap around his waist.

"Please," I moan, because he's hard between my legs and pressed right where I need him. I rock into him as he takes my breast in his big hand and grazes my hard nipple through the layers of wet cotton and lace.

"Please what?" he asks. He draws back and meets my eyes.

"Touch me."

"*Fuck.*" He lowers his mouth to mine, but it's as if our whole bodies are part of the kiss. Everything moving and searching and rocking. He squeezes my breast then pinches my nipple between two fingers. When I roll my hips, his cock presses so perfectly against my clit that my whole body shudders. My thighs flex, pulling him closer, and I thread my fingers through his hair and tug.

"Tell me to stop," he whispers against my ear. "*Fuck*, you feel so good, Alex, but I don't want to hurt you."

"Then don't stop."

"Jesus," he hisses. I roll my hips, unable to resist that delicious friction, and he groans. He brings a hand to my face, cupping my jaw in his big palm. "I feel like I've spent my whole life wanting to see you like this. Turned on. Undone."

His words are intoxicating. I'm lost in the sound of his voice and the thrill of his touch. He nips at my bottom lip, cups my breasts, presses his hard cock against the needy ache between my legs.

"More." I want to feel him inside me. I want to know the weight of him and see his eyes when he's as close to me as two people can get. "Please. I won't break."

"Maybe I want to see you break." He wraps his hand around my hip and curls his fingers. "Maybe I want to make you fall apart with my mouth and put you back together one piece at a time."

Suddenly, he's lifting me onto the side of the pool and spreading my legs. He slides his hands under my ass and pulls me to his face.

"Oh," I gasp. Because he's kissing me. His mouth is between my legs and his lips and tongue and *oh my God*. I've never felt anything like this. The air is cool on my skin, but I can only focus on the heat of his mouth and the scratch of his beard between my legs.

I put my hands behind me to prop myself up and stare in disbelief at the image of him there, his hands gripping my hips, his mouth working delicious magic against me.

But then he pulls the strip of lace to the side and there's nothing between his tongue and my clit, and I can't keep my eyes open anymore. I can't do anything but hold on as my body scales some invisible cliff. I cling and I rise, and his hands grip my hips tighter, his mouth relentless. I climb, and I stretch, and then there's nothing but release and cool air as I fall.

CHAPTER 23
ALEXANDRA

Slowly, Sebastian lowers me back down into the water, his eyes locked on mine as my body slides over his. "You okay?" he whispers, his voice a little gruff. His mouth tilts into a lopsided grin that makes my heart squeeze.

"I'm…" I take a breath and shake my head. "Yeah. I'm good."

He studies me and tucks my hair behind my ear. I'm equal parts loose-limbed satisfaction and awkward energy. I've never done that before, and I didn't expect it tonight. My old boyfriend wasn't interested, and if I was curious, I wouldn't have had the courage to ask. Does Sebastian expect me to return the favor now?

The idea makes my heart kick into another gear—pounding faster and harder. Because this is Sebastian, and touching him in any way makes my whole body hum, but the idea of putting my mouth on him makes my nerves rattle.

I skim my hands down his chest and to the waistband of his briefs. He hisses out a breath and squeezes his eyes shut.

"Hey, Alex! Are you out here?"

Just as the patio lights click on, Sebastian and I both spin toward the back door and the sound of my brother's voice.

Dante's gaze shifts between me and Sebastian. "What the fuck?"

"What are you doing here?" My voice squeaks. "Jesus, Dante. Have you heard of knocking?"

His jaw hardens and his hands flex to fists at his sides. "I called. I knocked. No one answered. The front door was unlocked."

"What are you doing here?"

"Mom wanted me to check on you." He narrows his eyes on Sebastian, and in the gleaming patio lights, betrayal is all over his face. "But I guess you're not alone."

He turns on his heel and goes back inside. Thirty seconds later, I hear the roar of his Harley.

I turn to Sebastian. "I'm so sorry. I should have locked the door. I should have…" Suddenly, I realize how much worse it would have been if Dante had walked out here even two minutes earlier. "Oh God…"

Sebastian drops his hands to his sides and turns away from me. Bowing his head, he rests his arms on the edge of the pool and catches his breath.

"I'll talk to Dante," I promise. "I'll make sure he's not angry with you."

"I'm not worried about Dante," he says quietly. "I can handle him."

But he's worried about something. "Then what's wrong?"

He drags a hand over his face and pulls in a ragged breath. As he moves to the shallow end, water runs down his hard chest in rivulets that I want to follow with my fingertips. But I can't, because the second Dante appeared, Sebastian withdrew. It crushes me to watch him put as much space between us as possible, and my throat grows thick.

"I shouldn't be here with you," he says. "I know that. Dante knows that."

"You're both wrong." I feel like I've been cut in two. How could we back-pedal so quickly?

"You say that like you know me." He shakes his head. "It wasn't any different in high school, either. You never saw me for who I was. You always thought I was better."

"And who were you?" I ask, my voice rough with unshed tears.

"I was a fuck-up, Alex. A user."

A user. "You mean drugs?"

He shrugs. He keeps his eyes cast forward on nothing, but frustration rolls off him. "Drugs. People. Whatever would get me ahead. Anything that would make me feel good for a minute." He drags both hands through his hair. "Fuck, I even used you." The words are a smack in the face. I don't want to believe what he's saying. "You think I could have passed English with all the school that I missed if you hadn't gotten me through it?"

"And who are you now?"

He turns to me, and suddenly I wish we were in the dark again, because Sebastian's eyes land on my scars. I've never wanted to cover them more than in this moment. "I don't know what you want from me, but I'm afraid it's something I can't give."

I take a deep breath. "What if I just want sex? What if I want you to take me inside to the bedroom and finish what we started?"

SEBASTIAN

I squeeze my eyes shut at her suggestion. It's too easy to imagine. Too tempting. Alex in my arms, warm and willing. I need to get out of here. She's soaking wet and so fucking sexy, and all I can think about is how damn sweet she tastes and how good it felt to make her fall apart.

I'm walking a tightrope tonight of being as honest with her as I can be without hurting her. Honesty without breaking any more promises.

"What happens tomorrow?" I ask. "Can you look me in the eye and tell me you're fine with tonight being some one-time thing? Because even if you don't know it, you're worth more than that."

I climb out of the pool, find my clothes, and struggle to pull my jeans over my wet legs.

When I head back into the house, she follows me in, her clothes in a ball held tightly against her chest. She's shivering.

The water itself was warm, but the air's cool.

"You need a hot shower," I say, dragging my gaze over her. "And I'm going to get out of here before I decide I need to help you with that." Hell, I'm already going to have blue balls for the next month.

"I never felt used," she blurts before I can turn away.

I blink at her. "What?"

"In high school, you said you used me, but I never felt used."

"That's because it never occurs to you that you should be getting something back from the people who take from you." I lower my voice. "You've been that way as long as I've known you. Always doing for someone else. Never getting shit in return. Good night, Alex." I turn toward the front, but I barely make it two steps before she stops me.

"Sebastian? Wait a minute."

Before I can turn back to her, her hands are on my back, skimming down my lats and making my gut knot.

"It's a phoenix," she says, touching me. I don't have to see what she's doing to know her fingertips are tracing along the flames that cover my lower back. I know the artwork well, and as she examines it, I imagine her hands grazing the spirals of smoke that wrap around the bird's feet. She uses both hands to follow the bird's wingspan to the tops of my shoulders and backs of my triceps, where the intricate pattern makes the feathers look like a design all its own. The last thing she touches is the human hand reaching from the fire, reaching for the phoenix.

I stay frozen through her examination, listening to her

breathe, feeling the slight trembling of her fingers and the soft puffs of air against my inked skin.

When she drops her hands and steps back, I turn to face her. Her face is pale and her eyes are wide.

I wait for her questions, but she doesn't ask any.

Her chest rises and falls with her breath. "Good night, Sebastian."

CHAPTER 24
ALEXANDRA

I wait for the sound of the front door closing before I head to the front of the house to lock up and set the alarm. I go straight to the master bathroom and run the steam shower on hot before stripping out of my wet panties, tank top, and bra. My head is spinning and it's been hours since I've had any wine, so I can't blame it on that.

Sebastian has a tattoo of a phoenix, and I didn't even know. The phoenix is the talisman for burn victims. It's a symbol I've been drawn to since those first days in the hospital when I was in such a deep, dark place that only the power of the mythical could reach me. Does that tattoo have anything to do with the night my sister died? Or is it just a coincidence? My hand goes to my side and the tattoo of the phoenix I had inked there when I was in Colorado.

He says I don't really know him. Before tonight, I wanted to know anything about Sebastian that he'd tell me, but now I have this cold, sick feeling in my stomach, and I'm not sure I want to know anything.

SEBASTIAN

I'm not surprised to find Dante waiting for me in front of my apartment when I pull in. He's in a leather jacket and boots, standing by his Harley like some badass biker cliché, ready to throw a punch.

If that's what he wants, I can take it. Fuck, I deserve it. I can still taste her on my lips.

I park in the space beside his bike and climb out.

"Not Alex," he says. He doesn't look angry anymore, just weary.

"It won't happen again."

"This isn't what I had in mind when I asked you to help her come out of her shell. What the fuck were you thinking?"

That she was so soft and smelled so damn good that I wanted to kiss her and touch her more than I've ever wanted anything else. "I wasn't."

He turns away, his jaw ticking. "We almost lost her too."

"I fucking *know*. That fire—"

"I don't mean in the fire. After we buried Martina, it was as if Alex just shut down. She was with us, but she was gone. If she had to deal with the fact that—"

"You don't need to say anything else. I get it."

His exhale is heavy and loaded with worry, and I wish he'd just punch me in the face. It would hurt less than having a friend point out that I've fucked up immeasurably. Again.

Martina's Journal

I met someone today. I'm gonna call him Mr. Bedroom Eyes. Because damn. Such good eyes, and when he looks at me, I wish we were in the bedroom. Move over, Sebastian Crowe, I've found myself a Real Man.

I was about done chasing after Sebastian anyway, and the minute I met Mr. Bedroom Eyes, I knew my days of chasing a boy were over. I've always preferred men to boys anyway. He's older than me, but that's the way I like it.

Sebastian spent too much time trying to keep me in check. Trying to pull me back from partying too much or too hard. He was more interested in being my babysitter than my lover.

Mr. Bedroom Eyes knows what's going on. I met him at a party, and I think he's important, because everyone acted different when he arrived. They all scrambled to make sure he had everything he wanted, and when I saw him I decided I was going to make sure I was on that list.

He caught me watching him and sent one of his boys over to invite me to join him upstairs. He headed for the stairs before I even had a chance to answer. That kind of confidence is so fucking hot, as is the rest of him.

I went upstairs, and Mr. Bedroom Eyes was waiting for me. When I stepped into the room, he closed the door behind me, ran his thumb over my lips, and before he even kissed me, he told me to get on my knees. See? A man. Don't worry, he earned his nickname. And me? I earned my high.

This might be the start of something beautiful.

CHAPTER 25
ALEXANDRA

"Hey there, beautiful."

I look up from the ticket I'm writing up to see Logan Lucas standing on the other side of the service write-up counter. "Logan. Is everything okay? Nothing happened to your car, did it?"

He laughs. "No. I'm not here about my car."

"Oh. Did you need to talk to Sebastian?"

He scratches the back of his neck. "I'm here to see if I could talk you into going out to dinner with me."

"Oh." It's been over a month since my date with Logan, and I really did intend to call him once I sorted out what I wanted. Then, almost four weeks ago, I was half naked in a pool with Sebastian, who made it very clear things between us couldn't go anywhere. Instead of thinking of Logan, I've been burying myself in school and work and telling my love-sick heart to stop whining.

Logan winces. "*Oh*? Is that sweet girl for 'No, please get out of my life'?"

"No!" I shake my head. "Not at all."

He shrugs. "I know I said I'd wait for you to call me, but patience has never been my best attribute." He folds his arms on the counter and leans forward. "What do you say, Alexandra? Put a guy out of his misery?"

Logan's in a pressed, long-sleeved black oxford shirt and dress pants, and I'm in my work uniform—making me feel like the cheap beer to his expensive champagne. "I'm a mess. I can't go out with you looking like this."

He leans across the counter and says, "I like you just as you are."

As he pulls back, a smile curls my lips without permission. I can't help it. This guy says the sweetest things. Sebastian made it clear that nothing can happen between us, and I've had a month to attempt to forget about his mouth between my legs. It's time for me to give Logan a real chance. "I can't go tonight. What about Sunday? Or the next weekend?"

Logan cuts his eyes away from me for a split second, and I follow his gaze and realize Sebastian's watching us, standing in the corner with his arms folded. Determined to ignore him, I turn my attention back to Logan.

"Sunday works," he says. He lifts a small black bag to the counter. "I brought you a present. You don't have to open it now, but I saw it and it made me think of you."

I grin. "Seriously?"

"What can I say?" He points to his chest. "This guy's got a crush. I'll see you Sunday."

"I can't wait."

"That makes two of us." He lifts my hand to his lips and kisses my knuckles before releasing me and turning to leave.

I watch him go—the broad shoulders, the slight swagger of a man who oozes confidence—and when he's gone, I push past Sebastian and into the locker room to open my gift.

The bag is stuffed with purple tissue paper, and I bite my lip as I remove it. My nerves click to life when I pull black, sheer fabric from the bag. It's absolutely beautiful, but if this is lingerie—

I drop the bag, and the sheer material slides through my fingertips. It's a long scarf that's embroidered with flowers.

"Jesus Christ," Sebastian says behind me. "Now he's dressing you?"

I swallow back a thousand possible responses—about how at least Logan thinks about me, about how I can't wait around for a guy who doesn't want me.

Setting my jaw, I spin on my heel to face him. "You know what? Fuck you. Did you ever think I might want a guy who looks at me like a woman? Did you ever think maybe I don't want to be just one of the guys? Maybe Logan thinks about me when I'm not in front of him, and maybe I *like* that. And if you don't, that's too bad." I force my hands to relax where I've wrinkled fistfuls of the beautiful fabric. I wince as I study it. I'm not being fair. I told him I wanted one night, promised we could go back to friends after, and I'm breaking my promise. "Fuck you, Sebastian," I mutter, even though it's not fair. It's always him, and I don't know how to make my heart let go.

"Alex." The sound of my name startles me, and when I lift my head, he's right there, inches from me. He places his palms against the lockers on either side of my head and leans forward. "Do you think this is easy for me? Do you think I like walking away when you offer yourself to me?" His gaze dips to my lips, and he studies me so intently that he might as well be touching me. My skin tingles, and everything inside me seems to dissolve. This is what Sebastian does to me. He turns me to liquid, weakens my defenses, and makes me melt from the inside out. And then he walks away.

"I don't know what to think about you anymore. I'm just trying to move on."

"Does it have to be with him?" His voice is low, rough, and he drops one hand from beside my head and cups my face. "A guy who tries to cover up your scars? You deserve better."

"Who do you think is better, Sebastian? Because let me tell you something about women: we want to be with someone who wants to be with us. I just want to be *wanted*."

The intensity in his gaze falters. He smells so damn good this close to me, and God help me, but I want to feel the rub of his beard against my neck again. I want to know if his lips could possibly feel as good as I remember. I have a date with a beautiful, kind, thoughtful man, and I'm standing here silently saying a shameful prayer for Sebastian to kiss me. To prove me wrong and insist that he wants me more than anyone else.

Sebastian steps back, and his eyes drop to the sheer material that's fallen from my hands and pooled at my feet. "He'd better not fucking hurt you." He shakes his head before pushing out of the locker room. The door slams closed behind him, making the room shake, and I lean back against the lockers and slowly sink to the floor.

SEBASTIAN

I use my key to let myself into Mom and Dad's, and walk to the den where Dad pays the bills.

The good news? Dante said Dad's been paying him again. He still insists I'm worried over nothing.

The bad news? Dad bought Mom a Camaro. A fucking *Camaro*.

I lost my mind today. I'd just found out about the car and it brought all my old worries to the surface, and seconds later I was faced with Logan Lucas arranging a date with Alex. It was too much at once, and after four weeks of being on my best behavior where Alex is concerned, I slipped again.

"*I just want to be* wanted."

Those words twisted the knife that's been in my gut since she got home, but I remembered the fucking Camaro Dad just bought Mom and I walked away.

Mom's dreamed of that car for as long as I can remember. The only reason he didn't buy her one back in the dealing days was because he didn't want her to be suspicious. He didn't want Mom carrying the burden of the lines he'd crossed to take care of his family. That was "a man's burden," he said, for him and me alone. In retrospect, he was giving a boy a man's burden, and even though I thought I could handle it, I wish he never had.

I just need to know for sure that he isn't back in that world, and need to see it for myself.

The checkbook is on the desk, and I flip to the register, scanning the deposits and withdrawals. Everything looks normal, except that his deposits from the shop are more in the last two months than they were before. He gave himself a raise, and the cash-flow situation at the shop certainly supports that the raise is coming entirely from Crowe's Automotive funds.

Dad's not stupid enough to deposit big chunks of cash, but if he bought the car with cash, it would have been a red flag.

When I see it, I sit taller. He wrote a check for the Camaro—a deposit paid to a local dealer. When he was dealing, he bought everything he could with cash from people who weren't going to leave a paper trail. He'd buy a car from a guy for five grand, pay cash, and the guy would write a receipt that said he'd paid a hundred. People do it all the time to avoid paying taxes on their vehicles, but Dad did it as an easy way to launder drug money.

I flip through a stack of papers and stop when I find a folder from the dealership. Inside are details about the loan for the car and the payment plan. My shoulders sag with relief.

"What exactly did you think you'd find in there?" Dad asks from the hall.

My pulse races at the sound of his voice, and my face heats from the disappointment in his tone. "I was worried." I put the papers back down and return everything to neat stacks. I should apologize. I've invaded his privacy and broken his trust. But I don't feel fucking sorry.

"Worried I broke our promise?" He steps into the den and flips on the overhead light. "Worried that I'd gotten greedy?"

I close my eyes. "The time away from work. The trips out of town. You bought Mom a fucking Camaro."

"I'm not allowed to spend time with my wife? I'm not allowed to buy her nice things? I've worked hard my whole life."

I stand and wipe my sweaty palms on my jeans. "I needed to see for myself." I know he's waiting for my apology. I know I owe him one. But it's stuck in my throat, tied down by bitterness for the man who used his fifteen-year-old son as his own personal drug mule.

"Get out of here," he whispers.

I keep my eyes cast down as I leave, and with every step I feel the fissure in our relationship grow wider, a chasm I'm not sure either of us is capable of spanning.

Martina's Journal

Mom confronted me after school today. She sat

me down at the kitchen table with a snack like a six-year-old and asked if I was depressed. "If you need to talk, I'm happy to listen." She flashed that watery mom smile that told me she was way more worried than she would admit. "Or if you're not up to talking to me, we could find someone outside the family, maybe."

I know "someone" is code for a shrink.

I insisted that everything was fine and she doesn't need to worry. She doesn't want to know anyway. There are things that I won't even write about here—because why relive the shittiest experiences? And because I'm scared some day she might read this, and I don't need her to beat herself up.

Are you reading this, Mom? Fucking stop. It's not your business. There's shit I don't tell you BECAUSE I LOVE YOU, BITCH.

Do I look depressed? Because I feel great. Mr. Bedroom Eyes bought me a diamond necklace. It has three-quarter-carat diamonds, each situated on a trio of golden petals.

It's so beautiful, and I spent the whole night in nothing but my sparkling gift and a pair of heels. I don't need a shrink. I have him. Not that I can tell Mom that. Her sixteen-year-old daughter with an older man? The horror.

You see, I think normal sixteen-year-olds are

more like me than they are like Alex. They spend a lot of time with their friends, hiding out in their rooms, and avoiding their parents. Surely Mom should know this by now, but Alex gets my parents confused. She likes spending time with Mom and Dad. She likes making sure she's home for dinner every night. She likes laughing at Dad's corny jokes and watching Mom's old VHS tapes of Murder, She Wrote. Alex is always setting unrealistic expectations that I cannot be expected to meet. She sets the bar for "perfect daughter" really high, and Mom forgets that I'm not like Alex.

I wish I could be…

CHAPTER 26
ALEXANDRA

Sebastian and I stare at each other from the table in Mr. Patterson's massive kitchen. "They're not gonna show," he says. "They didn't even bother coming for the test yesterday."

We've procrastinated as long as possible on this group project, and it's do-or-die time.

We were supposed to meet with our group tonight to come up with questions to ask the curator we're interviewing in New Hope. I thought meeting here would be a great idea. We could work around the big island in the kitchen, and I could feed the stoners to make them happy.

Instead, our group members have ditched us, and Sebastian and I are back in the same house where things changed four weeks ago. It's like everything that happened that night is hanging in the air between us.

"So much for my dreams of playing hostess," I mutter. "I even cooked."

"I'm sorry they stood us up," Sebastian says, closing his notebook and grabbing another pastry-puff-wrapped hot dog from the tray. I think that's his third. "The mummies are delicious."

"Don't look at me like that," I say, biting back a smile. "They're festive. Halloween is just around the corner."

He waves his hot dog at me. "You really think Beavis and Butt-Head would have appreciated the theme?" He shakes his head. "Never mind. It's food. You'd be their goddess." He swallows the last bite and frowns up at the cabinets. "Is that a raccoon?"

"The whole house is full of taxidermy," I say. "If I thought Mr. Patterson wouldn't care, I'd give it all away so I didn't have to live with it. But he's a little obsessed, so I'm pretty sure he'd notice."

"I can't get over this house," he says. "It's insane. I didn't even know there were people this rich in this city."

"Do you want to see the rest of it?"

He cocks a brow. "Like, a tour?"

"Sure. I'll be your tour guide." It's gotta be better than sitting here thinking about what would have happened last month if Dante hadn't shown up. I leave the kitchen and head into the foyer. Sebastian follows me up the stairs. "When I was little, I always wanted to live in a house with two sets of stairs. This place has *three*."

"Why?"

"Because it's so fucking huge, I guess."

He laughs. "No, why did you always want to live in a house

with two sets of stairs?"

I shrug. "Because it was cool. Then, when I was older, probably because I imagined sneaking boys up to my room on the back stairs." All those fantasies were specifically about Sebastian, but I'm not going to tell him that.

At the top of the stairs, I show him the two guest bedrooms, each with its own king-size bed, five-piece bathroom, and walk-in closet. Then I lead him to the end of the hall.

"This is my favorite room," I say, swinging open the double doors. The library has floor-to-ceiling bookshelves, vaulted ceilings, and a stone fireplace.

"Goddamn," Sebastian whispers. There's a look of wonder on his face.

"That's where he drinks his favorite scotch." I indicate the center of the room, where there are four leather armchairs around a circular coffee table. "And stairwell number two," I say, pointing to the wrought iron railing off to the right.

He arches a brow. "And this is where you'd sneak up your boyfriends."

"Why not?" I grin. "Can you even imagine growing up in a place like this?"

"Honestly? No. I don't even know what that would be like." He turns a slow circle, his gaze pointed at the ceiling. "Not a fucking clue."

"Me neither." I keep my tone light because his mood has gone dark. "Your kids will be able to tell us what it's like." When he frowns, I say, "Come on, you're amazing, Bash. What are you guys now, five and one? That's insane."

He grins, and their season has been so impressive, it *should* make him smile. "I'm not the only one on the team. We couldn't have done it without Chris and Mason and, hell, everyone else. The team works together to make it happen."

"Sure, but what you do on the football field is like magic. You just go and push and churn your legs like there aren't three giant dudes trying to pull you down at the same time. If you wanted to go pro, I bet you could."

"I…" He shakes his head. "Thank you. I put myself at the disadvantage by coming back here, so I'm not sure what's going to happen."

"Why do you say that?"

"If you play D1 ball, there are rules about transfers. They don't want people hopping around from school to school, so they require you to sit out a year. Now I'm in my junior year, but it's my first season playing with this team."

"You're already making such a big impression. The fans go crazy when you have the ball." I grin. "I sit in the stands and want to tell everyone that you're my friend. It's like knowing a celebrity."

He studies my face, and his chest rises as he draws in a deep breath. "I won't pretend I don't dream about it. We'll see, I guess."

Suddenly, it's all I can do not to throw my arms around his neck, rise onto my toes, and press my mouth to his. Sebastian is so modest when it comes to his game, and it's almost as if he's afraid that hoping too much will make his chance disappear.

What is it like going through life afraid to hope? The idea makes my chest ache for him.

"What about you?" he asks.

"What about me?"

The side of his mouth hitches up in a lopsided grin. "What do you dream about?"

Your mouth on mine. Your voice in my ear. Your hand in mine. But I dream about more than Sebastian, don't I? I lift my hands and turn up my palms. "I don't know. I feel like everyone knows what they want to do with their life but me. My brothers think I should spend the rest of my days working on cars, but as much as I love to drool over a hot classic, I don't want to be a mechanic forever. Does that make me a snob?"

He shakes his head. "Not at all." He releases a puff of air that's more frustration than laugh. "I tell my dad all the time that loving cars isn't the same as wanting to make a career with cars."

"Exactly, but that's always the thing I've been good at, ya know? It was what made me special, so if that's not what I want to do with my life, I'm not sure which way to turn."

"When you left to work for your aunt, I thought you were leaving Blackhawk Valley for good," he says.

"I guess that was the plan at first."

His eyes skim my face, like he's trying to figure something out. "Why did you want to leave?"

"It was just too much, you know? I saw her everywhere I looked. Every morning I woke up in the bedroom we've shared since we were kids. Every meal, I ate at a table where we grew up fighting over who'd gotten the bigger serving of ice cream. Everything reminded me of her, and everyone looked at me with so much pity in their eyes. It was just too much." *Some days I could barely breathe.* "Leaving seemed like the right thing to do, and at first it was kind of a relief. Aside from my aunt, no one knew my story. No one looked at me and saw my dead sister. But it didn't make the pain go away. I missed my family, and after two years I realized that I wasn't moving on with my life at all. I was in homeostasis. Hibernating until I could heal up enough to come back home."

"And now you're ready to be back?" he asks.

"Have you ever seen *Saving Private Ryan*?"

"The war movie?"

I nod. "Yeah. So his brothers have died and they're supposed to pull him out of the war and send him home. They go through hell, and all these people die in their attempts to rescue Private Ryan from the war and send him home safely. At the end, Tom Hanks' character is dying. In his final breath, he tells Private Ryan, 'Earn this.' I don't know if I was ready to jump into college or not, but I knew I wasn't earning anything doing what I was. I want my life to have some sort of *purpose*. But it's almost as if the wish itself paralyzes me. What if I was spared from the fire but I don't ever make anything of my life? What if I'm just a girl who has a meaningless job and leads a meaningless life? I was given a second chance, and it feels like I should do something profound with it. But what? I don't know if I'm ready for anything." It's never felt more true than tonight. "I just realized there are some things you can't run away from."

He draws in a ragged breath and ducks his head so I can't see his face. "True."

"What about you? You said you took a penalty for your transfer to BHU, but are you glad to be back?"

"Mostly." He clears his throat, and I can tell that whatever he wants to say is important. "When I left, it wasn't just about football. My dad and I have a complicated relationship, and I felt like I couldn't be my own person with him looking over my shoulder."

"And now here you are, working for him. That must not be easy."

He studies the row of books in front of him, running his fingers along the stiff spines. "I love my dad. I'm proud of the hard work he's done, and I know he's made a lot of sacrifices for his family, but..." He drops his hand, turning away from the books and meeting my eyes. "Sometimes I hate him just as much as I love him. Is that even possible? And what kind of son admits that out loud?"

My heart twists for him. "No one said family was easy or that love wasn't complicated."

"I don't want love to be complicated," he says. "I just want it to *be*. No fears. No doubts. No fucking regrets." His eyes stay on mine as he says this, and I wonder if we're still talking about his dad. When he looks away, his shoulders tense. "I should go."

"Are we still on for Sunday, driving to New Hope?"

"Definitely," he says. "I'm looking forward to it."

"We can be home by five, right?"

"Sure. Why? Hot date?" he asks, and when I just look at him, his grin falls away and I see that he remembers. "I'll have you back by five."

Martina's Journal

One of the things I've learned about Mr. Bedroom Eyes is that he is insanely private. The rare times he goes to parties, he stays in the shadows. He keeps his hands clean for the sake of public appearance and doesn't like people looking at him. He's a businessman, you see. Gotta have a front or everyone might think your money comes from—gasp—drugs or something. He seems to have everyone around at his beck and call, and yet he doesn't want any attention.

I found out he's married, which came as quite the shock. His wife must be completely clueless, but when I asked about her, he got angry. No personal questions. Fine. I get it.

I skipped school a few times last week to be with him. One day he took me to his apartment in Indianapolis. He bought me this ridiculously expensive lingerie, and when I modeled it for him, we got high and drank champagne and he fucked me from behind while I looked out over the city.

I don't understand why I have to stay in school. He's loaded and could totally take care of me. But he insists that I carry on with my normal life.

"Be a good little girl," he said when he dropped me off, and it would have pissed me off, except then he smacked my ass and whispered some really dirty promises into my ear, so I let it slide.

CHAPTER 27
SEBASTIAN

Alex is so close, it hurts. Except for our intense conversation on Thursday night, we've hardly spoken in the last month. She's avoided me at the shop, and in women's studies she's taken seats across the room from me. If she's been by the apartment to see Bailey, I wasn't there. And now we're in my truck on the way to the art exhibition in New Hope, Indiana. I can't decide if I want to go back in time and thank twenty-year-old me for buying this truck that's too damn small inside or if I want to punch him in the face for it.

Because with Alex in the passenger seat, it's torture. Her short black dress inches up her thighs every time she shifts. Her smell invaded my senses the moment she slid into the cab, and I can't stop thinking about having her propped up on the edge of the pool and the sweet sounds she made when I kissed between her legs.

"Thanks again for driving today. I would have driven myself if my car didn't act like it's on its last breath." She shakes her head. "I shouldn't say that out loud. If people in Blackhawk Valley find out one of the mechanics at Crowe's can't fix her own car, you'll lose so much business."

"You said it's the transmission?"

"I'm sure of it, but I've been in denial. It'll cost more in parts to fix than I paid for the thing to begin with."

"There's no reason for us to take two cars anyway, especially since Cheech and Chong dropped the class." I keep my eyes on the road, but I can feel her watching me. The truth is, I can't believe she's here. I can't believe she's *willing* to be this close to me after what a dick I was about the whole Logan situation. I just hate thinking about her going out with him. I hate that he bought her a fucking scarf when she's finally found the courage to go without them. And I hate that he gets to be with her without guilt over his mistakes eating him alive.

My knuckles turn white as I clench the steering wheel. I signal to take the next exit, and after pulling into an abandoned gas station, I climb out of the truck. We're in the middle of fucking nowhere, and the air is fresh and clear. It smells like cut grass and blue skies and not at all like her. Maybe that should be a relief, but it's not. Nothing about stepping away from her has ever felt like a relief. Keeping my distance is the burden I've carried for five years, and I'm fucking exhausted.

Leaning against the truck, I tilt my face up to the wispy white clouds floating across the bright blue sky. The day they buried

Martina wasn't too different than this one. The bright, happy sky mocked the storm brewing in my chest. If I close my eyes, I can almost imagine those years of my life never happened. Guilt thrives in darkness. It shrivels in the light, and this sunny day seems to promise a new beginning I'm not convinced I deserve.

I focus on the feel of the sun on my face, and I'm not surprised when I hear her door snap closed or when her hand slides over my bicep.

"Hey," she whispers. "What's wrong?"

I open my eyes. I don't know if it's the relief of finally believing Dad's clean or the ache of staying away from her, but I don't want to dodge the truth. "Honestly? I'm scared I'm going to lose you."

"I'm right here, Bash." She squeezes my arm. "Just because I had a crush on you doesn't mean we can't be friends, right?"

I swallow hard. "Sometimes I wish I'd been someone else when we met. A good guy. Someone who deserved you."

"But then you wouldn't have been *you*." She gives a sad smile, and the words pull at something in my chest, a thread threatening to unravel. For once, the idea of unraveling doesn't terrify me. Today, the idea I find so frightening is shoring up all this shit inside me. I'm sick of holding back. I'm sick of casting my emotions in solid steel until they suffocate.

"Are you looking forward to your date tonight?"

She bites her bottom lip. "I'm nervous. I haven't dated much since the fire. When I was in Colorado, I went out with this guy a few times. He was nice, but on our last date, he stroked his thumb over the side of my mouth, shook his head, and said, 'This kills me, because you'd be so fucking beautiful without it.' I knew then that I had to end it. I think he meant it as a compliment, but I couldn't see having a relationship with someone who constantly thought about how I'd be without my scars."

My body tenses. "He was a fucking idiot."

She smiles. "You're always good for the ego boost, Crowe."

"Nah. I just don't understand how there are guys who don't recognize real beauty when it's staring them in the face. At least I can give Logan credit for that. He loves looking at you. I see it in his eyes."

"He makes me feel pretty." She looks up to the clouds and sighs. "I really want to give him a chance, but it's scary."

I swallow hard, realizing just what road we've detoured onto and where it leads. Pulling a hand over my face, I draw in a ragged breath. "Alex, what we did in the pool…"

Her cheeks blossom red. "Oh, so we're going to go there?"

There was something about the way she reacted when I parted her legs, something about the way she moved when I pressed my face between them. "Are you a virgin?"

"I— What?"

I know she heard me.

Maybe it's Neanderthal. An old-fashioned idea that the first time a woman is with a guy it should mean something and should be headed somewhere. Maybe it's just something else I can beat myself up over—the idea of her first time being with Logan, when every cell in my body screams it should be with me. I don't fucking know why I care. Just that I do.

"It's none of my business, but I want to know," I say.

"Yes and no." She flips her hair over her shoulder and heads to the car, away from me.

"Yes *and no?*" *What the fuck?* She's already opening her door. "What does that mean?"

She gives me a sad smile. "It's complicated, Sebastian. Would another answer change anything between us? Would it mean you'd be sleeping with me tonight? Would it make you stop apologizing for kissing me?"

I blink at her. Would it? If she confirmed my suspicions and told me she was a virgin, would I back away? Or would I push Logan out of the picture as fast as I could?

She climbs into the car, leaving me confused about her answer and my own thoughts.

ALEXANDRA

New Hope has to be one of the cutest freaking towns I've ever seen. It sits right off the highway and along the widest point of the New Hope River. Sebastian parked on the street downtown, and we're walking along the wide sidewalks that showcase adorable storefronts.

Since we're a few minutes early despite our unplanned stop, we wander down the street side by side.

"I have to turn in my proposal for my photography project

tomorrow," he says, his eyes finding mine.

"Oh, how long does it have to be?"

"Not long." He takes a step closer and tucks my hair behind my ear. "I wasn't sure until today exactly what I wanted to do."

"And you know now?"

"Yeah, but I'm going to need some help. It's okay if you don't want to, but I…"

"I'll help you any way I can. What do you need? What's the subject matter?"

"You."

I freeze. I've never felt comfortable in photos, but even less so since the fire. I made the woman who did my senior pictures take them in profile on my good side so my scars wouldn't show. More often than not, when I'm out with friends and they pull out their phones to take pictures, I duck my head to disguise the scarring visible on my face. Sebastian's asking to take photos of me, and I'm guessing they'd show my scars.

"You're so beautiful, Alex. And not despite your scarring. To me, your scars are evidence of how deeply you love." His voice and eyes are soft as he leans toward me. "And when you told me about that guy you dated in Colorado, I started thinking about showing that. I promise you, if you let me do this, I won't submit anything you're uncomfortable with."

"If I'm in the pictures at all, I'm probably not going to be comfortable with them."

His chest rises with his deep inhale. "Maybe you could finally see you the way I see you." His eyes lock on mine, and they're full of tenderness and sincerity. It's as if he has no idea that the things he says to me are so much at odds with his refusal to take our relationship beyond friendship.

"Do you remember what that girl at the party said to you?" I ask.

He frowns. "What girl?"

"The girl who called me Freddy Krueger. She asked you why you'd want to be with someone like me, someone whose skin is disgusting when you could be with someone beautiful. I have to admit, when you touch me, I wonder the same thing."

"Do you remember what I told her?"

I take a breath. "You told her she'd just shown everyone how ugly she was."

"Alex, who made you believe that you weren't beautiful? I know you blame it on your scars, but I knew you before the fire, remember? You've always been insecure."

I can't answer that question. I'm not sure any woman can. I'm pretty sure ninety percent of girls my age walk around believing they're ugly—with or without scars, with or without makeup, with or without the extra ten pounds we gained during freshman year. We all believe ourselves to be ugly ducklings who spend every day hiding our flaws so we can try to pass for swans.

"I'll do it," I say. "I trust you. So I'll do it."

He grins. "You have no idea how long I've wanted to take pictures of you. This is definitely something to look forward to." He pulls his phone from his pocket and checks the screen. "Our meeting's in five minutes. We should probably go."

I nod and fall into step beside him as he leads the way.

A minute later, we're stepping up to the most beautiful art gallery I've ever seen—not that I've seen many. Inside the glass doors, we're greeted by the view of the river through the picture windows on the far wall. Even in this simple space in this tiny town, the building is as much a piece of art as the works it houses.

A woman with curly red hair and a wide smile greets us when we enter. "Are you the BHU students?"

"We are," I say. "Are you Maggie Thompson?"

"I am."

"It's great to meet you," I say. "We did a little research, and your achievements are so impressive for someone so young."

She chuckles softly. "I have to be honest, it's a little bizarre imagining myself as an option for a research project on any college curriculum. I can't say this has ever happened to me before."

"Your gallery is amazing," Sebastian says, waving a hand. "I'm not surprised our professor respects your work so much."

"This isn't my gallery. It belongs to William Bailey."

"Yes, we've met before," Sebastian says. "We talked photography."

"Oh, great. I'm sorry he's not here right now. His wife just had a baby, and he's taking some time off. I can answer any questions you have about the collection, as I'm the one who curated it. We're incredibly lucky to have a collection of this value in our little town."

"Is it pottery?" I step forward to examine a piece on a pedestal under a glass dome.

"Yes," Maggie says. "It's called Kintsukuroi."

I dip my head to get a better look at the urn. There's a huge crack up one side and a few smaller cracks branching out at the top, but cracks are now an almost-shimmering gold from whatever was used to repair the broken urn, and it adds a dimension and interest to the piece that makes me take a moment longer to examine it. A simple, unbroken urn, and I'd keep walking. "Kintsukuroi?" I ask. "Does that mean pottery?"

"This is Japanese pottery, and it's a classic example of Kintsukuroi, but the word itself means something that is more beautiful for having been broken. I've named the whole collection with that term, though it's not all the traditional pottery."

"It's incredible," Sebastian says, ducking his head to study the piece.

"I'm a little obsessed with concept, to be honest," Maggie says. "I did my undergraduate thesis on mosaic work, which I like to think shares some of the same principles as Kintsukuroi. I've included some mosaic in this collection as well as some decoupage, and you can see those over here."

I follow her to the other side of the gallery, examining the pieces as she speaks about them and talks about why each is so special. With each she shares with us, something fills my chest—a heavy emotion I don't want to feel today but can't block out. By the time she's shown us the whole collection, my throat is thick and I don't trust myself to speak. I'm not sure how I'm going to get through my half of the interview questions we've prepared for her.

"Are you okay?" she asks. She puts her arm on my shoulder and squeezes.

I nod. "I didn't expect..." I swallow, but it's too late. A tear slips from my eye. *Shit.*

Maggie gives me a sad smile. "Don't be embarrassed. Art can and should evoke emotion. Maybe that's why this collection is one of my favorites." She nods to the stairway in the center of the gallery that leads to a lofted area above. "Can we talk upstairs? I have some fresh coffee and chocolate croissants from my sister's bakery."

I wipe my cheeks and look to Sebastian. "Actually, we have interview questions for you if that's okay."

Maggie nods. "We'll get there. Come on." She leads us upstairs to the loft area, where there's a kitchenette and a small but cozy-looking seating area. Before we can protest, she pours us coffee and gives us each a plate with a croissant.

I can't eat. My stomach's too much of a mess, but I take a few polite sips of the coffee.

"In our culture," Maggie says, when we're all seated around the coffee table, "we too often assume that things lose their value if they're broken. It's obvious, right? Why would a glass that can't hold water be worth as much as one that is unbroken and can help us quench our thirst? Why would a car that can't run be worth as much as one that can?"

Sebastian and I exchange a look, and he grins before speaking. "But just because the car doesn't run now doesn't mean it can't with some work."

"Right," Maggie says. "But when we repair something that's been broken, it's different. The idea of Kintsukuroi is that in that process, it gains value. Just like us." She looks at me and her gaze drops to my neck, where my dress has shifted and shows more of my scar than I like. "We break, and we heal. Our scars can make us more beautiful than we were before."

Sebastian takes my hand in his and squeezes my fingertips. His skin is warm and his touch reminds me to breathe.

CHAPTER 28
SEBASTIAN

Alex is quiet when we leave the art gallery, and her silence makes my chest ache. The look on her face when Maggie talked about Kintsukuroi was enough to break my heart. Anyone could see—and Maggie clearly did—that the concept hit close to home for Alex. All I could do was sit there and hold her hand. We asked Maggie our questions and walked silently back to the car. I don't know if I should just let her be or get her to talk about it, but I want to say something—anything—because I hate seeing so much grief in her eyes.

I choose silence, and reach across the console to put my hand on her leg.

She squeezes my fingertips. "I'm sorry I kind of lost it in there. I wasn't prepared for that."

"You don't need to apologize. I'm just glad you see it."

Her brow furrows with her frown. "See what?"

"The connection—Kintsukuroi—and your scars..." I don't know how to say it without sounding like a corny greeting card. "You're beautiful, and your scars are too. It's exactly why I want to do my photography project on you."

"You think I was crying for myself?" She looks away, watching the landscape roll by outside her window.

It seemed so obvious to me, and I think Maggie thought the same. "No one would blame you if you were."

"I was thinking about my sister." She closes her eyes and squeezes my hand hard. "She wasn't just some crazy party girl. I know that's what everyone thinks." She's quiet a beat before adding, "That's even what my parents think. Martina was just trying to cope."

"Cope with what?"

She releases my hand and wraps her arms around herself, as if she's suddenly cold. The silence stretches for so long that I start to think she's not going to reply when she says, "I didn't know about it until a few weeks before she died, and if she hadn't been in such a dark place, I don't think she would have told me. Even as screwed up as she was at the end, I know she regretted letting the truth out."

"What happened to her?"

"When we were kids, we'd stay over at our aunt and uncle's house a lot. Mom and Dad were busy with our brothers' sports, so they'd take us there." She looks to me and back out the window, and my gut turns sour because I don't know where this is going, but I know it won't be good. "Martina said it happened the first time when we were ten. He came into the room after we fell asleep."

Bile creeps up my throat. Disgust. Horror.

"I always wondered why she insisted on sleeping on the side of the bed by the door," she whispers. "I always wondered why no matter how long I forced myself to keep my eyes open, she never fell asleep first there. It wasn't until she screamed the truth at me that I finally understood. After it happened that first time, she made sure he never had a reason to reach beyond her."

"God, I didn't know."

She shakes her head. "No one did. *No one.* When we were fourteen, the asshole died of a heart attack, and I remember her face at the funeral. She looked at the casket with a hard jaw, as if she hated him for being in the room even when he was dead. I had no idea. I couldn't even wrap my mind around something like that. I'd been so sheltered that it wouldn't have ever crossed my mind to guess what he'd done to her. But I could tell she was glad he was dead. I could *feel* it. So I was glad too." She shivers hard, even though the evening sun is beating down on the car and making it hot in here. "That kind of violation screws you up. That's why she was always looking for trouble. *That's* why she was always so desperate for the next high."

I know nothing can take this chill from her bones, but I turn off the air conditioner anyway. "Why did she finally tell you?"

"It was a few weeks before she died. Rehab was a big fail, and she was using again, only my parents were watching, and it was harder for her to get what she was looking for. It was a day shortly before she ran away, and I went off on her. I told her what a disappointment she was. I told her she was spoiled and selfish and needed to straighten up and realize she was throwing away a perfectly good life for no reason." A tear rolls down her cheek, and she bites her bottom lip. "I pushed her, and she snapped. She told me everything. She screamed at me—said she'd protected me over and over again from that sick old man, and I had no idea what it was like for her to wake up in the middle of the night in a panic thinking he might be coming." She draws in a deep breath, and it rattles as it passes in through her tears. "That broken pottery made me think of my sister. Of how beautiful she could be if she were still alive. Of how much she could give to the world if anyone had bothered to put her back together."

I turn off at the exit and park the car along the side of the road so I can turn to face her. "Alex." When she lifts her blue eyes to mine, they're shimmering with tears. "You can't fix someone who hides their broken pieces."

"I know. But I wish I would have tried." Her bottom lip trembles. "It could have been me, Sebastian. I ask myself, if I'd been the one closer to the door that first night, what would I have done? Would I have always made sure that he came for me and left her alone? Or would I have pretended I was asleep? Maybe I'd have told myself I didn't know what was happening when he took her? So, yeah, I ran into a fire to try to save my sister because she spent four years facing the fire for me."

I pull her into my arms, and her shoulders shake as she cries against my chest. "You did everything you could for her. You can't blame yourself for his crime."

"Some days I miss her so much it hurts." Alex and Martina may have been oil-and-vinegar opposites—soft and hard, tame and rebellious, innocent and experienced—but that never kept them from having a connection most people could never understand. I know I never understood it.

"She'd be proud of you," I whisper, and it's true. If Martina were alive and sober, she'd be proud of her twin.

Alex snorts. "For being twenty-one and having no idea what I want to do with my life? For trying to seduce a boy and failing miserably? For learning how to drink?" She shivers, her whole body shaking with it.

I look down to study her face, the running mascara making dark circles beneath her eyes, the scar on her mouth. "For going to school. For searching for your passion. For showing your scars."

Her hand goes to her face, and for a moment, I regret bringing them up and reminding her of them. I don't think many moments pass where Alex isn't conscious of her burns. Her fingertips trail down her neck and over her collarbone. "I'd do it again."

I squeeze my eyes shut. Talking about Martina is always dangerous, but I've never wanted to be one of the countless people who skirt around that terrible night. If she wants to talk about it, I'm going to listen. No matter how much it hurts.

"I know everyone thinks I'm stupid for literally running into a burning building, but they don't get it. I was walking home from a friend's house when I saw her, and I followed her without letting her know I was there. We didn't know where she was living, and Mom was afraid to go to the cops because there were rumors she was dealing drugs and she didn't want her to get arrested." She rubs her arms. "I followed her and watched as she went into that dilapidated old house. I was waiting across the street, trying to decide what to do next, when I heard the explosion."

I hold her tighter and squeeze my eyes shut. I can picture the house on Oak Street like I was there yesterday. The house was condemned and vacant, and it was only one of the places where Dad and I cooked meth. I still don't know why Martina was there, and right after it happened, I spent some dark weeks blaming her. She shouldn't have been there. She shouldn't have touched the lab. *She* must have done something to cause the explosion and subsequent fire. But as I processed my grief and my guilt, I had to accept what I already knew to be true. She shouldn't have died in that explosion. It wasn't her lab. If someone was going to die that night, it should have been me.

"I'd do it again," Alex says, and I loosen my grip on her, afraid I might be holding her tight enough to hurt. "If I thought there was any chance I could save her—even a *fraction* of a percentage of a chance—I'd do it again. I'd suffer through those horrible skin grafts again, the weeks and weeks of excruciating physical therapy." She pulls back to look at me. "The years of people staring when they see my scars. I'd do it all again just to try to get my sister back."

"That's not what she would want. You know that, right?"

"Oh, I know." Her smile is simultaneously sad and proud. It's a special smile she reserves for talk of her sister. "But it doesn't change anything. Because I fucking miss her and I'm angry with her. I want her to live so I can yell at her for being so stupid. I want her to live so I can be jealous of her being everything I'm not. But mostly, I want her to live because I want my best friend back. And I don't get that, because even though she kept me safe from a sick man for four years, I didn't save her when she needed it."

I feel like she's plucking out chunks of my heart and tossing them into boiling lava. "It wasn't your job to save her."

She shakes her head. "I don't mean from the fire. I mean from her addiction. I didn't even *try*. Not really. Once we hit high school, our differences were so obvious and painful to me…I got caught up in the petty things. She was prettier, more popular, more comfortable in her own skin. Boys loved her, and I was jealous." She pulls her bottom lip between her teeth. "When she first started using, I was upset. I told her she needed to get help. But part of me…" She lifts her eyes to meet mine. "Part of me felt vindicated because there was *one* thing where I was better. She was prettier, smarter, cooler, everything, but at least *I* didn't use drugs." She closes her eyes, and a tear slips through her lashes and down her cheek, bringing an inky streak of mascara with it.

I wipe it away with my thumb and leave behind a smudge on her cheek. I can't tear my eyes from that smudge, that evidence that I can't comfort her without consequence. My most well-intentioned interference with Alex's life will leave its mark.

"All that time that I was jealous of her for being so much

prettier than me, being pretty was her curse. All that time, she was walking around broken and we were all criticizing her for *coping*. It's like criticizing someone who's paralyzed because they never walk. I just wish she would have told me."

I stroke her hair from her face and draw in a ragged breath. "Sometimes we hide the truth to protect people we love. Sometimes it's the only choice we have."

ALEXANDRA

I don't know how long we sit there on the side of the road, Sebastian holding me in his arms while I sniffle against his shirt. I don't pull away until I finally feel like I might not fall apart, and the sun is low on the horizon, painting the sky in reds and oranges to match the autumn leaves.

I slide back over to the passenger seat and find a tissue in my purse. Pulling down the visor, I use the mirror and tissue to do the best I can to clean up my face. "I'm sorry about your shirt," I say with a soft smile. "And the total emotional breakdown. I don't think I knew how much I needed to talk about it until the words started spilling from my lips."

"You can cry on me any time you want." He attempts a smile; while I'm feeling reborn after my cry, he looks so damn sad.

"Are you okay?"

He wraps his hands around the steering wheel and squeezes

before meeting my eyes. "When I asked you if you were a virgin and you said *yes and no*..." He swallows. "If your uncle..." He grimaces and his knuckles go white as he squeezes the wheel harder.

I shake my head. "No, Sebastian. That's not what I meant. Not at all. Martina protected me." It hurts to think about, and yet after sharing it with him, it hurts a little less. "I've had sex before. I had a boyfriend in tenth grade—before the fire—and we..." I shrug. "We were together for months, and it just seemed like the thing to do."

He releases the wheel and exhales. "Then why did you say *yes and no*?"

I shrug. "I haven't had sex since the fire. No one but my doctors have seen me without the worst of my scars covered. I guess it kind of feels like its own kind of virginity. Maybe in a lot of ways it feels more important than having sex the first time. It's scarier." I have to laugh at myself. It's so damn dramatic. "I'm sorry. You asked a straightforward question. I shouldn't have answered it like that."

"No. No, I'm glad you did. You gave me your honest answer instead of the obvious, easy one. I know it's none of my business, but I just..." His voice cracks. "Don't let Logan push you to move faster than you want. I know you want to give him a chance, but it's more important that you take things at your own pace."

"I promise I'll let him know if he's going too fast, but this is our second date. I don't think I'm there yet." As soon as I say it, I realize I've never been on a date with Sebastian, and yet he's done things to me that no one else ever has.

We're quiet the rest of the drive home, and when he pulls up to Mr. Patterson's house, he surprises me by reaching for my hand. "Thank you for going with me today."

"It was a successful trip," I say. He grins at me, and my stomach flips.

"How's next Sunday for our photoshoot? I can get the studio in the evening if you're free."

I take a breath. "Yeah, I guess that works." I trace the scar on my neck. "If I chicken out, will you be screwed over?"

He shakes his head. "Nah, if you change your mind, I'll figure out something else. Wanna go grab a drink with me?"

I open my mouth to tell him I love that idea, then I remember Logan. "I have plans, remember?"

"Right. The Amazing Logan is waiting." His lips twist, and for a second I think he might tell me to cancel, to spend the night with him instead. "I hope you have a great time."

CHAPTER 29
ALEXANDRA

Logan picked me up at six thirty. He took me to dinner at a little place downtown, where we sat on their back patio and drank wine and held hands on top of the table. He talked about his new business and asked about my time in Colorado. It's been the perfect evening, except I've spent most of it thinking about Sebastian.

"Did you like your gift?" Logan asks as we leave the restaurant.

"I loved it. It's beautiful."

"Then it suits you," he says.

"Why are you so interested in me? I mean, why *me*?"

He arches a brow. "I assume you're looking for more than the fact that you're the kindest, sweetest, most beautiful woman I've ever met?"

I bite my lip and look into his eyes. Does he really mean those things? I draw in a breath for courage. "I want you to know the reason I didn't call."

He shifts and takes a deep breath. "Is this the part where you tell me you're seeing someone else?"

Guilt twists my stomach, but oddly, it's not as much over what I did with Sebastian in the pool as it is over letting him hold me today in the car. "It's complicated, but I feel like it would be dishonest for me to go into this with you if you were under the impression that you're my only romantic interest." I flinch at the phrase. *Romantic interest* feels like it implies reciprocation, when in truth Sebastian made the limits of our relationship clear. "I completely understand if you want to stop while we're ahead."

"What does that mean?"

"I mean maybe you want to end this before it begins."

Logan drags a hand over his mouth and tilts his face up to the sky before looking at me again. "Let me be honest, Alexandra. I've never dated a girl while she was involved with someone else—physically or emotionally. I've never been interested in that kind of arrangement, because I'm a selfish asshole and I don't share well." His jaw tightens, but when he exhales, some of the tension leaves his face. "And the fact that you're so fucking special doesn't make me any more inclined to want to share you."

This speech coming from this gorgeous man should have me swooning. Instead, I'm thinking of Sebastian's knuckles brushing mine as we walked down the streets of New Hope. I'm thinking of the way he held me as I cried.

I can't even tell if I'm relieved or disappointed to walk away from this—from something that could have turned into a real relationship, as opposed to Sebastian's incessant long glances and flirtations that go absolutely nowhere. "I understand," I say.

"Do you?" He releases a puff of air that was maybe supposed to be a laugh. "Because I fucking don't. I don't understand how you have such a hold on me already that I'm willing to keep things casual while you figure out what you want."

"You don't have to do that."

He turns away. "I don't have to, or you don't want me to?"

"Logan…" I wait until he looks at me again before continuing. "I like you, and I think there's a really good chance you're better for me than this guy from my past. I've just never been in this situation before. Ever. Come on, look at me."

He drops his gaze to my feet and slowly—so freaking slowly—brings it back up, skimming over my peep-toe wedge sandals to my black jeans and thin red sweater before finally settling on my mouth. "I am looking."

SEBASTIAN

After I dropped off Alex, I came home and took a long, hot shower, but it did nothing to get my mind off where she is tonight and who she's with. The sick irony of this situation isn't lost on me. Of the two friends I have who can understand why I can't have Alex, one is her brother and the other is the guy who's claimed her for himself. If Logan helped me climb out of the darkness to start a new life, Dante helped keep me there.

When I go out to the living room, Keegan's sitting on the couch, his back to Bailey as he frowns into a beer. "I don't know what else to do," he mutters.

Bailey's in the kitchen, draining her wine glass at a record pace. "That's awful, bud." Her eyes go big when she sees me, and she gesticulates wildly in Keegan's direction and mouths, *He won't leave. Do something.*

"Hey, man." I sit on the couch next to Keegan, positioning myself sideways to I can see both him and Bailey. "What's going on?"

"Your sister won't talk to me. I can deal if she doesn't want to be with me, but it's like she doesn't want me involved with the pregnancy at all." He sighs heavily and picks at the label on his beer bottle. "What does Chris Montgomery have that I don't?"

"Potential to make seven figures next year?" Bailey says from the kitchen, and I shoot her a look, but there isn't much I can say in Olivia's defense. Unfortunately, Bailey's right. Olivia's interest in Chris was always more about wanting to be an NFL quarterback's wife than it was about compatibility.

"Olivia's gotta figure this out," I say. "She had an idea of what she wanted her life to look like and she's been thrown for a loop. Just give her some time."

"Like *I'm* not scared?" he says. "Jesus. I'm terrified. I always wanted kids someday, but I didn't think that day would come for years."

Someone knocks on the door before it opens, and Chris

sticks his head in. "We're here to retrieve that sad drunk."

"Thank God," Bailey mutters. "Take him to a strip club or something. He's so pathetic."

Chris steps into the apartment with Mason on his heels. "Strip clubs aren't the solution to every problem," Mason mutters.

Keegan shrugs. "I mean, it isn't a *terrible* idea."

Chris rolls his eyes, and I bite back a grin. Keegan might be smitten with my sister, but he's still Keegan.

"We're going to Trent's," Mason says. He looks at me. "You want to come?"

"Hey, aren't I invited?" Bailey asks.

"It's guys' night," Mason says unapologetically. "No chicks."

"I'm staying in," I say. "Long fucking day."

"I'm not a *chick*," Bailey says with a flip of her long blond hair. "I'm one of the guys. I'm so dude-like, I practically have a dick."

Mason arches a brow. "Baby, we both know that's not true."

Her cheeks flush red, but either Mason doesn't care or is determined to act the part. After the guys leave, Bailey stares at the door for a long time.

"I miss him," she says, coming around to the couch. "We used to hang out *all the time* and now, nothing. It's like he doesn't like me anymore."

"You ever think that maybe it's just too hard on him?"

"What? Being my friend? I'm *easy*."

"Bailey." I wait until she looks at me. "The guy's been in love with you for as long as I've known you two. You want different things. At some point, that makes the friendship fall apart."

"Like you and Alex?"

I swallow hard. I'm not sure why I thought it would be a good idea to move in with someone who can see right through me. "She's on a date tonight."

She nods. "Right. Tonight she dines on apple pie a la mode."

I frown and imagine Bailey getting play-by-play texts about the date. I'm not sure if I want to know more or stop her while she's ahead. "She told you what they were eating?"

"No. Apple pie is… Never mind. I ran into Logan at the gym this morning."

I arch a brow. "You go to the gym? Like, to work out?"

"Um, yeah? You think this ass comes free?" She shakes her head. "Anyway, Logan and I chatted a little." She drains the rest of her wine and puts her glass down on the coffee table with a soft thunk. "I know more of your secrets than you realize. And I get why you think you can't be with her."

I can't decide if I want to shut down this conversation or pour myself a very large glass of that sickly sweet wine she likes so much. "What did he say to you?"

"Enough." With a heavy sigh, her shoulders sag. "You forget I dated Nic, and Nic knew everyone who was dealing in this town. Logan just filled in some blanks about you and Martina."

I stare at her, both shocked and horrified as I try to process her words. One of my few comforts about my dark past is that I stayed in the shadows, and when I pulled myself out of that world, I could do so more or less anonymously. When I told Logan about my history with Martina, it was in confidence, and

I'm a little pissed that he shared it without my permission.

"I'm not going to tell anyone that you and Martina screwed around. I'm just saying that I get it, and when everyone else sees the way you look at Alex and is confused about why you won't do anything, I'm not confused. Not anymore. But Martina made her own choices, and you can't torture yourself for her sins just because she's not here to take the punishment."

Martina's Journal

Sebastian Crowe came over to see me tonight. That's right. This time he came to me. I kind of wish Alex had been around to see it.

He's worried about me, he said. "I know you're dealing, and I saw you talking to Dad last week." He shook his head, all big-brother worried. "He's not going to look out for you like I do." He looked over his shoulder as if he thought someone might be watching us. "Guys like him, they're not just out for the deal, Martina. This is their life and they'll do anything to get a leg up. My dad is dangerous."

I grinned. "No, your dad is hot, Sebastian."

You should have seen his horrified face. What Sebastian doesn't know is that I don't need him to look out for me. I've got all the protection I need. A man who gives me red roses and fucks like a god.

Sebastian might think he knows my life, but he doesn't know about me and Mr. Bedroom Eyes—MBE is far too private to let anyone know about our relationship. He said it's for my own protection, and I get that, but sometimes I get a little jealous and think maybe he doesn't take me around because he's never going to leave his wife.

When I asked him if he was embarrassed by how young I am, he laughed at me. "I don't get embarrassed. I get what I want." I told him about Sebastian coming by, and he laughed. "Dangerous? He has no idea what he's talking about." Then he hiked up my skirt, pushed me against the wall, and fucked me hard and rough, his hand at my throat as he whispered that I was his and no one else's. So fucking hot.

When I got home, Alex asked about the bruise on my neck. I told her it was a hickey and laughed when she didn't believe me. She's pissed at me for skipping all the time. She's asked where I go. I've evaded.

She broke up with her little boyfriend. I wonder if Sebastian will make a move on her when he finds out. Not that it matters. He's old news.

CHAPTER 30
SEBASTIAN

"Are you fucking kidding me right now?" I've never seen so many drugs. Not even when I was dealing and making thousands a day. Not even when we were cooking our own meth and moving heroin, X, and everything else under the sun.

"Lower your voice," Dad says. He looks over his shoulder, as paranoid as the junkies who buy this shit.

I found him in the storage shed behind Grandma's trailer. I've been driving all over town looking for him today because I needed to talk to him. Bailey said I'm punishing myself for Martina's sins, and maybe she's right, and if Alex isn't going to read the journal, it's time for me to tell her myself. When the drugs and the fire were part of our past, I could imagine doing that, but finding him here with all this inventory brings the past screaming back into the present like a runaway train.

"I had an opportunity to turn a quick profit. This is temporary. I'm not using. I know better." His face is calm. He's really fucking serious right now.

I point my finger at Dad and jab him in the chest. "*You* are the one who told me we could be better than this. *You* are the one who stood by my side as we escaped it. We started over. And now what? All that shit you said about family first and valuing what we can get honestly, that means nothing now? You wanted a little extra money and so fuck everything and everyone else?"

He grabs my wrist and squeezes hard. "I have lived a hard life and I'm not going back there. I just want to give your mom all I can while she's healthy. We got a second chance. Do you have any idea what it's like to see the woman you love hurting and not be able to do anything about it?"

Oh, sweet fucking irony. "Yeah. I'm pretty familiar with that. If you can recall, I watched Alex suffer through burns on a third of her body because of an explosion this shit caused. Don't you fucking get it? Let's forget about the fact that you're breaking the law for a minute. Let's forget about the horrible, life-ending addictions you're enabling." I yank my arm from his grasp. "What about your family? What about *our* lives?" I point to Grandma's trailer. "You literally brought this shit into her backyard."

"Sebastian, this will be over soon." His voice is low, calm. He was always so good at rationalizing everything. If I started feeling bad about what we were doing, a short chat with Dad would fix me right up. "I ran into an old associate a few months ago and the opportunity fell into my lap. Trust me. It's not like we can count on your football career. I'm doing this for *all* of us."

I back away, shaking my head. "You're doing this for yourself."

~~~

I can't even start to wrap my brain around what I learned tonight, or what the hell I'm supposed to do about it. Do I call the cops on my own father? Do I put him away for a crime I was guilty of myself not long ago? Do I look the other way? Do I warn Mom what's coming and then make the call? I'm so fucking confused that I'm choking on it. So I play hard at practice. When Chris hands off the ball, I break tackles and push downfield like my life depends on it. I'm simultaneously numb and on fire. As if I'm watching the world from a distance and at the same time trying to punch my way out of a box without air.

As soon as practice is over, I take a quick shower, dress, and rush out to my truck through the pouring rain, but when I pull out of the lot, I don't head toward Mom's or my apartment. I know a bunch of them are hanging at Trent's tonight. Tomorrow's a home game, and I should be spending the evening with the team or resting for the game. But the only thing that sounds worse than having everyone ask what's wrong is being alone. I'm not even sure where I'm planning to go until I park in front of the house where Alex has been housesitting.

I don't know why I came to her. Maybe because I'm drowning. Maybe coming to the girl I can't have is the same as letting the water into your lungs before you reach the surface—because every instinct demands that you *try* to breathe.

ALEXANDRA

Note to self: When rich, do not buy home in subdivision. Find land. With no neighbors.

The doorbell rings a second time. With a sigh, I rub in the last of my moisturizer and head out front to answer it. I got out of the shower fifteen minutes ago, and I just finished drying my hair. I'm in my pink cotton robe and have approximately fifteen minutes to get dressed before I need to leave to meet Logan. He's going to show me around the Lemon Rind tonight, then they'll do a soft opening in a week and the grand opening the weekend after that.

The marble floor in the foyer is cold under my bare feet, and I take a deep breath, contemplating ignoring the bell altogether. The kids in this neighborhood always seem to be selling something—candy bars, magazines, trash bags—and when I tell them I don't have any money, they give me that face that says, "Yeah, right, lady. Look where you're living." Whoever's at my door right now must be seriously devoted to his cause, because it's raining cats and dogs out there.

I've adopted a new strategy of pretending I'm selling *them* something. I'm mentally rehearsing my sales pitch for jock itch ointment when I pull open the door, only to find myself face to face with Sebastian Crowe.

His shoulders seem to fill the doorway, and his eyes feel like they're trying to take in every inch of me all at once. Behind him, the wind blows rain onto the porch. It's one of those autumn storms that saturates the piles of leaves and turns them to sludge. The air is cool, and Sebastian is soaked.

"Sebastian. Come on in." I step back, but instead of going around me into the foyer, he comes right to me, backing me into the wall and kicking the door closed with his foot.

My heart races. He's so close, his eyes so intent on me. "Is everything okay?"

"No." He takes another step forward, closing what's left of the distance between us.

I'm trying not to overthink this, not to assume this is something it's not. But he's so close I can feel the heat radiating off his body, and I'm all too aware that we're alone in this big house. "What happened?"

"Shit day." His gaze drops to my mouth and his lips part.

I can hardly breathe. "Can I help?"

"Yes," he whispers. Then his mouth is against mine and his hands are in my hair, and it's so unexpected and everything all at once that when he positions his knee between my legs, I only shift to allow him closer. I'm trapped between the wall at my back and the hot wall of his chest, and it feels amazing.

His kiss is long and deep and steals my breath. His hands knot in my hair, and he's pressing so close that the slightest shift of my hips and I'm rubbing against his thigh, gasping against his mouth.

He tugs on my hair to tilt my head to the side and he whispers in my ear, "I need you." He shifts his thigh, and I instinctively cling to him and rock against him. "Fuck, that's right. Rub against me." Then his mouth is on my neck, all lips and teeth and tongue sliding and kissing and nipping. I couldn't stop my hips from moving if I wanted to.

Somewhere in the back of my mind, questions are stacking one on top of the other. What happened? Why did he come here? Why is he kissing me now when he promised he'd never do it again? But the questions are muffled by pleasure and too many years of wanting something I never thought I could have.

I tunnel my hands into his hair and lead his mouth back to mine. This time when he kisses me, he shifts again, only to sink lower and grab the backs of my legs. He lifts me up until my robe falls open below the tie at my waist and the hard length of him is nestled between my thighs. I wrap my legs around his waist and hook my feet at the ankles. His hands slide up my thighs and into my underwear to cup my ass.

"Let me feel you, Alex." His mouth against my ear. His demands release in hot puffs of air. "I need to feel you move."

Each time I rock my hips, something builds inside me like a wave out at sea. This isn't like what I felt in the pool. This is so big and intense that I'm as scared of it as I am scared that it might disappear.

The questions nudge again. Why this? Why now? Will this be something else for him to regret? But then he tucks his head and skims his mouth against my breasts, his teeth grazing over the thin cotton of my robe, and the questions sink deeper into the ocean as the wave rolls again, gaining strength and hurtling forward.

He shakes his head and inches back, lightening the friction and making me whimper. "I have to feel you. Please let me feel you." He slowly guides me back to standing on my own two feet, and my legs nearly buckle. His eyes lock on mine as he slides his hand between my legs and grazes his knuckles along the center of my panties.

I sway toward him, making needy sounds I don't recognize.

"Let me feel you," he repeats.

"Please," I whisper, closing my eyes.

"Fuck no, Alex. Look at me." His voice is as rough as the rocky sand, and I do as he asks. There's something different in his eyes tonight, or maybe it's just that he's never looked at me this way. Hungry. Determined. Half crazed.

I love it. And when I force my eyes to stay open, I'm rewarded with the rough pads of his fingers skimming down over my panties then sliding between my legs and underneath.

I gasp at the feel of his fingers finding me, but I have to grip his shoulders to hold myself up.

"Christ." He brushes his fingers over my wet clit then slides two inside me. My eyes water with the sudden stretch even as my muscles squeeze around him. He rotates his hand and presses my clit with his palm as he moves his fingers, loving me with his hand. He dips his head to whisper in my ear. "So good… So fucking beautiful… Lost in this… Love the sounds you make…

Alex."

His words coax the rolling waves, making them stronger, calling them closer to the shore, until finally everything inside me feels like it's bound up in one tight coil and it all releases at once. And I'm not the waves or the water anymore. I'm nothing but the salty sea air. Everywhere and nowhere. Nothing and everything.

I keep my eyes closed and focus on the feel of his thumb traveling along my jaw and his breath against my mouth, my ear, my neck. He nuzzles me there, his beard a thrilling scratch against the tender skin.

And still, I keep my eyes closed. I know what happens when I open them. The dream ends. The fantasy breaks under the weight of our imperfections. We've been here before.

He doesn't seem in any hurry to end the moment, either. He slides a hand into my hair and we cling to each other until our ragged breathing steadies. Even then, he holds me still. There's a distinct sweetness to the way his face is buried in my neck, a comfort and warmth that feels like home.

And maybe that's why I open my eyes. Why *I* break the spell. Why *I* pull away.

Sebastian is staring at me, but the heat in his eyes earlier has been replaced by something else.

He looks upset. No, he looks wrecked and filled with the last thing I want to see on his face: regret.

CHAPTER 31
SEBASTIAN

As I watch her open her eyes, my chest aches so much and my heart is pounding so hard that I'm sure if she listens closely she'll know everything. About Dad. About Martina. About how much I've fucked up and how desperately I need her to tell me it's all going to be okay. Somehow, if she's says it, I might believe it.

My hands are fucking shaking. There's too much noise in my head, and the thrill of touching her has left me wanting so much more.

She must see the panic on my face. She shakes her head and the softness leaves her eyes. "Don't do it, Sebastian. Don't stand there after touching me and tell me it was a mistake. I don't want to hear it. Don't you dare apologize for kissing me again. Don't you dare tell me this was a mistake."

I was nothing but wild need when I walked in the door, and

I didn't even stop to appreciate that she's in a robe. She's barefoot and her toenails are painted a soft, light pink. It's the color of innocence and femininity. God, she's beautiful.

"Don't," she repeats, her voice shaky.

I take a lock of hair between two fingers and shake my head. "I didn't say anything."

The light trill of her ringtone sounds from the other room. "Shit," she whispers.

"What?"

She lifts her hand to her mouth. "That's probably Logan. I was supposed to meet him…"

I slide my hand into her hair and graze her bottom lip with my thumb. It's red and swollen from my kiss, and I've only gotten started. "Tell him something came up. Stay here with me."

She catches my thumb between her teeth and bites down softly. I groan, long and low, at the feel of her lips around my finger, tongue grazing the tip. "Fuck," I growl before lowering my mouth to hers again.

She opens under me and moans into the kiss. I'm ready for everything her soft sounds promise. I want to take her in the shower, hold her in the bed, fill the tub, and get her off while she's wrapped around me in the water.

She's breathless when she breaks the kiss. "Stay here with you and what? Is this how we're being friends now?" I reach for the tie on her robe, and she grabs my hand to stop me. "Sebastian, what's changed?"

I need you.

Her phone rings again from the other room, and she throws a helpless glance in the direction of the phone before turning back to me. "Can you tell me this is going to end differently than last time? Can you promise me you aren't going to declare this a big mistake in five minutes or an hour?"

"I don't know what I'm doing, but I don't fucking *want* to analyze it right now."

"Logan's waiting," she whispers. "I should probably go."

"Right. Logan. Tell my friend I said hi." I know my sneer isn't fair, but I'm feeling selfish. I'm feeling cheated. I'm feeling like *life* isn't fucking fair, and I want a break. I want Alex.

She lifts her hand to her lips. "You don't get to be mad at me about this when I don't even know what you want from me."

I rake my gaze over her then back up to her face. "I think you know exactly what I want."

She lifts her chin. "You want to get me naked? You want to take me to the bedroom and spread my legs? Maybe you don't even want to bother going as far as the bedroom?"

"For starters." I nuzzle her neck. "Dammit, Alex, I promise I'd make you feel so good."

"And then what?" She gasps and arches into me when I suck at the skin beneath her ear. She slides her hand into my hair. "Sebastian… God, please, I…"

"Please what, Alex? Tell me what you want. Anything. Tell me, and it's yours."

She releases my hair and whispers, "I want you to stop."

My gut goes cold. I back away. "Right. Because Logan."

"No. Because this is *us*. What if I tell you to take me to bed? What are we after that? Fuck buddies? Ex-friends? Coworkers who can't look each other in the eye?" She licks her lips. "Maybe you did me a favor when you put on the brakes last month. Because you were right. I need more than just a hookup. I can't do this unless I know there's going to be more. With *you*, I'd need more." There's a note of hope in her voice, like she's waiting for me to say everything is different now. "Has something changed? Should I believe this is going somewhere?"

I swallow hard. "I can't change the past. If I could, I would have a long time ago."

"What's that supposed to mean? You think I care about who you used to be?" She shakes her head. "Sebastian, you aren't that guy anymore. I'm not even convinced you were ever as terrible as you believe."

"But I was. I was him long enough to fuck everything up."

"What did you fuck up? I want to understand." Her voice rises and echoes off the vaulted ceiling. "What did you do that was so terrible that I can't be with you?"

I stroke the scar at the corner of her mouth then follow it down her neck to where it widens and disappears into her robe. "I don't deserve you." My words come out the husky rattle of someone who's been trying to breathe water. "If you were with me, there'd come a day that you'd regret it." I lift my eyes to hers. "But if you say the word, I'll fucking fight Logan and anyone else in my way for every minute I can get between now and that day."

ALEXANDRA

Sebastian offered me what I've wanted for years, then left me standing in the middle of the foyer, trembling with some emotion I couldn't fully identify.

I texted Logan that I was going to be late, and by the time I finish getting dressed and make it to the Lemon Rind, my mind is fuzzy from a thousand thoughts traveling in a hundred directions. My hands are trembling, and I can still feel the scratch of Sebastian's beard on my neck.

Logan is waiting for me by the front doors, and flashes a concerned smile when I enter. "Everything okay?"

I touch my fingertips to my lips. Are they swollen? Are my cheeks red? When Logan looks at me, does he know what I've just done? Can he see that Sebastian just kissed me, touched me?

"Alexandra?" I've always loved the way Logan says my name without shortening it, but with the memory of Sebastian's exhale of "Alex" hot against my ear, the four syllables feel less like my name and more like this girl I've been trying to be. "What happened?"

"Before I left the house tonight, a friend came over and he…" I open my mouth and close it again. My eyes are burning. I'm so confused. Part of me wants to be angry with Sebastian for confusing me right when I was finally moving forward. And yet another part wants to back-pedal to the moment he put his hand between my legs and find a way to keep him there—to rewrite history and let him take me to the bedroom, feel him slide between my legs.

"He hurt you?" Logan steps toward the door, and I reach out to grab his wrist before he can push his way outside.

"No." I shake my head. "He kissed me."

Flinching, Logan drops his hand, his jaw going hard, and I avert my eyes. He's been nothing but kind to me, and I've never given him a real chance.

"I *let* him kiss me." *And I let him do more. And if you hadn't called, maybe I'd have let it go even further.* "It just happened, and I know you and I are new, and there's nothing exclusive here, but I wouldn't feel right if I didn't tell you."

He spins around, swings, and punches the wall. "Who is he?"

"Does it matter?"

He hangs his head and rubs his knuckles. "It does if you have feelings for him."

"If I didn't care about him, tonight wouldn't have happened." My stomach flip-flops. How *did* I let that happen?

Because it's Sebastian.

Because you've always loved him.

Because tonight something was wrong and he needed you.

Maybe it's the last that bothers me the most. I let Sebastian touch me because I wanted him to, and that would have been enough, but adding to that was the feeling that something was off with him tonight, the sense that he *needed* me, the sense that his offer to try to be more was rooted in a desperate attempt to escape something else. I don't want to be his new high of choice—a drug he indulges in to feel better and then feels guilty about later.

Logan steps toward me and reaches for my hand. I instinctively pull away, and he flinches and sighs heavily. "So it's over?" he asks softly.

I hate myself a little right now. Here's this sweet man who wants to give me everything I *should* want, and I'm so hung up on Sebastian that I can't accept it. But I'd hate myself more if I let this continue. "It's not fair to you, Logan. You're such a nice guy, and I really care about you."

He shakes his head as he looks away, but he can't hide the pain on his face. "Don't. Don't do that. I don't want to be the nice guy. I want to be the guy you want." He steps back and swallows hard. "But you don't. You want him. And if I thought fighting for you would change that, Alexandra, I wouldn't just fight. I'd fight *dirty*."

I squeeze my eyes shut, because his words are too close to an echo of what Sebastian himself said to me. The only difference is that Sebastian's bottom line includes his promised ominous ending. "I don't deserve that."

"Fuck that." He drags a hand through his hair then stops and goes behind the counter to pour himself two fingers of whiskey. He shoots it back and closes his eyes a beat before looking at me again. "Whoever he is, I hope he deserves you. But if he doesn't, you know where to find me."

"Thank you, Logan. I'm so sorry."

"Don't be sorry." He plants his legs wide and crosses his arms. "You don't owe me anything."

Martina's Journal

You know how every soon-to-be seventeen-year-old girl dreams of spending her summer vacation? Not in fucking rehab.

That's right. Mom and Dad are on to me. I got sloppy, and they decided I needed to spend my summer break at an in-patient facility in Indianapolis, where they can teach me why methamphetamines are going to fuck with my life and my future.

I don't know what they want from me. It's not like I've stopped going to school, and my grades have slipped but I'm not flunking out or anything. Despite the incessant appeals to female vanity at this facility, I don't look like those meth junkies on the billboards. I'm smart about it, and I'm definitely no fucking addict.

But they don't care. Their narrow view of the world is all black and white: All drugs are bad. Use once, and you'll end up on the street. Today you're having fun, but tomorrow you're spreading your legs for any guy able to supply your next high. As if.

Alex cried when they dropped me off. She

hugged me and said, "Please just get better." What, am I sick? Because I've felt more alive the last six months than I ever have.

I know she cares, but maybe she's a little jealous too, ya know? She's having such a hard time with me living my own life. Even when you're fraternal twins, people want to throw you together in every facet of your life as you grow up. They want you to dress alike, take the same dance class, wear the same clothes, love the same books. Alex and I have never been like that, but until lately we have been close. I just think a natural part of getting older is spending more time doing different things. But I'm not sure she sees it that way.

Of course, she doesn't know about Mr. Bedroom Eyes, and I'm not sure if knowing about him would make her feel better or worse. Probably worse. He's older, for one, married, for another, and he's not afraid of an occasional buzz.

Anyway, I'm here for the indefinite future to "get sober." As if I don't know what sober is like. As if I couldn't stop on my own if I wanted to.

So I guess I'll be back to writing in this stupid journal all the time, because God knows there's nothing better to do around here.

Time for me to go eat the shit they call food. Joy. More later.

CHAPTER 32
SEBASTIAN

On Saturday, I go to Mom's after the game. I haven't talked to Alex since I left her in her robe last night. Did she go to Logan? Did she tell him about me? Did she let him touch her? The questions are only drowned out by the questions about Dad and what the hell I'm supposed to do about that.

When I walk in the door, I hear Mom and Olivia arguing in the back of the house. They've been doing that a lot since Olivia started college, and maybe even more since she got knocked up.

I can't make out what they're saying at first, but then I hear Mom say, "Stop it! You don't know that. You're going to have a great life." Olivia mumbles something I can't make out, and then I hear my mom say, "This is my choice, Olivia. Please, baby. I need you to understand I won't live like that again."

My gut twists at the tremor I hear in Mom's voice. What are

they talking about?

Their voices are coming from Olivia's room, so I head in that direction, but I stop when I hear Mom say, "It won't be easy, but we'll get through it together."

"Haven't we been through enough?" Olivia says. "It's not fair."

I draw in a sudden sharp gasp and realize I've been holding my breath. Is the cancer back? *I won't live like that again.* My hand trembles as I turn the knob and push open the door to Olivia's bedroom. She and Mom are sitting on the edge of the bed, turned sideways to face each other.

Mom sees me and the blood drains from her face. She tilts her head to the side. "Sebastian…"

"But you got the mastectomy so it wouldn't come back." I shake my head. "The cancer…"

Olivia throws her hand over her mouth and tears spill from her eyes.

"No, Bash. That's not what we're talking about," Mom says. "I'm healthy." She looks to Olivia, but her brave smile cracks as she turns back to me.

"Then what is it?"

She takes a deep breath and schools her expression to reflect complete calm. "I can't do it anymore, Bash. Sometimes people need to take their punishment. I spent years looking the other way while he sold his soul." Her composure cracks when she lifts her gaze to mine. "While he sold *yours*."

She knew?

Olivia presses her hand against her mouth to stifle a sob, and

Mom takes her hand and squeezes it. "I found out what he was doing. He said he had an opportunity to make some fast money and he took it. He's spent the last month trying to buy my silence, trying to drown me in gifts so I'd stay." She stands and crosses the room to stand in front of me. She's almost a foot shorter than I am, but I feel like her little boy when she holds my face in her hands. "I'm ashamed that I ever gave him the impression I could be bought. I'm ashamed of so much, and I couldn't sink into that kind of shame again. It would kill me. I found an opportunity to escape him and I took it. Forgive me."

My eyes burn and my hands shake as I wrap my hands around her wrists and pull her against me in a tight hug. Her body shakes as she releases a sob, again and again and again. "Forgive you for what?"

"For letting him almost ruin your life," she says between sobs. "And for turning him in. Your father was arrested tonight."

"Do you want to tell me why you're so miserable?" Dante asks. I came to the Cavern to drink after leaving Mom's. I was going to hide from my feelings by drinking, but I'm on my second beer when Dante slides into the seat across from me.

"I'm not miserable," I lie. But maybe it's not a lie. Maybe I've sunk to a level that's worse than miserable. Because my father lost his mind, and Alex is falling for someone else. There's an ache that sits on my chest like a boulder slowly compressing my lungs. It's an ache I've felt before. I felt it after the fire, when Martina was declared dead and Alex was in critical condition. I felt it when I was at Purdue, and Olivia called to tell me Mom had cancer again and my parents didn't want me to know. Alex is the only person who's ever been able to make this ache budge, and now she's his. It hurts to imagine her with him, and I feel like an asshole for wishing she weren't, because I know he'll treat her right. I'm selfish and jealous and want every one of her smiles and laughs for myself.

Dante sighs. "You want to tell me another one?"

"Dad was arrested tonight. He had a shit-ton of inventory, and they found it. It's bad." I shake my head. "But it feels good, so I'm not sure what that says about me."

"Fuck." He grabs my beer out from in front of me, and downs half of it. "You were right. He was back in it."

"Maybe he was never out," I whisper. "I don't fucking know. I'm just glad..." *Glad it's over. Glad he can't infect my life again.* "It's like he didn't learn anything after the fire."

We're silent for a while. I finish my beer and Dante orders us two more while I try to sort out the tangle of emotions making a mess of my thoughts. Mom's guilt. Mine. Dad's arrest. The fact that she had the courage to do what I should have.

When the silence has stretched out for too long and our beers are empty, Dante looks at me. "Alex told Mom she had another date with Logan last night."

I squeeze my eyes shut. "Yeah. I'm aware of that."

"Is he an okay guy?"

"Yes." I rub the back of my neck, but it doesn't help the tension knotted there. "I don't think I could have turned my life around without him." Dad introduced me to Logan, who, like me, had battled his addiction in his teens. Logan was twenty-two when he became my mentor, but he'd gotten sober while he was still in high school, and he understood it was different for me than for my dad. *"It's good to have someone who's been through this before."* And he helped me through the worst of it, listening when I needed a confidant.

"But you don't want him with her," Dante says.

"It just sucks to see her with someone else."

"You never cared when Martina dated someone else." Dante bringing up my history with his dead sister only makes this weight on my chest a little heavier. Everything he knows, he learned from me. Some he plied out, other bits I told him freely, but eventually it was clear that he could forgive me and Dad for the part we played in the fire, but he agreed it would be different for Alex. Knowing would hurt her more than it was worth. Were we wrong about that?

"I wasn't in love with Martina," I mutter before snatching back my beer. "I wasn't *anything* with Martina."

"You're in love with Alex." It's not a question, but he leans back in the booth, staring at me as if he just had some great revelation.

"You're just figuring this out?" I wince. I'm being an ass. "I don't know how to *not* be in love with her. I've fucking tried."

"I'm not sure if I should hug you or punch you in the face, man." He exhales heavily and scans the faces in the bar. "I miss

Martina. She always kept everything in perspective. If some of us were fighting at the dinner table, Martina would be the one to crack a joke and make us realize whatever we were fighting about wasn't that important. Some days I forget she's not around. Something will make me laugh, and I'll think, *I've gotta text Martina about that.* Then I remember, and it's like being sucker-punched. Every time. And yet I know what I feel is nothing compared to what Alex feels. Two people couldn't have been more different or closer."

"What was their relationship like?" On one hand, I know they were close, but it seemed like Martina kept her twin at arm's length.

"She always thought Martina was better than her," he says. "Any mutual friends they had, Alex assumed hung around for Martina. She thought boys were more interested in Martina, and some were. But she never saw how much people loved her for being *her* and not just for being Martina's sister."

That much was clear from the first day I met her. Alex had no idea how much I liked her. The two classes where I sat next to her were the best parts of my day, but if I'd admitted as much, she wouldn't have believed me anyway. "Martina didn't tell her anything."

"She had her secrets." Sighing, Dante drums his fingertips on the table. When he lifts his eyes to mine, they look tired and older than his twenty-three years. "But then, so do you."

"You and I both know that keeping secrets from someone doesn't change how much we love them. Lying isn't always cruel.

Sometimes we hide the truth to protect people we love." I said the same thing to Alex when she told me about her uncle, but I flinch when I realize it was the speech Dad used to give me about making sure Mom never found out about our "side business." Maybe I've been trying to convince myself of something that's never felt right.

Dante scratches his jaw. "We lie to the people we love for two reasons—because we're trying to protect ourselves or because we don't believe they can handle the truth." Dante swallows hard and pulls his hair out of his face. "Maybe you need to give Alex more credit. She's strong. She can handle it."

"But I thought you agreed I shouldn't tell her."

He props his forearms on the table and leans forward in the booth. "That was when you wanted to keep your promise to your dad. When I believed his bullshit about being a better man." He shrugs. "And maybe I was protecting myself too. What if she couldn't handle it? I didn't want her to be angry with me for working with you guys, for being your friend, for knowing and not telling her. I lost one sister. I couldn't face losing the other one."

"But now?" My heart beats double time at the thought of telling Alex the truth, and I'm not sure if it's with fear or something else altogether.

"Now I'm not interested in protecting your father, and I don't think you are either." He draws in a breath and studies me. "I think Alex can handle it. Martina was my sister too, and I forgave you. You were a kid, Bash. Your dad was the one who started it all. He pushed you right in the deep end."

"I can't do that," I whisper. "I can't put it all on him. I made my own choices."

Dante folds his arms and leans back in the booth. "Then own up to them."

CHAPTER 33
SEBASTIAN

By the time I leave the Cavern, news of Dad's arrest is all over the radio, and instead of going back to the apartment and sleeping on Dante's advice, I drive straight to Mr. Patterson's house to see Alex.

I ring the bell three times and knock on the door twice before I can accept that she's not home. Does that mean she's still out with Logan? Will she stay with him? Will he be the first person she lets see her scars?

The idea makes me so sick to my stomach that I can't leave. I sink into one of the chairs on the porch and wait.

It's after eleven when Alex gets home. She parks her car next to mine in the driveway, and she looks so gorgeous walking toward me in the moonlight that I wish I had my camera to capture this moment.

"What are you doing here?" she asks as she steps onto the

porch. She looks at her watch.

I stand and study her in the porchlight. I'm torn between the need to protect this moment, to preserve the peace between us, and a guilt so heavy it feels like gasping for oxygen and pulling water into my lungs. "Dad was arrested today. The cops got a warrant on a tip and found evidence. They found drugs. He's dealing again." The words tumble from my lips, and when I hear them I'm stabbed in the gut with the reality. I swallow again and again once the truth is free, gasping for air as if I could suck it back in and make it not so.

Alex lifts onto her toes and loops her arms behind my neck, pulling me down to her. I breathe her in as she tunnels her fingers into my hair and whispers against my ear. I'm so lost in the sensation of being entirely unraveled that I only process some of her words. "I'm so sorry... Had no idea... Not your fault... Allowed to be scared."

Then she turns her head and sweeps her lips over mine. She's kissing me and I'm kissing her. Not because I want to—though I do, I always want to kiss Alex—and not because she's so close and the sounds she makes when I touch her make the rest of the world slip away—but, fuck yes, that too. I kiss her to stop the compassion spilling from her lips. I don't want her to comfort me. I don't deserve her comfort or even her presence, and her sweetness is destroying me.

When I break the kiss, we're both breathless, and I back away. "Last night, you asked me what I did that was so horrible that I couldn't be with you." I take a deep breath and nod. "This is it. The same shit Dad's involved in now."

She frowns and takes a hesitant step toward me. "You already told me about the drugs. Remember?"

"But I didn't tell you I killed Martina."

ALEXANDRA

You know those dreams where you're in one place and then suddenly and with no explanation, you're in another? I had one last night. I dreamed of my sister. It was autumn, and we were sitting on Mom's deck playing cards and drinking from Mickey Mouse straws. The leaves on the trees seemed to change in front of our eyes—from green to every color of orange and red and yellow and in between to brown. We were laughing because when the wind would blow, they'd fall into our hair.

Suddenly we were standing by a pile of leaves like the big mounds we'd rake up as kids. Martina giggled and jumped right into the middle of the pile, sinking to the bottom. I could still hear her laughter when her hand darted out and grabbed my hand. She tugged me down and pulled me under with her.

But then her laughter stopped. And we weren't in Mom's backyard anymore. It was dark and hot, and we were stuck and couldn't get out. She was unconscious, her face bloody and unrecognizable. I was trying to wake her up, but the leaves were too heavy and they were suffocating me. Then suddenly they were on fire.

I don't think I'll ever forget what it feels like to feel my skin bubble and melt while it's on my body. It's the stuff of nightmares, and the only thing more painful was putting her in the ground while I had to go on living.

I wonder if this time of year will ever get easier for me. If someday the changing leaves might make me think of football, bonfires, and hot cider. I wonder if I'll ever again see a pile of leaves and first think of our childhood. Of feeling them crunch beneath us as we jump in, of throwing handfuls into the air and giggling as they fell into our hair, of the unadulterated joy of a candy apple from a festival. Someday, I want those to be the memories that surface when autumn rolls around. Because they're there too. They've just been singed by the flames.

Sebastian stares at me, waiting for me to say something. Are you supposed to say something when the guy you've loved for five years tells you he killed your twin sister? Are there words for these moments when, like in those odd dreams, you're suddenly somewhere else? It's as if the ground has disappeared from beneath my feet, as if I've left my body and am floating here watching these two kids stare at each other. When he speaks, I'm slammed back into my body with a violent crash, and I'm not sure I want to be here.

"It's my fault Martina started using to begin with." He sinks onto the steps and drops his head in his hands. "I met her at a party back when I was using. She was looking for a good time and I…I offered. I could sit here and tell you that I tried to keep her from getting too deep, but I know I was the beginning for her."

I don't want to believe what he's saying. The idea of Martina and Sebastian using together makes me want to crawl out of my skin. "No."

"It's true. Maybe she was looking for trouble, but I showed her the goddamn map. And the night she died, the meth lab explosion, that was my fault."

"Stop talking," I blurt. "Sebastian…"

He lifts his head and stares at me until I sink onto the step beside him. "I don't know what went wrong or why the fire started. Hell, I don't even know why she was there. We think maybe she broke in to steal drugs, but I didn't have to set the fire to be responsible. It was my shit that blew up."

I stare blankly ahead, clenching and unclenching my fists just so I have something to think about other than the horrible things he's saying. I want him to stop. I want him to take it back.

"All this time I've been keeping quiet to protect Dad. We worked so hard to leave that life behind. I've been suspicious for a while now, but tonight I found out that the greedy asshole went back to it. He doesn't deserve to be protected."

My hands are shaking and I'm afraid to look at him—as if looking him in the eyes will make this all too real. As if, if I can just avoid his gaze long enough, this will all be some terrible joke. "I think I want you to leave now."

Martina's Journal

Mr. Bedroom Eyes hit me today.

I don't know what set him off. Things have been so good since I got out of rehab and moved into this apartment he got for me. Sex, booze, gifts, and everything else he knows I love.

I was just teasing, joking around about the times I fucked around with Sebastian. I don't know why I did it. I was bored and sometimes it's like he goes for days forgetting I exist and I...

I shouldn't have done it. I shouldn't have said anything.

He apologized, and I really think he is sorry. He's never done it before. I just love him so much, but sometimes I think he gives me drugs just to keep me controlled.

He doesn't know I keep this journal. I hardly write in it anymore, so that helps, but I don't know what I'd do if he took this away from me too.

Mom wants me to come home. Last time I talked to her, she begged me. She said she's going to file a runaway report, but I know she's too afraid of me getting arrested for drugs and that's what keeps her from doing it. As long as I check in regularly, *she won't. I told her I was fine. I want her to believe that, but some days I'm not sure. He doesn't let me out much.*

That sounds crazy—like he's keeping me his prisoner, and of course that's not it. It's just that he's so private and wants to protect me. I understand that he deals with a lot of dangerous people. But still, I get lonely.

I wonder if Alex misses me as much as I miss her.

CHAPTER 34
ALEXANDRA

I'm supposed to hang out with Bailey and Mia today, but I text Bailey and tell her I'm not feeling so great, then I go to Mom's without bothering to change out of my pajamas.

She pulls me into her arms as soon as she answers the door. "Did you see all this with Sebastian's dad? It's so terrible, isn't it?"

I nod, and a fat tear rolls down my cheek.

"Hot chocolate and *Murder, She Wrote*?" Mom asks, and I nod again.

I curl into a chair in the family room and stare vacantly at episodes of the TV mystery series I've seen a hundred times.

Part of me wants to be angry with Sebastian for what he admitted to, for showing Martina the trouble she was looking for, for giving her the escape she craved. Another part of me knows Sebastian was a means to an end for her. If it hadn't been him, she'd have found it somewhere else. She was broken and trying to cope, and none of us can be blamed for not knowing that.

A few hours into our marathon, my phone buzzes in my lap, and I realize I've fallen asleep. My phone tells me I have a text from Bailey.

I'm so clueless. Just found out about Sebastian's dad. Fucking crazy. Call if you need me?

"You want some dinner?" Mom asks.

I shake my head. "No thank you. I'm going to go back to Mr. Patterson's."

She reaches across the end table and squeezes my hand. "I'm here if you need to talk. I know this time of year is hard on all of us."

"I'm okay," I promise, my voice a little shaky. I swallow hard. "I think I'm going to read her journals."

Mom's eyes soften. "You sure you're up for that?"

I shrug. "I guess we'll find out."

"Alex, there are things we never told you about your sister's autopsy." Her grip on my hand tightens. "I just couldn't add another layer to your grief."

I study the lines around her eyes. She's still beautiful, but it was as if she aged ten years in the month after the fire. "What do you mean?"

Her exhale is choppy and her eyes are sad. "When your sister died, she was pregnant."

Martina's Journal

I'm pregnant.

Well, that didn't help—spelling out the words, reading them for myself. The four tests I took in the Walmart bathroom didn't help. The reassuring feel of Mr. Bedroom Eyes' fingers in my hair when I told him didn't help. Nothing will help me make sense of this.

I'm scared.

"You have nothing to be afraid of," he said. "I'm going to take care of everything."

What do you do when you're seventeen years old and get knocked up? Do you move out on your own? I imagine going back home, sleeping with a crib tucked along the wall between my bed and Alex's. I imagine her helping me change the baby's diaper, and the thought almost makes me smile. Almost.

I don't need to worry, of course. My man will take care of me. He always does.

But the whole thing makes me miss Mom. She'd know what to say. But then she'd cry and beg me to come home. No, neither of us needs to go through that.

I'm pregnant and I'm scared, but I have my man. Things are about to change, and maybe that's good. Maybe this is a good thing.

CHAPTER 35
SEBASTIAN

The BHU photography studio is a big space with a bunch of lights and tarps of various shades, and right now it feels so fucking empty because Alex didn't show.

I don't know why I came here. I haven't heard from her since Saturday night, and I didn't expect her to come. I can't stop thinking about the look on her face when she begged me to stop talking.

It would have been logical to send her a text to confirm she wasn't coming and that I needed to find another subject for my project, but I didn't want to ask. I just wanted to be here in case by some miracle she can look me in the eye after what I told her.

So when she walks in the door, I can't say it's totally unexpected, but it still makes everything inside me slow down. That's the way I always feel when she's close—like the whole world is going on at normal speed around us while she and I are wrapped in this bubble where nothing outside can get to us.

"You came."

She hugs herself and scans the room. "I need to tell you something," she says. "I've been trying to figure out how to say it."

I instinctively step closer. "What? Are you okay?"

"Okay?" She breathes in deep and closes the distance between us, staring into my eyes. *Fuck* but it feels good to have her here. "No. I'm not okay."

"What happened?"

"You. You happened. You showed up in my life five years ago, and I haven't been the same since. Do you have any idea how awesome Logan is?"

Logan? Why are we talking about him right now? I expected her to bring up Martina or my dad, but Logan? He is awesome, a great fucking guy. But I sure as fuck don't need to hear about it. Not from Alex. Not when she's this close to me. "I'm sure he's great," I say in a monotone.

"He's perfect. He's handsome and successful, and he treats me like a princess. He wants to be with me."

Then why are you here? My heart feels like it's trying to break out of my chest. Maybe it wants to claim her before Logan can.

She takes a breath. "And it sucks because instead of giving him a chance, I keep wondering why he can't be you."

Fuck. My chest aches. "Alex—"

"Don't *Alex* me. I'm broken. You ruined me. I don't want to be broken. I want to be with Logan, feeling beautiful and letting him kiss me and touch me the way I let you."

I could do without the specifics. My gut is in knots of need tangled up with guilt and frustration, and hearing her talk about Logan like this is only making that knotted mess burn. I'm on my way to an ulcer, but I deserve this torment. I deserve worse.

"But instead I'm here." She tilts her head to the side.

I want to ask her why. I want to know why she's willing to be close to me after my confession, to know how she can look at me without anger or hatred in her eyes. But I'm afraid to ask, afraid to say anything that might bring her to her senses. "Does Logan know you're here?"

"No."

I'm not sure what to make of that. Should I be glad he's not part of this in any way, that she didn't seek his permission before coming? Or does it just mean that her being here means more to me than it does to her?

My chest feels too full and my mouth is a jumble of words that defy order. *Thank you, you're so goddamn beautiful, I've missed you,* and *why him and not me?*

"Where do you want me?" she asks.

In my arms. I point to the black backdrop. "Standing to start, if that's okay."

"Sure."

She takes her position, and I survey her outfit. Tattered jeans, knee-high boots, and a button-up flannel shirt with only the top button undone.

She wrings her hands in front of her and looks up at me through her lashes. "Should I pose, or…"

"Try to relax." I adjust the lights so they highlight the side of her face. "Just turn your head toward that light right over there."

She turns her head, bringing her scars into the light, and I take the shot. *One, two, three* pictures before adjusting the light again. This time pulling it to the other side of her face and allowing those scars to be cast in shadow.

When I pause, she turns to me. "Should I…" She unbuttons the top two buttons on her shirt then pulls it to the side so it falls off one shoulder and exposes the scars on her chest. "This doesn't seem right. This isn't what you need."

"What isn't? You're beautiful."

"No." She looks down at her chest then back up at me before slowly lifting her shaking hands to the next button, then the next, and the one beneath that. My breath sticks in my lungs, burning, and she squeezes her eyes shut. "Help," she whispers.

She's so fucking vulnerable. I could tell her to button back up, that we don't have to do this, but I can see in the determined set of her jaw that she needs to. I step forward and help her pull the shirt from her shoulders.

I've never seen the full extent of her scars before, and it's like having the wind knocked out of me. When I reach out to touch, my hand trembles. I've read that skin grafting is incredibly painful, and I can't imagine how excruciating it must have been for her to have this much of her torso treated. The bulk of the scar is almost triangular, with its narrowest point starting on her neck and widening as it travels down, and the widest part stretches from her navel to under her jeans.

As I trace the uneven surface with my fingertips, she slowly opens her eyes. I follow the scar along the waistband of her jeans then unbutton them and slide them down her hips. I help her out of her boots, and she swallows hard as she steps from her jeans. And there she is.

My most beautiful Kintsukuroi standing at my fingertips in nothing but a black bra and matching panties.

I drop to my knees and press my mouth to her belly as I wrap my arms around her waist. When I lean my forehead against her hip and hold her tight, I feel her ragged inhale.

"I was dealing when I met Martina. I was the reason she was an addict." I feel like I have to say it again, like I have to make sure she heard me and her being here now isn't some terrible misunderstanding.

"I know," she whispers. Two words that break my heart.

The ache in my chest turns sharp. "Then why are you so close to me? Why are you letting me touch you?" My hands frame the scars on her belly. "Don't you understand I'm no good? Don't you understand *I* am the reason she was caught in the fire? Don't you understand *I* am the reason you almost died with her?" I reach up and press my palm flat against her chest. "Your pain, your suffering, your loss, it's on me."

"I don't blame you. I blame Martina. I blame *myself*. But I don't blame you," she says softly. A tear runs down her face. "Oh, Sebastian… You've been carrying around all this guilt."

I feel as if a dull blade is slicing right through the middle of me. "No. Don't do that. Don't you dare feel sorry for me. I made my own choices."

"But your father…"

"I made my own choices," I say again. "My father asked me to help, and I did. Don't you see why I had to stay away from you? From the very beginning, you were goodness and light, and I was darkness and ugliness. I couldn't do anything but bring you down into my hell, and I wouldn't do that. I was never supposed to fall in love with someone so good, but I did. And then you ran into that fire like a fucking superhero."

"What kind of hero am I?" She shakes her head, sadness filling her blue eyes. "I didn't save anyone."

"But you are. You saved *me*. I thought that world was my life. I thought I was stuck, but your bravery, your strength as you recovered, you saved me."

When I finally stand, it's to cup her jaw in my hand and lower my mouth to hers.

Maybe it was supposed to be as simple as a kiss. Or maybe I knew it would be more. Maybe I'm a selfish bastard who will use any excuse and any opportunity to touch her. The next thing I know, I'm spinning her around and propping her on the work desk so I can spread her legs and stand between them, so I can slide my hands beneath her ass and pull her against me.

I kiss her and nip at her bottom lip with my teeth when she moans.

"I'll stop," I whisper. I don't want this to be something she regrets. I won't ask for something she isn't ready to give.

She shakes her head. "No. Don't stop." She threads her fingers into my hair. "Touch me."

I kiss down her neck, and she arches into me. I slide my hand over her stomach. She's warm and soft, and my breath rushes from my lungs as I cup her through her bra. I scrape the pad of my thumb over her nipple, and she gasps and takes a handful of my hair. She holds my mouth against her neck and whimpers as I suck her earlobe between my teeth.

I'm not doing this to drown out the world or to make her stop talking. I'm doing this to feel her pleasure, to feel what it's like for her to fall apart in my arms. I'm doing it because I fucking can. Because she fucking *wants* me to—and that's a gift in a life that lately feels to be taking more than it's giving.

She unzips my jeans, and I draw in a ragged breath. She slides her hand down and cups me through my boxer briefs, ripping a groan from my chest.

"Not here," I whisper. Because if she starts touching me now, I won't stop her. I don't want to even now. But I need to.

Breathless, she withdraws, leaning away from me and pulling her hand back. "I think it's my turn to say sorry now."

I squeeze my eyes shut and wait a beat, praying for patience before opening them again. "You're fucking kidding me, right?"

"I got carried away, Sebastian." Biting her lip, she shrugs.

I trail down her arms and cuff her wrists in each hand. "Fuck it, Alex. I *want* you carried away. I want you wild. I'm dying to know what it feels like to have you touch me."

"I want to. I want more."

I squeeze my eyes shut again. "I want more too."

She runs her fingertips over my beard. When she looks at me like this, I almost can't remember why I've stayed away so long. I almost can't remember why I'm all bad for her. Being with her is like swimming to the surface for air. It's coming up from a dark and clinging abyss. She's fresh air. She's sunlight. She's the wind on my face and the reason I fought to free myself from the darkness.

"I keep waiting for you to apologize." She scans my face again and again. "That's what you do after you kiss me."

My heart sinks. "I was only sorry for kissing you because it made me want to do it again."

She sucks her bottom lip between her teeth and shakes her head. "Should we take some more pictures?"

"Yeah." But I want to breathe her in. I'm not ready to let go.

She smiles tentatively and peers up at me through her long, dark lashes. "Or you could just lock the door." The way she says the words—soft, low—makes me want to do just that. Lock the door, strip her bare, and touch her until her moans fill my ears and block out all the ugly fears that fill my mind. She grins. "It's almost like you're considering it."

"I am. But you deserve better than an old photo studio." I reach for a silky black sheet. "Cover anything you don't want in the picture."

Her cheeks are flushed, and she nods as she wraps it around her waist and over one shoulder. The next forty minutes, I take as many pictures as I can. I can't take my eyes off her. The smooth, soft skin of her stomach, the perfect curves of her breasts in a black lace bra, the wrinkled skin of her scars. She watches me through each shot, moving this way and that, sitting with her knees drawn to her chest for one shot and stretched out on her side for another.

Every click of the camera feels like a promise of how I want to touch her, and by the time I'm putting my camera in its case, I'm desperate to get her home, where I can make good on each of those promises.

CHAPTER 36
ALEXANDRA

When Sebastian is done with his pictures, he waits for me to dress, then we walk side by side out of the art building and toward Mr. Patterson's house. Sebastian never reaches to hold my hand, but every time his arm bumps mine or his knuckles brush the back of my hand, he winks at me. The look in his eyes sends a flurry of flutters through my stomach that's better than any warm and fuzzy feeling handholding has given me before now. This is better. This is a secret, ours alone right now, something special and private that we get to figure out before we make it vulnerable to other people's eyes.

And I can't wait to figure it out.

Martina's journals gave me the courage to come. I haven't read them all, only the first two from before her life spun out of control. She was so young and the subject matter was trivial, but it was like having my sister in the room. I could practically hear her telling me to go to him, to forgive him, to let myself be happy.

We pass a bakery that has a large wedding cake as well as croissants and baguettes in the display in the window, and my mouth waters. I press my hand to my stomach. "I'm so hungry."

Sebastian runs his eyes over me, from my head all the way down to my toes, before slowly moving back up. "Tell me about it."

That flutter in my belly transforms into a low and slow shimmy, and I swallow hard. *Patience.* That's all I need now. Patience will get me back to the house. Patience will give me Sebastian.

I grin at him. "I'm nervous," I whisper.

His chest rises as his gaze skims over my face and lands on my lips. Then he holds up a hand for me to see, and it's shaking.

My heart trips and then does a few happy back-tucks to cover its awkwardness. *Please don't pull away from me again.* "But the scariest part is over, right? You saw my scars. Even the worst of them."

His tongue wets his bottom lip as he drags his gaze down my body. "For the record, I fucking *pray* that was the first time of many."

SEBASTIAN

We make it back to the house through a stretch of long sighs and meaningful glances, and as soon as she disables the alarm and closes the door behind me, she's wrapping her arms around my neck and giggling against my mouth.

"Is this real?" she asks, yanking my shirt off over my head and tossing it onto the floor.

"You'd better believe it." I slide my hand into her hair and tilt her head back so I can kiss her long and full and with everything I've been feeling since she walked into the photography studio.

"Bedroom," she says, breaking the kiss. She leads me to a room at the back of the house that's bigger than my grandma's entire two-bedroom trailer.

She unbuttons her shirt and drops it to the floor then toes out of her shoes and peels off her jeans. My heart pounds faster with every inch that's exposed, as if we didn't just do this in the studio.

"Sorry about the taxidermy." She frowns at the stuffed jackrabbit mounted above the bed. "Hope it doesn't kill the mood."

I arch a brow and stalk toward her, shedding my own shoes and jeans. "There could be an entire forest of live animals watching us, and I'd still want you more than anything. Then again..." Grinning, I scoop her shirt off the floor and toss it over the rabbit's head. "I'm gonna do things to you that Little Bunny Foo-Foo doesn't need to see."

She bursts into laughter and I kiss her, grinning against her mouth.

I lay her back on the bed, and she draws up her knees and parts her legs as I settle on top of her. I kiss her mouth, kiss my way down her neck. I use tongue and teeth and lips to taste her, to feel her, and the sounds that slip from her lips make me crazy.

I trail my hands down her arms and lift them over her head, holding them there as I draw up onto my knees to take her in. "You are so beautiful."

I release her hands so I can unclasp her bra and slide it off her arms. She lifts her hips, and her fingers tangle with mine as we work on her panties—both of us impatient, desperate. I pull them down her legs and off her feet and toss them to the floor.

She reaches for me and I have to stop, catch my breath, and force myself to slow down. I need to commit every second of this night to memory. This isn't the fantasy. It's Alex, real, soft and willing, and as hungry as me.

"What are you doing?" she asks.

I shake my head and trail my gaze over her—the flush of her cheeks, the swell of her breasts, the ridge of her hipbones…lower. "Looking."

She draws in a deep breath, and her chest rises and falls. "I like the way you look at me. But I want you to touch me."

I feel greedy and terrified all at once. "Do you have any idea how many times I've thought about this?"

"You're not the only one," she says, and the words send a rush of heat through me.

I trail my knuckles down the center of her body, between her breasts, circling her navel, then dipping between her legs.

She arches and rocks her hips into my touch as I put the slightest bit of pressure there before finding her clit between two fingers. She gasps. "Yes. Please."

"I love the way you sound when you're turned on. And the way you taste." I work my way down the bed and lower my face between her legs, relishing her gasp as I taste her first with a light flick of my tongue and then with the hungry press of my open mouth against her. I explore, lick, taste, delve until she lifts her hips and arches into my face, her hands finding my hair, her gasps making me greedy for more.

I want her to dissolve in this bed. I don't want her to define herself by the night she ran into the fire. I don't want her to limit herself or her life to *survivor* when she's so much more. I want her to lose herself here and see herself as I see her: beautiful, brave, *everything*.

I slide a finger inside her and then another, and she tugs on my hair as she cries out and comes apart against me.

I pull away gently and kiss the inside of each thigh before kissing my way back up her body. I climb off the bed to strip out of my briefs and grab the condom from my wallet.

When I look up, she's rolled onto her side, watching me with hungry eyes as I slide it on. Maybe I should be embarrassed by my trembling hands, but I want her to see who I really am and I want her to see what she does to me.

She rolls to her back as I settle over her. "Are you ready?"

"Please." Her hands slide down my back as her teeth find my neck and I settle between her legs. She holds my gaze as I sink deeply, and my breath catches. There are too many emotions battling in my chest. Lust tangles with years of longing and friendship. Affection and adoration push something even stronger to the surface.

"You're so beautiful," I whisper in her ear. "You feel so good."

She moans, and I position an arm under one leg, hitching it higher, driving into her deeper, and when I feel her tighten around me, feel her body tense and then release again, I follow her, and instead of drowning in her, it's like I'm finally coming up for air.

CHAPTER 37
ALEXANDRA

We're still in bed. When the light coming in the windows dimmed with the setting sun, Sebastian went to the kitchen and brought back a tray of food and a bottle of wine, and now he's feeding me olives, crackers, slices of cheese, and chunks of hard salami.

"Tell me about your childhood," I say after swallowing a mouthful of food. "You told me you couldn't imagine growing up in a place like this, but what was it like how you grew up?"

Sebastian takes a deep breath and refills our wine glasses. "There were some rough patches. Times I couldn't even imagine wearing a pair of shoes that didn't belong to some other kid first." He studies his wine, and his brow wrinkles in concentration. "Dad didn't just suddenly decide that he was going to get into drugs. The world had beaten him down one day at a time. He worked hard to make Crowe's Automotive a viable business. It didn't start as what it is today. Mostly, it was Dad picking up odd jobs in his garage for a lot of years. Mom busted her butt as a nurse's aide, and Dad did side jobs anywhere he could, but there were times that the only meal Olivia and I could count on was the one we got at school."

I'm surprised to hear him reveal all that. Even in high school, when I suspected his home life wasn't that great, I never asked, because I didn't think he'd want to talk about it. Maybe before tonight he wouldn't have. "I didn't realize you had it so hard. I'm so sorry."

He shrugs. "It is what it is. My parents didn't have any family to fall back on, and that meant eviction notices and nights sleeping in the old shop. My parents would scrape together all they had just to get the car running so Mom could get to work. People throw around the word *poor* when they can't afford a vacation or a new car, but we were the *hungry* kind of poor."

"You never showed it." I finger my scars. In the light of Sebastian's childhood, I feel shallow as hell for all the hours I've wasted with self-pity over something so trivial. "I thought you were just a normal kid."

"By the time I met you, Dad and I…" He drops his gaze to the fluffy down comforter we've used to make our little nest. "We'd figured out how to make ends meet."

"Drugs," I say, filling in that blank.

He winces but doesn't deny it. "My parents weren't irresponsible. They just didn't have any safety net. Mom got cancer the first time when Olivia and I were in elementary school. She was really sick and couldn't work. When you have nothing and you're living paycheck to paycheck and half your income disappears, it's catastrophic. It was for them."

I tilt my head and study his face. "But that's all behind you now, right? The trouble your dad is in... If you were involved, you'd tell me, right?"

He cups my jaw in his hand. "I lived in that dark place and I don't ever want to go back there." His thumb skims over the scar at the corner of my mouth. "I wish I could tell you it was a surprise that Dad did, but I never really believed he'd changed. I wanted to, but at the back of my mind I was always waiting for him to go back."

"I think a lot of people never escape that world."

He studies me for a long time, as if he's trying to memorize my face. "It haunts you. Even when it's out of your system and you don't need to get high to feel normal, you're never really free of it. I sold a piece of my soul with every deal, and I don't think I'll ever get those pieces back."

I set my glass down on the end table and move our platter of food to the floor, then I straddle Sebastian's lap and comb my fingers through his hair. "Maybe the pieces aren't missing at all. Maybe they're all right there and you just needed to tell someone you're broken so she can fix you."

He sets his glass down and his gaze dips down to my mouth as his hands slide under my T-shirt. "Are you volunteering?"

"I'll put in overtime," I whisper against his mouth. He guides my arms up over my head and pulls off my shirt before throwing it to the floor, then his hands are on my breasts and his mouth is on my neck and my voice hitches as I say, "Nights, weekends, whatever it takes."

"You have a deal." He turns and lowers me to the mattress, and when he settles over me, the weight of him is so sweet, I gasp and shift my hips. "Because I'm broken as hell."

"And more beautiful for it." The words are a murmur and nearly lost as he kisses his way down my body and marks my breasts with his beard.

SEBASTIAN

"I can't take another minute of these animals staring at me," Alex says, staring at the menagerie of taxidermy over the fireplace. "Will you take me out for a drink?"

It's Monday, and we both played hooky today. I never miss practice without a damn good reason, but since my father was just arrested, Coach didn't question it. As for class, Alex and I figure we can get away with missing one day.

We made the most of it, staying in bed until half past ten and then taking a long shower under the rain head of Mr. Patterson's walk-in steam shower. I keep thinking about Alex telling me that I'll have a house like this one day, her quiet confidence that I'll be able to make it in the NFL. Usually, I don't let myself think about it, too scared I might jinx my chances, but when I had her in that shower with me, all I could think was that I want to be able to give this to her. The fancy house, the overpriced clothes and loaded car. I don't think any of that means anything to me until I think about Alex enjoying that life with me.

"Of course. Want to check out Logan's new bar?"

She makes a sour face. "You want to take me on a date to the bar owned by the *other* guy I've been seeing?"

My stomach drops. "You're still seeing him?"

"I wouldn't have come to you if I were."

"Then yeah. I want to take you there. I wouldn't mind kissing you in front of him, either."

She rolls her eyes. "How about the Cavern instead? I'm craving nachos."

I shrug. "Sure. Do you want to change or anything?"

She's in a simple white dress that she pulled on after our shower, and when she looks down at herself, her face goes pale. She's quiet for a few beats too long.

"Alex." I tilt her chin up until she's looking at me. "It was just a question. I wasn't suggesting that you need to. You look amazing in that dress, but I'd be happy to have you with me wearing anything." I pause. "Or nothing. I could go for you wearing nothing."

Her eyes go wide and she bites back a grin. "I'm not wearing *nothing* in public."

"Okay, I guess we can stay here and get naked again. If you insist." I reach for the hem of her dress, and she smacks my hand away.

"I do want to change, now that you mention it."

Before I can say anything else, she's heading into the master bedroom. "You don't need to change for me," I call after her.

"If I'm going on a date with Sebastian Crowe, I want to do it right."

"A date," I say to myself. "Damn straight." I settle back into the leather sofa and try to ignore the leopard that's been staring at me from its second-story perch all day. Rich people are weird. The walls are covered with art that probably cost more than my parents' whole house, and the coffee table has stained glass inlays. Yeah, if Alex and I are this rich, I think we'll do something good with the money. Maybe build shelters where homeless families get their own rooms with locking doors, or create afterschool programs. Hell, with NFL money, anything is possible.

Alex's books are stacked on the glass, and there's a soft blanket folded on the arm of the couch. This must be where she studies. The idea makes me grin.

I grab the stack of textbooks. Calculus, communications, the reader for our women's studies course. My heart stutters when I get to the bottom of the stack and the pile of well-loved journals waiting there.

"Those are Martina's diaries," Alex says, surprising me. "I actually thought I had them all until someone sent me her last one out of the blue."

I feel like I've been caught snooping through her drawers, and I restack the books—including the journal—and put them back where I found them. Every time Martina comes up, it's half shock and half relief to be able to speak freely. "That was me."

She frowns and looks from the stack of journals to me. "Why did you have it?"

"She left it at my house. She was supposed to come by for it but..." I shrug. "She never got the chance. I never read it. I didn't feel right."

Alex's brow creases. She takes a seat on the couch beside me and pulls the bottom book from the stack. "But I got this before you told me the truth."

"I know," I whisper. "I thought I had to keep my secrets to protect Dad...to protect you. But I knew that journal didn't belong with me."

"Then your dad got arrested and you decided it didn't matter?"

I rub the back of my neck. "I was only protecting a guy I thought was trying to turn it around." I run my finger along the tattered spine and wish I'd had the courage to read it. I wonder what she wrote in there. My stomach churns at the idea of Alex reading about what Martina and I did together. "Have you read it?"

"No." She leans her head on my shoulder, and I close my eyes with guilty relief. "I brought the whole stack over here to read, and when I sat down to start, I only made it through the first one and a little of the next. I can't decide if she'd want me to keep reading. I mean, the whole pinky promise didn't outline what was allowed in the event that one of us dies too fucking young, you know?" She wipes at her cheeks and shakes her head.

"I don't think you have to read them now, but you should eventually. Otherwise you'll always wonder."

"She was always braver than me, too."

I cup her face in my hands and graze her scar with my thumb. "I've never met anyone braver than you."

ALEXANDRA

"You're all smiles tonight," Bailey says. She grins at me from across our table at the Cavern. Sebastian is at the bar ordering drinks, and she's right. I can't stop smiling.

"So what?"

"Oh my God, girl. If there was a facial expression for *I've spent the last two days coming my brains out*, it's the one on your face right now."

I bite my lip to stifle a giggle. I feel giggly. I feel *giddy*. This morning I woke up with Sebastian's arm around me. He was holding me tightly, my back to his chest, like he was afraid I might disappear while he slept. I've never felt so cherished in my life.

"Totally unrelated," Bailey says, "but Sebastian didn't come home last night. Hmm. Crazy coincidence."

My cheeks heat and I duck my head to hide my face, but she laughs so hard that I'm sure my embarrassment is clear.

"So you two are a thing, then?"

I shrug. "I don't know. Yes? Maybe?" *I hope.*

"What about Logan?"

"I broke up with him Friday night."

She sighs dramatically. "You're going to tell me you didn't even dip your *spoon* into the apple pie before throwing it away, aren't you?"

I shrug. "What can I say? I'm a chocolate girl."

"Sounds reasonable." She tilts her head and her grin falls away. "So did you and my roommate work out whatever was keeping you apart before?"

"We did." I shrug. "Or, I don't know, maybe we're still working through it, but it's going to be okay."

"It's the man of the hour," Bailey says.

My pulse ticks up a notch as Sebastian steps up to the table holding our drinks, his expression solemn.

"Hey, Bailey." He sets his beer and my margarita on the table. "Could you keep Alex company? It looks like I have to run."

"What's wrong?" I ask.

He meets my eyes, and there's so much worry in his that I feel guilty for being so carefree the last twenty-four hours. "Dad's lawyer couldn't get him out today. They're holding him until the court date because of some related crimes." He shakes his head. "I don't really know what's going on. I just want to go home and make sure Mom and Olivia are doing okay."

"Do you want me to go?" I ask.

Leaning forward, he presses a kiss to the top of my head. "This is something I have to do alone."

CHAPTER 38
ALEXANDRA

Sometimes your life transforms from not much more than tolerable to a dream so fast that you're not sure that bad stuff ever happened. Did I ever have a twin sister named Martina? Did I ever survive a house fire?

That's how I feel at the shop Tuesday with Sebastian throwing long glances at me my whole shift.

I flip the sign on the door to *closed*, and Sebastian grabs me from behind, spins me around, and presses me against the glass. He grins into my hair, his hands moving over my shirt. He cups my jaw in one big hand as he lowers his mouth to mine. His kiss is sweet and firm, gentle and demanding all at once. And by the time he pulls away, I'm breathless.

"I have to go to practice," he says. His voice is low and husky, and he trails his thumb along my jaw before nipping at my bottom lip. "I don't want to go anywhere."

Smiling up at him, I shake my head. "I have plans anyway, so you need to go to practice like a good boy."

"I don't want to be a good boy," he says. The hand that's at my waist slides under my shirt, his thumb circling my navel. I gasp, and he lowers his mouth to my ear. "I want to be very, very bad."

I groan. Arching into him, I contemplate making out with him in the locker room. The loud knock on the glass brings me to my senses, and we both swing our attention around to the man standing on the other side.

It's Logan. His jaw is hard as he stands there staring at us, his hands tucked into his pockets. His eyes shift between me and Sebastian, and guilt crawls over my skin like a thousand tiny ants. We were never really together, and I cut things off completely on Friday. He knew I had feelings for someone else, but that doesn't change the hurt in his eyes. It doesn't change the guilt eating at me when he stares at us.

I'm frozen, but Sebastian seems unfazed. He opens the door and extends a hand. "Logan! Is everything okay, man?"

Shit, shit, shit. This can't be good, and judging by the anger on Logan's face, it's definitely not.

"I was coming to check on you," Logan says to Sebastian. "With everything with your dad… But I guess you're busy." Grimacing, he turns to me. "Sebastian must be the old friend you were telling me about."

"Yes." God, this moment couldn't be more awkward.

All three of us are silent. Sebastian looking between me and Logan, Logan looking between me and Sebastian. The only noise comes from out front and the hum of cars buzzing down the street in front of the shop.

"I really like you, Alex," Logan says. He shifts his gaze to Sebastian, and his nostrils flare as his eyes go dark. "Jesus Christ, Crowe, are you for real about her?"

Sebastian closes his eyes like he can't look Logan in the face, and I'm not sure what that's supposed to mean.

"Real smooth," Logan says. "Martina dies, so you just move on from her to her twin? One sister's as good as the other?"

Sebastian's eyes fly open. "Fuck. *You.*"

Logan arches a brow and lifts his hands. "Are you going to deny it? Because from what I just saw, it looks like I'm right."

"What?" *Oh, God.* "Martina?"

Sebastian closes his eyes.

"You and Martina? You told me that you... But you were together?"

"It was complicated." He seems to know how bad that sounds, because he flinches. The words are as damning as an affirmation. With the kind of trouble they were involved in, I'm sure everything about their life was *complicated*.

My stomach surges into my throat. "How could you keep that a secret from me?"

Sebastian looks to Logan, who looks almost pleased with himself. "I would have told you," Logan says, "but I didn't know he was the asshole you had feelings for. You can do better, Alex."

"Get the fuck out of my shop," Sebastian says. His voice is quiet, but no one can miss the razor-sharp edge of it. He seems more dangerous in this moment than I've ever seen him.

Logan looks at me one last time. "This doesn't change how I feel about you, but it sounds like you two have some things to figure out." He turns on his heel and walks down the street away from us, leaving me alone with Sebastian. Leaving me alone with my dead sister's former…what? Boyfriend? Lover?

"You two must have gotten a real kick out of keeping that from me," I say, my voice shaking to match my insides. "Was it funny? Did you and Martina laugh together, watching me moon over you when you were fucking around with her?"

"Alex."

"You were *broken* after the fire, and I let myself believe that you cared so much for me that seeing me hurt broke you. Everyone I cared about was grieving her death and no one could really grieve for me, for what *I* lost that night. I thought you were the one exception. But that's not it. I was wrong. You were broken about *her*."

He steps forward, his eyes desperate. "I was broken about *you*."

"Why? Why the secrecy? Why leave me in the dark and make me feel like a fool?" He reaches for me, and I push him away. "No. Don't answer that. I don't want to talk to you right now."

I rush to my car and drive away as quickly as possible, but it still hurts like I'm moving in slow motion.

―――

The worst thing about having a broken heart is that you never really know if you're being rational. I mean, I've always wanted Sebastian, and as soon as I walked out of the shop tonight, I wanted to turn right around and tell him to forget everything I just said. I wanted to tell him I'd be okay and I'd take him any way I could get him. Yes, it hurts to know that he was with Martina first, to know he was the secret boyfriend who was going to take care of her. *"We're soulmates, Alex. Don't stress so much."* But maybe I'd take that hurt in exchange for being with him.

I know that's the wrong thing to do. I'd be selling myself short and selling him short. Our relationship is too new to survive the weight of that kind of doubt.

When my phone buzzes an hour later, I'm afraid it's Sebastian. I don't trust myself to talk to him right now. But it's not him, it's Bailey, and I'm glad, because I really need a friend.

> *Bailey: Mason said that Sebastian was a mess at practice. What happened?*
> *Me: Logan came by the shop and told me Sebastian used to be with my sister.*
> *Bailey: That's awkward. What did Sebastian say?*
> *Me: Not much. I didn't give him a chance. I walked away.*
> *Bailey: Where are you now?*
> *Me: At the house.*
> *Bailey: You can't stay there. Do you want me to pick you up or meet you?*
> *Me: I want to climb into bed and stay there for a*

week.

Bailey: *Exactly. So which will it be? Pick you up or meet you at the Cavern?*

Me: *I'll meet you there.*

I take a quick shower before climbing into my car and heading toward the Cavern. Maybe I should have had her pick me up. Drinking until I don't remember my problems sounds pretty incredible right now.

When I pull into the lot and climb out of my car, Bailey is already there leaning against her car. "I'm sorry, sweetie," she says. "I thought he told you."

"You knew?" I ask. It feels like another betrayal, and I understand it's not her fault, but it hurts. "Why didn't you tell me?"

She steps forward and tilts her head, studying me. "Should I have? Because I wondered, but I honestly didn't think it was mine to tell."

I look away. She's right, but *dammit*. Am I the last one to know? "He told me about the drugs, but I didn't know that they..."

She waits for me to finish, but when it's clear I can't choke out any more, she wraps me into a hug. "Mia's on her way. Let's go drink irresponsible amounts of alcohol and talk about why all boys suck."

Bailey makes good on her promise, and I'm sitting with the girls and either on my third or my fourth vodka cranberry when Logan walks up to our table. He looks tired. His hair is mussed and he hasn't shaved today. His hands are tucked into his pockets and his shirt stretches tight across his chest.

"Alexandra," he says, and his gaze skims over me in such a sweet and gentle way that I'm reminded why I wanted to give this guy a chance.

"Hey, Logan."

"I'm glad I found you here. I wanted to apologize for earlier."

I shake my head. "You don't owe me an apology."

"I do. I spoke out of anger, and even if you'd already known, it was wrong of me to talk about it like that. It made you feel bad, and I regret that. My anger was with Sebastian, and I feel like you took the blow."

Bailey and Mia exchange a look before Bailey points toward the bar with her thumb. "I think Mia and I are going to grab another round. We'll give you guys some privacy." She reaches across the table and squeezes my hand. "We'll be right over there if you need us."

Then they slide out of the booth, and Logan watches after them before turning back to me. "May I sit?"

"Of course."

He takes a seat across from me and rubs the back of his neck. "I'm glad I saw you."

"I'm surprised you're not in your own bar tonight."

"I thought I might find you over here, so I ducked out for a little bit."

"Sebastian's the one who never told me." *Not the whole story.* "You don't owe me an apology."

"It's nice of you to feel that way, but I'm not sure it's true."

"You know," I say, "I'd expect that kind of secrecy from Martina. She was all about that. Keeping something a secret made it more exciting. But Sebastian was my friend. We sat next to each other in class and worked on lab reports together. Even if he and I hadn't been involved, it would have hurt to find out from anyone but him."

"I'm not going to sit here and defend his choices. I probably could, but I don't want to. I think you're better with me," he says. When I open my mouth to reply, he holds up a hand. "Just hear me out?"

"Okay."

"I know you're not in a place for a relationship right now, and honestly you made that clear to me the very first time we went out." Running a hand over his jaw, he shakes his head. "I'm sorry I thought I could change your mind."

"It's flattering. You don't have to apologize for that either."

"It's just that…" He studies the old Budweiser sign on the wall above our booth. "I don't think I ever told you I got married young."

"I didn't know you used to be married."

"We were a couple of kids." He thrums his fingertips against the table. "I screwed up with her and we divorced a couple years ago. I regret the mistakes I made, and I'm trying to be a better man. I guess what I wanted to say is right now if you need a friend, I can be that. And if you ever want something more, I'd like that a lot. I just don't want to lose you because of him. I don't want *us* to lose a chance at something—even if it's just a friendship—because of his screw-ups."

Am I that dumb girl who threw away her chance with a good man to be with a liar? "That means a lot, Logan, thank you."

"And..." He reaches for my hand and toys with my fingers. "I was hoping you'd still come to the grand opening at the Lemon Rind this weekend? As friends. It's a big night for me, and I could use a friend by my side."

He holds my gaze, and I have a fleeting thought of how pretty his eyes are—all the warmth there directed at me should be something I want. I can't stop thinking of Martina and Sebastian together, and I want desperately to stop thinking about it. And here's Logan, offering me something that might get my mind off the mess of emotions in my head for a couple of hours. "I think that could be fun. *As friends.*"

He exhales heavily, and his eyes drop to my mouth. "Try not to look *too* pretty, okay?"

My cheeks heat. I'm not used to getting the kind of compliments he and Sebastian deliver, and to get them from both of them in such a short time frame, I feel like I need to check to make sure I'm still in my own body and not someone else's. "That's not a problem," I say.

He huffs. "We'll see about that." His gaze dips to my mouth one more time before he stands. "I'll pick you up Saturday night. Around seven?"

"Sounds good."

"I'm looking forward to it." He turns to leave.

"Logan," I say, stopping him. "Thank you. For being so kind."

He grins. "I'll be anything you want me to be, Alexandra."

CHAPTER 39
SEBASTIAN

We won, and after last weekend's embarrassing defeat, we needed to, but I don't even care. I'm numb. I played. I ran hard when I got the ball. I did my job. But that's it.

Somebody told me once that when nerves don't make you feel like you might throw up before every game, then you're done. You shouldn't play anymore, because if you don't care, you won't play hard enough. According to that logic, I'm going to have a nice, long career, because I'm always nervous when I put on my uniform. The nerves fizzle away once I'm on the field and working for the win, but up until that point I always feel like I should carry a bucket with me or something.

Tonight, on the other hand, maybe they shouldn't have let me go out there, because I didn't fucking care. And when Chris leaned more heavily on the pass game despite playing a team with a weak defense against the run, I should have been pissed, but I didn't care.

A few disappointed glances have been thrown my way since we got in the locker room. They know I'm not myself.

"We're going out tonight," Mason announces, giving me a hard look.

"I think I'll pass."

He sets his jaw. "We are going out tonight."

Chris bumps me on the shoulder with his fist. "Come on. A bunch of the team is going. Make an appearance. You don't have to stay long."

Honestly, I'm not sure I want to be at home alone with my thoughts, so I agree. I shower, dress, and follow the guys when everyone's ready.

"We're walking," Mason says when I turn toward the parking lot.

I frown. "Campus bar?" Of course we're going to a campus bar. Tonight we're fucking rock stars for winning the game. But I don't want to be a rock star. I want to be a loser sitting in a dark corner. I want to feel sorry for myself and drink until I can't feel my face.

"The Lemon Rind," Chris says.

I stop walking, and the guys turn to look at me.

"What's the problem now, Crowe?" Mason asks.

"No. I'm not going there."

"Is there are reason?" Chris asks. "Or are you just being a dick on general principle tonight?"

"Alex is seeing the guy who owns that place."

Chris and Mason exchange a look before Mason says, "All the more reason for you to go."

"You're fucking kidding me, right?"

"I'm surprised at you," Chris says. "I thought you'd fight for her."

"It's complicated."

"It's always complicated," Mason says. "Life is complicated. Football is complicated. But chicks?" He shakes his head. "Complicated barely scratches the surface, so you're going to have to find a better fucking excuse."

"Isn't that hypocritical of you?" I ask. "Are you fighting for Bailey?"

He takes a step toward me, his nostrils flaring as he points at me. "You're having a shitty week, so I'm gonna let that slide, but you don't know jack about how I've fought for that girl. Don't pick a fight with me just because you're too scared to face your own problems."

He backs off, and the guys turn and start walking again. I follow—not because I don't think they'd take no for an answer but because now that the idea's in my head, I want to go. I guess I'm a fucking masochist, because if she's there with him, I want to know. I need to see them together for myself.

Will she be the woman by his side as he opens his bar? Maybe seeing it will help me let go. Or maybe it'll be another knife in my gut to keep the other one company.

The bar is one of those hip places with lots of "handcrafted," overpriced drinks and craft beers. A popular local band plays at the back of the building, and the place is already packed.

"You want a drink?" Mason asks.

I shake my head. "I'm fine."

"I'm sorry," he says. "I said that wrong. I meant, *you want a drink*. It's not a question."

"We'll find seats," Chris says.

I give him a look. There isn't a table available, but a group of middle-aged patrons wave at us from a booth adjacent the bar and motion us over.

"The champions!" they shout.

Chris treats them to his Southern boy charm as Mason places an order at the bar, and the next thing I know the group is giving us their table.

"We were leaving anyway," one of the ladies informs me. "We wanted to save seats for the team though."

"You're too kind," Chris says. "We really appreciate it."

"We appreciate *you*," the lady says. "What a great game. Can't wait to see what you can do when Arrow Woodison is back on the field."

Since I'm currently playing in Arrow's position, the statement is a bit of a low blow, but I earned it after my lackluster performance tonight and last week. Chris flinches slightly before looking my way, but the lady seems oblivious.

"We'll be glad to have him back for sure," Chris says. When they leave, he looks at me. "Sorry about that."

I shrug. "I deserved it."

"You deserve *this*," Mason says, shoving a glass of dark liquid into my hand.

"What is it?" I sniff it.

"Fancy whiskey. I can tell you now, this won't be our regular watering hole. I'd be broke before the semester's over."

"You won't get any argument from me," I mutter.

There's a bit of a cheer as everyone turns toward the stage, but when I follow their gazes, I realize they're not looking at the band. Logan just stepped out onto the balcony that's positioned just to the right of the stage, and he's waving like he's some sort of celebrity.

Alex steps onto the platform to stand by his side, and my stomach twists into a knot. She's wearing a yellow, high-necked dress that hugs her curves, and a matching pair of scrappy fuck-me heels. From my seat, I have a great view of her, and a perfect view for when Logan slides an arm possessively around her waist.

Jealousy tears through me, and I drain the drink faster than I intended.

I thought coming here might help me let her go. The idea is laughable. Nothing has helped me let go of Alex. Not two years in different states, not kissing her and holding her all night long, and not even being responsible for the worst night of her life. The only way I can let go of her is if I stop breathing.

After the first round of drinks, the guys left for the Cavern in search of cheaper beverages, but I stayed. I can't leave when I know Alex is here, not if there's any chance I can get her to talk to me.

I wait all night to get her alone, and it's after midnight before I find my opportunity. She's at the bar in front of three shots of tequila. I put my hand over the second one when it's halfway to her mouth.

"What do you think you're doing?" I ask.

She narrows her eyes and frowns at me. "I'm having fun. Isn't this how you do it?" She pulls the glass out from under my hand and brings it the rest of the way to her mouth, shuddering faintly as it goes down.

"Why are you trying to be like her?" The music is so loud that I have to shout to be heard, but I know she hears me because she freezes.

"What?" Her eyes are hard as she turns them on me.

"Why are you trying to be like your sister?"

"Are you *trying* to pick a fight?"

"No. I'm asking you a question, because I really don't understand why you can't just be *you*."

"So, what? I'm not allowed to have a drink? You're sure about that? Or is it that your picture of me as the good little girl is shaken by the fact that I enjoy a little buzz from time to time?" She clunks the glass on the counter and makes a face of mock horror. "Ooh! I like to party a little! So what?"

Party. That was always Martina's word for it. *Party* meant alcohol. It meant late night drives on back roads pushing a hundred and ten miles an hour. It meant going down on me in the restroom at school. It meant drugs. It meant anything she could do to get a cheap thrill.

When I meet sixteen-year-olds now, I'm blown away by how young they look. That's how old Martina and I were when we met, and I'd already been dealing a year. If I saw a sixteen-year-old today doing the things we did, I would drag them home by their hair.

But by the time I was sixteen, I was already in too deep, and Martina was spending every spare moment looking for trouble. I know why I made the choices I did, but until Alex told me about their uncle, I never understood Martina. Especially when I compared her to Alex. She was such a contrast to Martina—as if Alex got all the good decision-making skills and Martina none.

"I couldn't be her if I wanted to," Alex says, and I feel like a dick, because all the joy I saw on her face earlier is gone and she looks so damn defeated.

"Alex…"

"I'm just trying to catch up, okay? I haven't done a lot of living in the last couple of years." She draws in a shaky breath then puts her hand to her cheek before grabbing hold of the bar with the other.

"Unsteady?"

"Little bit."

"That's what happens when you take three shots of tequila in a row."

"It feels good." She stares at me defiantly. "If the rest of my life didn't suck right now, I might just like it." Then she turns and heads for the door, swaying slightly in her heels.

I go after her, telling myself I'm only following her because she's been drinking and someone needs to look out for her.

She's standing on the sidewalk, leaning against the building. She's studying her feet, her arms crossed over her chest, and when she lifts her head, there are tears in her eyes.

This is my fault. That broken expression on her face right now. The pain in her eyes. It's my fault, because I didn't tell her what needed to be told. I thought I told her the part that mattered, but maybe I left out the rest because I knew how much it would hurt her. Maybe I was too ashamed of the part I can't blame on my father.

Now here she is, staring at me like I've broken her heart when all I ever wanted to do was protect it.

"Can we talk?" I ask.

"Yeah," she says. She straightens, stepping away from the building and toward me. "Let's talk. Let's talk about what it's like to have a twin sister who's better than you in every single way."

"Alex—"

"No, I want to talk about it. I want to talk about what it's like to be twins but be so very different. I want to talk about what it's like growing up and having everyone naturally compare you to someone who's smarter than you, prettier than you"—she lifts her hands and makes air quotes—"'more *fun*' than you. I want to talk about what it's like to be the sister boys use to get closer to the other. Let's talk about growing up without any scars and finding a quarter of your body hideous at the age of seventeen and feeling like the only thing that's changed is that the better version of you is gone forever." She takes another step forward and slams the palms of her hands into my chest. "Let's talk about what it's like to watch your sister become an addict and to feel *grateful,* because at least in this one area you aren't the crappier sister. You want to talk about that? What a mind fuck it was for me to watch her spiral?"

She slams her palms into my chest again, and I let her, letting the blow land so it rocks me back on my heels. She's so close, and I desperately want to hold her until the stubborn tears in her eyes flow down her cheeks, to whisper in her ear that it's going to be okay.

"I think..." She tilts her face to the sky and growls in frustration. "I think I've been in love with you since sophomore English class. You went out of your way to make me laugh and make me smile."

"Because I liked you," I say softly. "I liked seeing you smile, and I thought someone should make you do it more."

A bachelorette party files out of the bar and stumbles toward the Cavern, and Alex waits until they're gone before she speaks again. "If she were still here and you chose me, maybe I could do it. Maybe I'd still be jealous of whatever time you'd had together, but I could do it."

This ache in my chest is too big. Too much. "I've always wanted you, Alex. But we can't have everything we want, and I couldn't have you."

"She's dead, Sebastian. And when she was alive, you never

showed any interest in me beyond friendship."

"I wasn't good for you."

"Wasn't that my decision to make?" Her eyes shimmer and her hands are in angry fists at her sides. "I never asked you to be anything more than you are. You were good enough for *her*. I can't be her. I'm tired of trying to be. I just want to be me, and I want to be enough."

That chisel she keeps poised against my heart makes impact, and this time it's not just a crack. The rock in my chest crumbles into heavy shards that settle into my burning gut and leave my heart vulnerable and unprotected. "You've always been enough," I whisper. "You're better than enough. You're all I've ever wanted, and you're more than I deserve." I close my eyes and look away. The pain on her face is too much to bear when I know no information I have will make it better.

"It wasn't until after she was in the ground that you ever gave any indication you were interested in me. And I don't blame you for that. No one would. But I know what that information will do to me, and I just can't lie to myself. I can't tell myself you'd be with me if she were still alive."

I don't know what to say—not when I can see on her face that every apology will fall short. "If I could go back in time… If I could change the decisions I made… But there's no point. I can't. For the record, you were always precious to me. Maybe you were her opposite. Maybe that's what drew me to you, and during one of the most selfish times in my life, you were the only one I cared enough about to make a decision that wasn't entirely selfish. I made a decision to stay away from you, a decision not to let you close, a decision not to kiss you before you went to Colorado and not to beg you to stay to be with me. You *saved* me, Alex. This life I have, every good fucking thing I have? I wouldn't have any of it if it hadn't been for you. I told you I didn't deserve you, and now you know why."

She presses the flat of her palm against her chest. "Why didn't you just tell me the truth to begin with? Why pretend to be my friend and keep your relationship with her a secret?"

I shake my head, willing her to see it the way I do...the way I *did*. "The secret was the drugs, the dark path I set her on and she never escaped. The other stuff was meaningless. *To me,* it was meaningless. We fucked around, it's true, but it was never like what I felt with you." She won't look at me, and I'm falling apart inside, each of those chunks from the rock around my heart digging its way out through my stomach. "I want you to understand the secrecy was to protect my family. It was never because I was in love with her. Tell me why you won't believe that. Tell me why you can't forgive me for this when you forgave me for everything else."

She wraps her arms around herself and lifts her chin as she looks me in the eye. "Because she was pregnant when she died. Because she was having your baby, and I'll never be able to look at you without thinking about that."

CHAPTER 40
ALEXANDRA

It's been almost four years since I've had this horrible darkness sitting on my chest. It reminds me of those early days after the fire, when I was still in the hospital—days when I couldn't decide if I was happy they got to me in time or resentful that I had to continue with this pain, these scars, this body while Martina was free of it.

In those early days, my grief was like poison in the air, and breathing felt like torture. Grieving was anger and selfishness and resentment, and so fucking much self-pity I thought I might choke on it.

But at the same time it was a heavy, unwieldy beast I had to carry on my shoulders. It was forcing myself to thank God for sparing me when I wanted to curse him. It was watching them lower half of my heart into the earth and being still when I wanted to jump in after her. It was the guilt of living and the heart-stopping reminders that there would be no more Christmases, no more laughter, no more fights.

And today my grief is watching the shock on Sebastian's face after saying that Martina was pregnant. Did he not know? Or is this horror in his eyes from his realization that *I* knew?

"It wasn't mine," he says when he finally speaks.

"Don't." My chest aches so much that I rub it as if that might soothe the hurt. "Don't throw shade on a dead girl by denying—"

Shaking his head, he takes my shoulders in his hands. "We never slept together."

"What?"

"We never had sex, and when Martina died, I hadn't been involved with her in *months*. I wasn't messing around with her or getting high with her. Nothing."

"Then who was she with?"

"I don't know." He presses a kiss to the top of my head, and the tenderness in the gesture threatens to break me into pieces. "I'm so sorry. I should have protected her. I should have done something to keep her from getting too deep."

It wasn't his baby.

"Let me take you home." He cups my face in his hands and tilts it up so I'm looking at him. "Please, I fucking love you more than air."

I gasp. I should be deliriously happy at those words. Instead, it's the most painful thing I've ever heard because it's a love I can't accept.

"I need you," he whispers. "Let's talk this out. We can get through this."

"I can't, Bash." I shake my head. "I'm sorry if my feelings

don't make sense to you, but I'm not okay, and I can't just let you take me home and kiss away all these doubts." I step out of his grasp, and his hands fall to his sides, his chest rising and falling in measured breaths.

I love him, but if I disregard my heartache now, it'll always live between us. I have to walk away.

SEBASTIAN

I wait until closing time and follow Logan up to his office. The door's unlocked, and when I go inside, I find him behind his desk working at the computer.

I close the door behind me and lock it so no one will interrupt us.

Logan looks to me and arches a brow. "Can I help you?"

"Yes."

Sighing, he stands. "What do you want, Sebastian?"

"I want you to stay away from her."

"Why? So you can have her for yourself? So you can come clean about what happened and convince her to forgive you and live happily ever after? You think that's how it'll work?"

"There aren't any secrets between us," I say. "Not anymore."

He steeples his fingers and watches me over them. "You can trust me with her. I won't hurt her. And if you really care about her, you'll step back and let her live her life without her sister's mistakes hanging over her."

That's the knife that cuts into me every night when I try to sleep. "I want her to be happy."

"Then let her be with me. I can take care of her. I can make her happy."

I want to punch him in the face and tell him to stay away from her, but that's only because the logical part of my brain knows he's right.

CHAPTER 41
ALEXANDRA

My hangover on Sunday morning is nothing compared to the hollow ache in my chest that comes every morning since I learned about Sebastian and my sister.

I have a text from Logan, checking in on me. He wanted to drive me home last night—he was worried about me—but I got a ride with Bailey. I didn't want to talk and I knew she'd understand, whereas Logan seems determined to get me to open up. It's sweet, but I'm not ready.

Everything I told Sebastian last night is true. As much as I want to believe that it doesn't matter that he was with Martina first, there's a part of me that'll always wonder if he'd choose me. Maybe that makes me the lowest kind of petty. Maybe I'm looking for excuses. Because I'm scared that if he was with her for any period of time, he knows how good she was—without the drugs and without the addiction, an amazing person who made your life feel fuller just by being close to you. Maybe deep down inside I'm afraid he'll spend time with me and realize that I won't ever be her, realize that I fall short.

Or maybe it all comes down to this dark secret I carry. That I should've been the one by the door when we were ten and our uncle came into our room. That I should've been the one searching for an escape all those years.

The secret fear that if fate were fair, *I* would've been the one to die in the fire.

Maybe that dark, horrible secret won't be a secret anymore. Because there's only one thing worse than having all that ugliness hiding behind my thoughts and waiting for me when the nights are long and sleep is elusive—the idea that someone else might agree.

"You're pathetic," I mutter. I wash my face and make myself a cup of coffee. I pad out to the living room, where I take a seat on the couch and stare at the stack of journals.

If Sebastian wasn't with Martina in the end, why did he have her journal? And why does he have that tattoo on his back? And who is the father of her baby? It never mattered to me before I knew about Sebastian, but now it feels significant.

I grab the journal I left off with, skimming the pages and reading about movies we saw and how much she hates our big brothers, and on the next page how much she loves them. I shake my head as I flip through, then I shove the whole stack to the side and let it spill to the floor as I grab the bottom journal. This is the journal she wrote in the year before she died. This is the journal Sebastian had.

I thought I needed to start at the beginning. But maybe for Martina I need to start at the end.

Taking a deep breath, I open the cover and frown when I see the sticky note on the front page.

> Dear Sebastian,
> If anything happens to me. Please make sure Alex gets this. I'm scared. I screwed up a lot of things, but mostly not sharing my life with her lately. If something happens, I want her to know my story. I trust you to do the right thing.

Seeing his name in her handwriting does something to me, and I have to close the book, put it back on the coffee table, and focus on my breathing for long minutes. Suddenly this isn't about jealousy. It isn't about who Sebastian would choose if we were both here. Because seeing his name in her handwriting made me imagine for a moment a life where I get them both. I remember Martina warning me off Sebastian, but she was trying to protect me from the life he was involved in. I want to tell my sister that he's changed. I want her here next to me so I can tell her I'm in love. I want to tell her about how he makes me feel when we're in bed together, the way he held me as I fell asleep.

I want the life where I get to be with Sebastian and I get to share my happiness with my sister.

I just fucking miss her.

"Just do it," I whisper. I grab the journal, open to the first page, and start reading.

***

Martina's Journal

I'm scared.

That's probably a bad sign—two entries in a row with those words. But I didn't know scared last time. This is a whole new level of fear.

Mr. Bedroom Eyes told me that he was taking me for an abortion. An abortion? I don't even understand how he could say it so callously. He said it the way he'd say, "We're going to stop for gas on the way home."

I come from a big family. There were six of us, and my parents treated each kid like a miracle. Call me naïve, but that's the way I see this pregnancy. A miracle.

I understand that some women and some situations call for abortions, but this isn't one of them. He has plenty of money. We'd be fine, we'd make it work. Maybe he'd need to step away from the drug scene but…that would be a relief, wouldn't it? He could finally leave his wife. We could be like a normal couple.

I told him no.

And he hit me again.

I swung back this time, a bad-ass woman who won't be a victim. I'm so sick of being a fucking victim. I nailed him. Right in the jaw. Then he tackled me to the floor and sat on my chest, his knees on either side of my arms, his hand around my neck.

He squeezed. I thought he was going to kill me. I couldn't breathe. And those beautiful eyes that I fell so hard for looked right into mine as he said, "You'll fucking do as I say, or I'll be done with you."

I went crazy. I told him I was going to go to the police. I told him I'd tell them everything, that I knew enough to put him away for years.

"Like hell you will," he said. He pulled my hair, and some came out. I tried to fight him, but he was too strong. I tried to get him off me.

The last thing I remember is the back of his hand against my cheek.

I woke up with a sore jaw, a fat lip, and an eye that was already swelling shut. He beat me unconscious, and I can't even remember anything beyond the first blow.

When I found the strength to get out of bed, there was a note. He left me a diamond bracelet on the counter beside a vase of red roses. He always gets red roses. Never anything else.

I love you, baby, the note said. *Please don't disobey me. It hurts me so much.*

I'm scared, and I don't know how to get away from him. He called and told me I need to meet him tonight at this house where I know some of his guys cook meth. I don't know if he's going to have some black market doctor there to cut out my baby or if he has something equally horrible planned, but I'm going. Not because I want to see him or because I accept his fucking apology, but because I'm afraid if I don't, he'll kill me.

I'm going to drop this journal off at Sebastian's house. Because if he finds it, I'm dead.

CHAPTER 42
SEBASTIAN

After class Monday, I go to the jail to see Dad. He asked for Mom, but she told me she doesn't want to look at him. I wish I could be so lucky.

"Thanks for showing up at court last week," Dad says with a sneer. He's dressed in the orange jumpsuit the jail gave him. It's weird to see my dad like this, but the vindictive part of me feels like the uniform suits him.

I take a seat at the table across from him and nod to the guard. "You thought I was going to come support you?" I shake my head. "Been there. Done that. No. We had a deal, and you broke it."

He stares at me for a long beat. "I've worked hard my whole fucking life, Sebastian. You have no idea the things I've sacrificed to take care of this family. I risked everything so you could have clothes on your back and hot food in your mouth."

I've heard this speech before. I used to buy it. This time, I want to spit his words back at him. "What was your excuse this time?"

"I don't have one," he says between clenched teeth. He eyes the guard before looking at me again. "I've agreed to work with the FBI in exchange for a lighter sentence. It'll happen this afternoon, but until then you need to look out for Alexandra. That man's got his eye on her."

"What man? What will happen this afternoon?"

"They'll get the arrest warrant for Logan Lucas."

"What?"

"I'm small potatoes, Sebastian. He's the man they want."

ALEXANDRA

I'm halfway through Martina's journal when there's a knock on the door. I don't want to put it down. I feel like my sister's next to me telling me a story, and how dare someone interrupt me when I'm talking to my sister?

I run my finger over the words *Mr. Bedroom Eyes* and frown. When Sebastian told me he hadn't been with Martina for months before she died and the baby wasn't his, I believed him. Believing him wasn't the problem. But now that I've read two entries about "Mr. Bedroom Eyes," I want to know who this guy is whom she refers to only in code.

She talks about going to Indianapolis with him, about their days away together and their extravagant weekends, and I wonder, if I keep reading, will I find out where she went when she ran away? Was she with him? Will she tell me who he is? He's older and married, and I have this sick feeling in my stomach that it might be Sebastian's dad. The idea makes my stomach churn.

The bell rings again, and with a sigh I close the journal and go to open the door. Logan's standing on Mr. Patterson's front porch with a bouquet of red roses and a jewelry box. He offers me the flowers, and I grin, shaking my head. "What are you doing here?"

He lifts one shoulder in a sloppy shrug. "You were sad last night," he says. "And I couldn't stand it. Can you blame a guy for wanting to spoil the girl he's really into?"

I soften. "Logan, you're so sweet, but I can't…"

"Can't what? Can't take these flowers and put them in a vase? Can't wear this necklace?" He opens the box, and the sunlight catches on the diamonds inside.

Mr. Bedroom Eyes bought me a diamond necklace. It has three-quarter-carat diamonds, each situated on a trio of golden petals.

"What's wrong?" he asks, stepping into the house. "You don't like it?"

I shake my head and lift my eyes to his. This is a coincidence, right? The jewelry? The roses? This guy who has the most beautiful eyes? But the piece is so unique, and my skin crawls with the way he's looking at me.

"Alex?"

"How do you know Sebastian?" I ask.

His smile falls away and his jaw goes hard. "Why are we talking about him again? He just makes you sad."

"How do you know Sebastian?" I ask again, my voice teetering like it's balancing on a razor-thin edge. Turning, I step back and onto the front porch, only because it's the easiest way to put space between us.

"I helped him turn his life around when he was battling his drug addiction. I helped him."

I swallow hard. That's not something Mr. Bedroom Eyes would do, is it? The man Martina described wouldn't help anyone. "How do you know Sebastian's dad?"

His gaze is steady on mine, but I see anger rising in his eyes.

You're imagining things, Alex. You've been spending too much time reading Martina's journals.

"He's Sebastian's dad," Logan says.

"No. He's more than that. When you picked up your car that first day I met you, there was no invoice. Mr. Crowe insisted you didn't pay. It was a lot of work. Thousands in parts alone. But you didn't have to pay a cent. How do you know him?"

My phone rings, but I keep my eyes on Logan.

"Get in the house, Alex," he says. His voice is low and calm, almost mechanical.

I shake my head. "Not until you leave. I want you to leave."

"Just get in the house. We need to talk."

"I don't know you. I don't want you here."

He grabs me by my ponytail and yanks me forward. I stumble into the foyer as he slams the door, his hand still wrapped around my hair. My eyes water. "You're such a pretty girl," he whispers in my ear. "Don't be like this. We're gonna be so good together."

I squeeze my eyes shut as if not seeing him might make him disappear. "You were with Martina."

My eyes fly open again as he spins me around and pins me against the wall, his hands on either side of my head, his body so close I can't move more than half an inch in any direction. "I'll give you *anything*," he says, anger inching into his voice and his eyes. "*Everything.*"

"I don't want anything from you."

His eyes drop to my mouth. "I've been so fucking patient with you. Come on, baby. Your sister liked me. You should too."

I shake my head wildly, but he still has a hold of my hair, and it barely moves. Words, fear, and regret all clog my throat and make it hard to talk. "I want you to leave now. I won't tell anyone you were here."

Logan nuzzles the side of my neck. "I think I picked the wrong sister to begin with. You're so much sweeter." He licks my scar, a full animal lick from the top of my sleep shirt to my jaw. I shudder, nausea rolling through me. "I've watched you. Waiting for you for four years. I thought I'd get over this little obsession I have about you, but you see, I have what they call an addictive personality." My skin is wet from his tongue, and he traces down the path with one knuckle. "Please, baby. We can do this the easy way or the hard way."

His hand drops to my waist and tugs at my shirt, then someone's pounding on the door.

"Shh," Logan whispers against my ear, a hand over my mouth.

I bite down on his hand, and the second he pulls it away, I scream.

The door flies open, cracks against the doorjamb. Then Logan's off me and on the floor, and Sebastian's there, tackling Logan to the ground, fists swinging. Logan gets in a few shots and Sebastian reels, but he caught Logan off guard and he has the advantage.

"Son of a bitch," Sebastian says, pinning him down. "You don't fucking touch her."

I scramble for my phone and dial 911. Soon, there are sirens, and it all happens so fast. This is how it's supposed to be. The night of the fire, I called 911 and waited for what felt like hours. Maybe it was only seconds. But there were no sirens. No one was coming to save the day, and my sister was in that burning house.

This is the way it's supposed to be. Something bad happens, and the good guys come. The good guys win.

The next hour goes in a blur. Logan's in handcuffs, and the police question me and Sebastian about what happened. I hand over Martina's journal with tears, shaking hands, and more questions than my clumsy, shocked brain can properly form. Only after all that do I think to ask Sebastian, "How did you know?"

He's sitting next to me on the couch, a cold cloth against his swelling eye. "How did I know what?"

"How did you know that Logan was here?"

"I didn't. I called and you didn't answer, and I just..." He shakes his head. "I just had a feeling that I needed to check on you. Maybe I would have had a feeling the night of the fire too, but I was too busy getting high." Shame and guilt hang on his words, pulling them lower. "I swear, I didn't know about Logan until my dad told me today. He was supposed to be my friend, but he was really just there to keep me in check and make sure I didn't go to the police about Dad's whole operation. I never would have let him near you if I'd known."

"It's not your fault, Sebastian."

"The fucker had you pinned against the wall, Alex. If I'd been two minutes later, he would have—"

"Don't do that to yourself." I swallow hard, mentally compartmentalizing the chaos of questions and fears all fighting for my attention so I can focus on Sebastian. "You saved me."

"You got that backward," he says, tucking my hair behind my ear. "*You* saved *me*."

CHAPTER 43
ALEXANDRA

"I'd like to call to order the first weekly meeting of the We Don't Get Enough Dick club," Bailey says.

Next to me, Keegan clears his throat. "Um, no offense, Bail, but I wasn't actually wanting to hang out because I don't get enough dick."

I bite back a giggle, and Bailey grins, telling me she was absolutely aware of the way she phrased that. "Fine. The Undersexed Friends Unite club, also known as UFU." She turns to Mia and wriggles her brows. "Get it, 'You Eff You'? It's a masturbation pun."

"Oh, I get it," Mia says, straight-faced. "It's hilarious."

"Don't quit your day job," Keegan mutters.

"Do I still get to be a member?" Mia says. "Because, um… yeah…not exactly undersexed."

"Bitch," Bailey mutters.

I laugh again.

"I've never been to a support group before," Keegan says. "Is this how it goes? A bunch of chicks talking about how they need more dick? Because maybe I could make some room in my schedule…"

"UFU rule number one, group members don't fuck each other." Bailey turns to me. "Sorry, hon. I like you, but it's for the integrity of the group."

"I'll get over it."

"You're all hilarious," Keegan says. "If this was really about sex, you could pretty much end your problem tonight with just about any single guy here."

She arches a brow and makes a show of looking him over. "As could you. With the girls, I mean."

He grins, grabs his beer, and leans back in the booth. "So true, so true." His grin falls away. "Too bad Olivia's treating me like I have the Zika virus."

It's been two weeks since they arrested Logan Lucas. Sebastian's dad agreed to cooperate with the authorities in exchange for lighter sentencing, and he provided them with evidence of Logan's longtime drug-trafficking business. Between what Sebastian's dad provided, evidence they found at Logan's apartment, and Martina's journal, they think they'll have enough to tack on Martina's murder to the rest of his charges.

I don't think that knowing the explosion was rigged by Logan has relieved any of Sebastian's guilt. But I do know that he's glad to see his dad on the right side of the law, and the prosecutor is pushing for the harshest sentencing possible for Logan.

They kept the journal in police custody for the trial, but Sebastian got someone to pull some strings at the police department, and they let me go in and sit in a quiet room to read the rest of it. Everything I read there was as profoundly upsetting as it was touching. Because in the end, Martina was still my sister. That never changed. She made terrible choices, but when I read about those choices from her point of view, I could almost understand how easy it was to follow that dark spiral down into the fire where it ultimately led her.

There's no way I could read what Martina wrote and have any doubt about Sebastian's feelings for me, but imagining them together was still painful. I've been working through it, taking my time to process everything and figure out how *I* feel.

Bailey's in the middle of a sentence when Mason and Chris walk into the bar, and she stops talking and stares at Mason.

"You're absolutely ridiculous," Keegan says. "The both of you are ridiculous. He's in love with you; you're obviously in love with him. *Do something.*"

Bailey's face cracks with a self-pity I've never seen her show before, but then she looks down at her hands and back up at us and it's gone. "That's not an option."

"Just tell him what you did," Mia says softly, and even though her voice is low enough that I'm pretty sure I'm not supposed to be listening, I look up to see Bailey shaking her head.

"And lose him completely?" She grabs her beer and gulps down half of it before taking it from her lips. I wish she'd open up to me about her relationship with Mason, but maybe I wish even more that she'd just open up to Mason.

Sighing, Mia takes a sip of hers and raises her glass. "Here's to impossible relationships," she says. "And to love *always* being bigger than our mistakes."

"I can toast to that," Chris says as he steps up to the table. "So why wasn't I invited?"

Bailey holds up a hand. "Excuse me. This table is only for sex-deprived single people."

"And me," Mia says.

"Right," Bailey says. "Sex-deprived single people and Mia because she gets to go wherever I go."

"I might not be single," Chris says, "but my girlfriend living in New York makes the other part pretty damn applicable." He brings his beer to his lips. "Already counting down until Thanksgiving."

"So you're saying UFU"—Bailey pauses dramatically, and Chris coughs on his beer—"is for you?"

"Undersexed Friends Unite," Mia explains.

Keegan and I scoot over in the booth, and I pat the bench beside me. "Join us," I tell Chris.

Next, Mason walks up to the table and, without saying anything, Mia and Bailey scoot over to make room for him.

"Where's Sebastian?" Everyone looks at me like I'm not supposed to ask that question, but can you blame me?

Chris clears his throat. "I think he went to see his mom tonight."

"Good." He's been spending more time over there since his father's arrest, and I like to imagine him mending all his broken family ties.

"Are you doing okay?" Chris asks. "After…everything?"

"Yeah, actually, I am. It's been intense, but I have closure I didn't realize I needed."

"Well, there's a bar for sale next door if anyone wants to go into business," Mason says.

Keegan rubs his jaw. "That's not actually a bad idea."

"You're kidding me, right?" Chris asks.

"What? My baby mama lives here. What am I supposed to do? Just carry on with my life like I don't have a kid out there? After I graduate in May, I'm staying in Blackhawk Valley."

"And you're gonna run a bar," Chris says in disbelief.

Mason shrugs. "I don't think it's a terrible idea, but you have to change it from the uppity shit he had for sale."

"Oh yeah," Keegan says, "It needs to be a sports bar. Obviously."

"Let me know if you need help with financing," Mia says. "I know a guy who might be interested in the investment."

"But you have to have at least one karaoke night," Bailey says.

"Well, damn." Keegan rubs his hands together. "Let's start a business."

We all order another round of drinks and talk about everything and nothing. It feels almost like my life has finally fallen into place after all these years, except there's this one piece missing and I can't stop thinking about him.

Bailey catches me staring off into space and taps on my glass to get my attention. "Go to him." She fishes her keys from her pocket and hands them to me across the table. "I can make myself scarce. I owe you more than that after being so fucking wrong about asshole Logan. Go on now. You've waited long enough."

I bite my lip. She's right. Sebastian's been giving me the space I asked for, but it's time to tell him that I love him, miss him, am miserable without him. "I'm nervous."

"You don't need to be. You've got this."

I stand and say my goodbyes to everyone.

Chris winks at me. "Tell Sebastian we said hi."

CHAPTER 44
SEBASTIAN

"How are you doing?" I ask Mom. We're sitting on the couch in the living room like we have so many times since Dad's arrest. In a lot of ways, it's been good for us. I've been over more, and she looks good, maybe a little tired, but the dark circles under her eyes aren't anything compared to what I've seen before—during the hard times, during the cancer.

"Bash," she says, "I'm fine. I've wanted to leave your father for a long time now, and I didn't have the courage to do it before. He got in my head, you know? He convinced me I couldn't do it without him, and since I know what it's like to have nothing, I was scared." She takes a breath. "There's a silver lining in everything, and the silver lining in your father's greed is that it gave me the push I needed to be brave."

I wince. All this time I thought the best outcome was keeping the family together. Even during the days when my bitterness with my father was at its worst, I never stopped to consider that Mom might be better off if the family fell apart. I never stopped to consider that, like Maggie Thompson's broken pottery, maybe breaking would have allowed my family to build something better.

"You won't ever have to worry about money," I tell her. "I'll make sure you're taken care of, even if it means I have to work two jobs. You won't have to struggle again."

She huffs. "That is not your responsibility. I'm a grown woman and I'm not sick anymore. God has given me another chance, and I can take care of myself." Smiling, she pats my shoulder. "Now, when you become some bigshot NFL player, then we can talk about you buying something for your mom. But until then, just trust that I've got this. Okay?"

"Okay." It's not an easy promise. Dad, despite all his flaws, instilled in me this belief that we need to take care of our family. He took it too far, but at its core, it isn't a terrible thing to teach a kid.

Mom shakes her head. "If I could have a redo and change the way—"

"Mom, don't."

"You always carried too much of our struggle on your shoulders. It shouldn't have been yours, but I know I did the best I could." She sighs, stands, and stretches. "Now, your sister…I'm not sure what we're going to do about her."

I rub the back of my neck. Olivia is almost five months along now, and while her pregnancy is starting to show, she has yet to make any plans for how she's going to live after the baby's born.

"I've offered to set up a nursery here or to help her fill out paperwork for low-income student housing if she wants to do it on her own, but she won't make a decision. It's as if she's in denial about the whole thing, and I'm not sure if this situation with your father is making it better or worse."

"She's taking it really hard."

Mom nods. "Yeah. She was his little girl. He always spoiled her as much as he could. Now she feels like she's screwed up. She's going to be a single mom with no college degree living in her mother's house, and now she doesn't even have her daddy there to hold her hand. It's tough."

"I'll talk to her."

Mom wraps me into a big hug and squeezes me tight. "You're a good boy." She reaches up to ruffle my hair. "I'm proud of you."

I walk to Olivia's room and knock on the door before cracking it open. "May I come in?"

"Go ahead," she says. She's sitting on the bed, her legs folded under her, her iPad propped on a pillow in front of her.

"What are you looking at?"

"My Pinterest boards. Did you know I have a board for every room of my dream home? Decoration ideas, colors for the walls, furniture. I even have an entire board dedicated exclusively to master bathrooms."

"It can be fun to dream." I watch as she taps the screen and scrolls through images of perfectly polished houses. "But you know that's not what those places look like while people are *living* in them, right? Unless you spent all your time cleaning and never lived your life, it only looks that good for the holidays."

"I hated being poor, Sebastian. I hated the kids thinking I was dirty because I wore the same clothes all the time, and I hated feeling like when Mom and Dad bought something for me I was cheating them."

"I know." I sit on the edge of the bed and put my hand over hers.

"I'm not shallow." There are tears in her voice. "I didn't want to be poor, but I never would have wanted him to make the choices he did."

"Of course not, Liv."

She places a hand on her rounded belly. "It makes me realize my priorities have been all screwed up."

"Does this mean you're going to give Keegan a chance?"

She shrugs, and a tear rolls down her cheek.

"He's the father of your baby, Liv, not just some guy you're blowing off at a party."

"That doesn't mean I have to marry him, does it?" Her voice hitches with panic.

"Of course not."

"I don't want to get married. I'm already having a baby I'm not ready for, I can't pile a sudden marriage on top of it." She speaks so fast that her words tumble into each other. "When he talks to me, he wants to plan our whole life out. Not in the fun Pinterest board dreaming way but in a super-practical, 'This is how we're going to pay the bills and run our lives' boring way. I don't want that."

"Okay," I say. "Then tell him that. You don't have to decide yet whether or not you and Keegan are going to be an item, but you're going to have to make some decisions about your future after this baby comes."

She bites her bottom lip and shuts off the screen on her tablet before looking up at me. "I'm not freaking out about Dad. For the record. Because I know my baby will have his uncle Bash, and you'll be a better role model than Dad could ever be."

My exhale is jagged, but I feel good. For the first time, the idea of a niece or nephew feels real to me, and I'm excited about the prospect and glad I can be here for Olivia. "I'll help any way I can."

"Did you work things out with Alex?" she asks.

I lie back on the bed and stare up at the spinning ceiling fan. "She's not mad at me anymore."

"But she's not *with* you either?"

I swallow and place my hand on my chest, on that ache by my heart where it feels like a piece of me is missing. "I'm giving her space. She's been through a lot, and I can wait."

She shakes her head. "If I ever feel about a guy the way you feel about her, I hope someone takes me out back and puts me out of my misery."

"Brat." I grab a pillow and throw it at her face, and she grabs it from the air and holds it against her belly.

She laughs. "You're pathetic."

I shrug. "I'm in love."

"Do you wish you weren't?" She bunches the pillowcase in her fist. "I mean, now that you know how much it sucks to love her and not have her, do you wish you could go back and have never met her?"

Sometimes I forget how young my sister is. Not just in years, but in experience. "Not at all. She's part of me, and whether or not she decides to let me into her life, I'll always love her and know that I'm better for loving her."

She grunts. "Oh my God."

"What?"

"I'm just thinking that if you haven't told *her* that, you're a fucking idiot."

"Watch your mouth," I say.

She sticks her tongue out at me. "I learned it from you."

"I don't know where I'd be if she hadn't run into that fire. Would I be in jail with Dad? Logan's second in command? Fuck. It's terrifying. I don't like to think about it."

"Would you just get out of here and go tell *her* all of that? The pregnancy gives me enough issues with nausea. I don't need your help."

I sit up and stand then pinch her nose like I did when we were kids. "You're not alone, okay?"

She nods. "And neither are you."

CHAPTER 45
SEBASTIAN

Alex DeLuca is naked in my bed.

I don't know how long I stand in the doorway to my bedroom blinking at her, trying to convince myself she's real, but it's long enough that her cheeks turn pink. She climbs out of bed and walks toward me. When she's close enough that I could touch her, she takes my hand and places it on her bare hip.

"She's with me too," she says, turning so I can see the inked skin where she's positioned my hand. I saw her phoenix tattoo during our two nights together, but we never got the chance to talk about it—or maybe I never asked because I didn't want to tarnish those moments with talk about the fire.

When she reaches around to touch my hand, her fingers skim the feathers of one wing then dip down to graze the ink at the base of my spine. "She'll always be with me. She's my biggest failure and my biggest regret, and I carry her with me. I carry her broken, imperfect heart in mine because it was too stubborn to die with the rest of her in that fire." She drops her hand and turns back to face me. "And it's okay if you carry her with you too. It would be wrong if you didn't, just like it would be wrong if I didn't.

"I don't want you to want me because I'm like her or because I'm different. I want you to want me because I'm me." Her voice cracks, but the lift of her chin is so brave it nearly breaks me.

Stepping forward, I cup her face in my hands and kiss the tears streaking down her cheeks. Then I brush my lips across hers. I've always thought of her as so fragile, but right now I can feel her strength, and it's bigger than mine. She's steady under my touch. The art that's better for having been broken. The phoenix who's stronger after rising from the ash.

"I got the tattoo for you," I tell her, and I realize I could have told her that years ago. I should have. I shake my head, studying her in wonder. "Maybe I'm not the one you meant to save by running into that house, but you did. You saved me. And God, what I'd do to be able to stand here with you and believe I deserved it."

"Sebastian." She takes my hand and guides it to her chest, pressing my palm flat against her steadily beating heart. "I am who I am in part because of my relationship with Martina. Just like you are who you are in part because of your relationship with your father. We can make mistakes and still deserve to be loved." She holds my gaze. "We both have the scars to prove it."

She places her hand over mine and guides it back over the length of her scars. "How can you believe that I can be loved with these scars, that I can be beautiful with mine, but you cannot? Are yours less profound just because they're on the inside?"

My chest feels too full and too tight, and when I pull her against me and press my mouth to hers, something releases in me. It's as if I've been chained to the ocean floor and I'm finally cut free from my tether.

She slides her hands into my hair and parts her lips beneath mine. I back her onto the bed, never pulling my mouth from hers as I lower her down. "I love you." I say it against her skin and into her hair and along every inch I touch.

"I love you too," she says when I settle over her. "Always have. Always will."

EPILOGUE
ALEXANDRA

The spring art exhibition is packed, and my stomach is alive with nerves. For a girl who, seven months ago, had never shown her scars to anyone but her doctor, tonight isn't just a step out of my comfort zone, it's in an entirely different solar system.

But even though I'm nervous and worried that people are going to look at me and know I'm the one in the photos, I'm also proud. For his fall semester photography class, Sebastian took those photos of me and put together the most beautiful album. When he showed it to me, I almost couldn't believe I was the one in the pictures. It looked like me, of course, but the way the light hit my scars and the way he had me sit and stand, it all worked together, and for once I could see myself the way he saw me—as beautiful, as whole, as someone whose scars are as much a part of her beauty as the rest of her.

It's a big deal to be asked to be part of the visual arts art exhibition, and it's rare that non-majors are given a spot. But Sebastian's professor was so blown away by his work that she insisted his work be part of it.

I'm proud of the way he put the pictures together and the way he represented my body in them. Somehow, he took dozens of pictures that tell a story about a scarred woman without glorifying the scars.

"Girl," Bailey says next to me. "You are *hot*."

My cheeks burn and I grin at her. "They're not supposed to be sexy."

She arches a brow. "Tell that to all the boys who can't keep their eyes off them. I think Sebastian's gonna blow a gasket when he sees that puddle of drool in front of those freshmen."

I shake my head. "He knows who I'm going home with."

"I can't believe the year is over." She looks around, a bittersweet contentment on her face, and I know how she feels. It's been a good year, and it's sad to see it come to an end. The guys made it to a bowl game for the second year in a row. They didn't win, but they did great. More and more high-profile players want to play at BHU, and the stands were full of NFL scouts who might be the ones to give these guys the shots they crave so desperately.

Mason, Arrow, and Chris all entered the draft in April and were all picked up. This is our last week all together before the three of them relocate and spread out across the country to train with their respective teams.

"Are you doing okay?" I ask Bailey. Mia has decided to go to Chicago with Arrow and finish her degree through BHU's distance program. Bailey may have encouraged this decision, but I know it kills her.

"I'm great." She smiles, but it's not her normal Bailey smile. She's been down lately, and I can't help but think that might be in part to Mason's impending move to Florida, where he'll train with the Gulf Gators.

Apparently whatever secrets Bailey has regarding Mason, she's decided to take with her to her grave. Nothing's changed between them, except that with each passing month, Mason's pushed her away a little more.

"God, would you look at that?" Bailey says when Keegan walks in with his baby girl in his arms. A group of girls rushes over to coo over his two-month old, and Keegan grins proudly. Not much has changed there, either. He's still trying to make it work with Olivia, and she's still avoiding any sort of meaningful contact with him. She lets him see the baby, thank God, but she's kind of a mess.

"Where's the star of the show?" Bailey asks, looking around for Sebastian.

"He's in the hall talking to Maggie Thompson." I grin, too damn proud to hold it back. "She wants to include his photography in the next exhibition at the New Hope Art Gallery. It's really an amazing opportunity, and he could make some money if he decided to sell any of the photos."

"Is he going to sell these photos of *you*?"

"Hell no," Sebastian says, coming up behind me and wrapping his arms around my waist. He kisses the side of my neck. "You doing okay?"

"Surprisingly, yes." I smile up at him. "You're a star tonight. An artist and a stud on the football field. I don't know how I'm going to keep the girls off you."

He grunts. "There's only one girl here I'm interested in."

Bailey groans and backs away slowly. "You guys, I'm sorry. I'm happy for you but I can't. I just can't."

Sebastian nuzzles my neck, and I'm guessing it's to hide his face, because I can feel his chest shake against my back as he chuckles silently. "I can't wait to get you out of here," he whispers in my ear when she's gone.

"Only one more week at Mr. Patterson's, and then I have to move out."

"Oh, the things those animals are gonna see me do to you this weekend."

My whole body goes warm with laughter and joy and arousal. "I love you." I spin in his arms so I can see his face.

"I love you too."

"What are we going to do next year?" I loop my hands behind his neck. "I'm going to miss the guys when they go. And Mia. It's made me think about us."

"Well, if I'm drafted—"

"Which you will be," I say.

He shrugs. "You can do the distance thing like Mia is, or you can stay here if that's what you want. I'll come back as often as I can."

"We've been through rough waters, and I know we can handle anything that comes at us," I say.

"Of course we can."

"Even the unexpected?"

"Even the unexpected." He laughs. "What are you so worried about?"

Sighing, I run my thumb over his jaw, my mouth dry with nerves and my pulse racing. "Even an unexpected baby?"

His grin falls away, replaced by shock and then slowly by open-mouthed awe. "You're pregnant?"

"Remember when I had that stomach bug last month? I'm thinking it screwed up my birth control."

Now he's outright grinning and shaking his head. "You're gonna be so fucking beautiful with my baby growing in you."

I draw in a ragged breath. He couldn't have said anything better. "I don't want to ruin your plans."

"The only plans I have that matter are the ones where I'm with you."

"You have the best lines, Sebastian Crowe. Are you trying to pick me up?"

He scoops me into his arms, and I screech and cling to his neck.

"What the heck?"

Everyone turns to stare at us, but he ignores them. "I'm picking you up," he says, walking toward the door, "and I'm taking you home."

THE END

Thank you for reading *Going Under,* **the third book in The Blackhawk Boys series. If you'd like to receive an email when I release Keegan's story in book four,** *Falling Hard***, please go to my website to sign up for my newsletter. If you enjoyed this book, please consider leaving a review. Thank you for reading. It's an honor!**

GOING UNDER
Playlist

"i hate u, i love u" by gnash, feat. Olivia O'Brien
"Chasing Cars" by Snow Patrol
"Something I Can Never Have" by Nine Inch Nails
"Stay With Me" by Sam Smith
"Jealous" by Labrinth
"Drunk" by Ed Sheeran
"Stay" by Mayday Parade
"Closer" by The Chainsmokers and Halsey
"Unsteady" by X Ambassadors
"Don't Wanna Know" by Maroon 5 and Kendrick Lamar
"Cold Water" by Major Lazer, MO, and Justin Bieber
"Say You Won't Let Go" by James Arthur
"Tenerife Sea" by Ed Sheeran

Other Books
by LEXI RYAN

The Blackhawk Boys
Spinning Out (Arrow's story)
Rushing In (Chris's story)
Going Under (Sebastian's story)
Falling Hard (Keegan's story, coming summer 2017)

Love Unbound
by LEXI RYAN

If you enjoy the Blackhawk Boys, you may also enjoy the books in Love Unbound, the linked series of books set in New Hope and about the characters readers have come to love.

Splintered Hearts (A Love Unbound Series)
Unbreak Me (Maggie's story)
Stolen Wishes: A Wish I May Prequel Novella (Will and Cally's prequel)
Wish I May (Will and Cally's novel)

Or read them together in the omnibus edition, *Splintered Hearts: The New Hope Trilogy*

Here and Now (A Love Unbound Series)
Lost in Me (Hanna's story begins)
Fall to You (Hanna's story continues)
All for This (Hanna's story concludes)

Or read them together in the omnibus edition, *Here and Now: The Complete Series*

Reckless and Real (A Love Unbound Series)
Something Wild (Liz and Sam's story begins)
Something Reckless (Liz and Sam's story continues)
Something Real (Liz and Sam's story concludes)

Or read them together in the omnibus edition, *Reckless and Real: The Complete Series*

Mended Hearts (A Love Unbound Series)
Playing with Fire (Nix's story)
Holding Her Close (Janelle and Cade's story)

Other Titles
by LEXI RYAN

Hot Contemporary Romance
Text Appeal
Accidental Sex Goddess

Decadence Creek Stories and Novellas
Just One Night
Just the Way You Are

ACKNOWLEDGMENTS

I need to thank my husband first. If he ever thought me leaving my job as a professor and writing full-time meant I was going to work less, he's certainly learned and accepted that's not the case. This man understands what it takes to get a book done to my standards. And when I text him to tell him everything I've written is awful and my career is over, he replies, "You're that far along already, huh?" Because he understands *me* too, and knows that enormous amounts of doubt are part of my process. The fact that *he* never doubts helps me push forward until the book finally becomes something I'm proud to share with the world. Thank you for encouraging me, Brian, and for always knowing what to say to make me laugh.

I'm surrounded by a family who supports me every day. To my kids, Jack and Mary, thank you for making me laugh and giving me a reason to work hard. I am so proud to be your mommy. To my mom, brothers, and sisters, thank you for cheering me on—each in your own way. I'm so grateful to have been born into this crazy crew of seven kids.

This book is dedicated to my sister Deb. We grew up as sisters and best friends who became two very different young women. She's not Martina and Martina is not her (thank goodness!), but there was a lot about Martina and Alex's relationship that I could better understand because of my sister. Deb, if you read this book, you're gonna cry. I'm sorry. Don't say I didn't warn you.

I'm lucky enough to have a life full of amazing friends too. A special shout-out to Mira, who gave me so many pep talks during the drafting of this book that I'm surprised she didn't quit me. Thanks to my lifting buddy Kylie, my coach Matt, and the entire CrossFit Terre Haute crew. Thank you for teaching me to love picking up heavy things and giving me an outlet I needed more than I ever realized. I've been blessed with so many amazing people in my life. You encourage me, you believe in me, and you know how to make me laugh.

To everyone who provided me feedback on Sebastian and Alexandra's story along the way—especially Janice Owen, Mira Lyn Kelly, and Samantha Leighton—you're all awesome. Thank you for helping to make this idea in my head into something worth reading.

Thank you to the team that helped me package this book and promote it. Sarah Hansen at Okay Creations designed my beautiful cover and did a lovely job branding the series. Sara Eirew took the *hot* cover photo. Rhonda Stapleton and Lauren McKellar, thank you for the insightful line edits. Thanks to Arran McNicol at Editing720 for proofreading. A shout-out to my assistant Lisa Kuhne for trying to keep me in line. To all of the bloggers and reviewers who help spread the word about my books, I am humbled by the time you take out of your busy lives for my stories. You're the best.

To my agent, Dan Mandel, for believing in me and staying by my side through tough career decisions. Thanks to you and Stefanie Diaz for getting my books into the hands of readers all over the world. Thank you for being part of my team.

To my NWBs—Sawyer Bennett, Lauren Blakely, Violet Duke, Jessie Evans, Melody Grace, Monica Murphy, and Kendall Ryan—y'all rock my world. I watch you all in awe as I plod along on my own career path. Thank you for sharing your wisdom. I'm so proud to call you friends.

To all my writer friends on Twitter, Facebook, Instagram, and my various writer loops—especially to the Fast Draft Club and the All Awesome group—thank you for being my friends, my squad, and my sounding board.

And last but certainly not least, a big thank-you to my fans. I've said it before and I'll continue to say it every chance I get—you're the coolest, smartest, best readers in the world. I appreciate each and every one of you. You're the best!

~Lexi

CONTACT

I love hearing from readers, so find me on my Facebook page at facebook.com/lexiryanauthor, follow me on Twitter and Instagram @writerlexiryan, shoot me an email at writerlexiryan@gmail.com, or find me on my website: www.lexiryan.com

Printed in Great Britain
by Amazon